I Hear You

Kay Mitchell

ISBN   979-8-9878282-1-2

A Note

This book is a spicy romance that deals with some subject matter that
readers may not want to engage in.
Content and trigger warnings can be found on author's website and on
the very last page of this book.

www.kaymitchell.com

To anyone who ever felt like they weren't worthy of giving or receiving
love. You are.

PROLOGUE

Three Years Ago

To: ravensfan4lyfe@gmail.com
From: madisrad@gmail.com
Date: September 5 21:27
Subject: New Poem... The Sparrow

Ender,

It's the middle of the night and I just finished writing this. I couldn't wait to share it with you. It's just a free verse, but I think this is the first time I'm really proud of one of my poems. Like, really proud. This is the first time I feel... connected to something I've written. Like I've written it just for myself and those that are truly meant to read it. Not for anyone and everyone.

The Sparrow

When all the world is filled with pain

And you feel like living isn't worth it
Like it's hard to take the first day's breath
When you're trying to find an ounce of gain

You'll look to someone you love
Someone you long for and ache for
To give you the same sense of belonging
That others seek from above

When you find it you hold on to it greedily
But at the same time you cradle it
As if it's a delicate sparrow
Hold it too tightly you'll hurt it easily

Instead you let the sparrow fly free
And hope that if it's destiny
Your sparrow will stay
Even when there's no guarantee

Your BFF,
Mads

CHAPTER ONE

MADISON

I am not running away from my past. I am running toward my future.

This mantra has been playing on repeat in my head for the last hour. There's a pit in my stomach the size of an avocado and I spent half the morning dry heaving. The seat creaks as I move around in it, trying to get comfortable, when I realize I've sat in gum. Great, these are new pants. Well, new to me anyway. They're from a second-hand store. I hadn't spent money on clothes in a *really* long time, but last week I finally decided to treat myself. This new adventure deserves new pants, is what I told myself. Unconvincingly reasoning with myself isn't something I shy away from when necessary.

The restaurant where I worked let me pick up extra shifts so I could tuck away some cash. It wasn't much after the expenses of moving across the country. Even with the extra shifts, flying, as opposed to taking the bus, wasn't an option. Now I'm suffering in the heat, with gum on my new pants.

I dig around in my backpack for a napkin, and start trying to pry off the gum. Most of it comes off onto the napkin and it's at least not sticky anymore. My shirt should be long enough to hide the stain when I stand up. I need to avoid drawing attention to myself as the new girl. Being the normal, average girl would be ideal. My desire to have an ordinary college experience is ardent. Enjoy my classes, study, and maybe make a few friends–that's the current agenda.

The gum isn't even the most irritating thing right now; it's unbearably hot on this bus. The air conditioning stopped working a couple hundred miles ago. Even with all the windows open as far as they'll go, the smell of everyone's body odor is getting stronger. A toddler a few rows back is hating the heat more than I am. His mom has him stripped down to just his diaper, but he's still fussing.

At this point, I'm just thankful the seats on the bus aren't sold out and I'm alone in this row. Otherwise, I'd be stuck rubbing against someone's sticky arms. Instead, I have the entire seat next to me to prop my leg up on and use my backpack on it as a barrier between me and everyone else.

The map on my phone says there are only two hundred and forty miles to go. Two hundred and forty miles until I become just another face in the crowd at Pinehurst College. Where no one knows me, where no one knows my past, where no one will look at me with pity or judgment. Two hundred and forty miles until I can sleep in an actual bed, even if it is a crappy dorm room twin mattress. It will still be an upgrade from the couches I've been surfing and damn near luxury compared to sleeping sitting up, with one eye open, in the mall parking lot alcove.

I open my email app and re-read the acceptance letter for the last time. Just to make sure it wasn't a fever dream and I'm not wasting my time on this hot, smelly bus.

To: madisoncartwright11@gmail.com
From: admissions@pinehurst.edu
Date: January 18 09:15
Subject: Application Decision

Dear Madison Cartwright,

It is with great pleasure that we would like to inform you of your acceptance at Pinehurst College of Easton, Maryland. We are pleased to offer you an academic scholarship; including housing and meal allowance, for a minimum of one year. Subsequent years' housing stipend is to be evaluated at a later date.

Please contact us at your earliest convenience to accept admission and plan the bright future we know you have.

Sincerely,
Pinehurst College

Pinehurst isn't a well-known college by any stretch of the imagination, but it's got an amazing writing program, and the best part–it's nearly three thousand miles away from home. Easton is a town smaller than I'm used to, which is saying something. Oceanside, the town I grew up in, only has a population of ten thousand. But Easton being small means not owning a car shouldn't be an issue.

Before I'm tempted to check my *other* email account, I tuck my phone into my bag. The email account that receives emails from only one sender outside of the occasional spam message. I finish zipping my bag before I do what I told myself I'd stop doing and read his email–his last email. Self-control is something I'm working on. I don't even need to see the email, though. It's ingrained in my mind, committed to memory. I must have read it thirty times the day he sent it.

My phone is safely tucked away now, preventing me from writing the millionth draft to him. The outbox currently holds over a hundred drafts. Some are drafts in response to his last email. Others are just telling him things that made me happy, sad or angry throughout my day. Some drafts don't even acknowledge any of the questions I left unanswered and are just catching him up on mundane aspects of my life. I write the drafts and pretend for a moment we never stopped talking. I told myself I was going to stop writing the draft emails; I was going to move on. Even now, sitting on this hot, smelly bus, it's easy to think back to the last email he sent. His last plea for a response.

To: madisrad@gmail.com
From: ravensfan4lyfe@gmail.com
Date: October 15 19:27
Subject: Is this the end?

Mads,

I told myself I would stop emailing you. That I would move on and give you the space you're so clearly demanding by not responding to me.
Sometimes I wish I could go back in time a few months. It's been over 2 months since I've heard from you. I hope you're okay.
I don't regret telling you what I've been wanting to tell you for years. There's a lot I regret, but sending you that email isn't one of those regrets.
Madison, I am sorry. I'm sorry it changed everything. I miss you.

Yours.
Ender
P.S.... I've written a new ending to one of your poems. You know the one, my favorite one. If you ever decide to respond, I promise to share it with you.

This email exists only online, but other emails–other emails I've printed and carry around the paper copies. The printed ones have my favorite poems he's shared with me or the short stories he's written. Ender doesn't think he's a talented writer, but he is. His fantasy stories are my favorite. The characters have so much depth and diversity. The writing itself paints the most beautiful pictures in my mind. Other emails I've printed are just ones that make me feel better when I'm having a bad day.

There's one printed email a little more worn than the others. It's worn from being opened and re-folded so many times. The creases where it folds are showing signs of cracking and tearing. That email has some of the most beautiful words I've ever read. Reading it makes my heart swell, ache and break all at the same time. It's the one email I usually carry in the front pocket of my backpack so I can re-read it when I'm feeling lonely, or sad, or when I'm missing Ender too much. The rest of the printed ones are tucked into the bottom of my jewelry box.

I pick up my notebook and pen from the seat next to me, open it to an empty page, and start writing. I'm not writing anything in particular, just jotting down thoughts and ideas. This is something I do a lot to deal with anxious thoughts or to help me when I have writer's block. Right now I'm doing it because of the former. Writing words that pop into my head as I do my best not to think about how long it's been since Ender sent his last email. Or how long it's been since I stopped replying to his emails.

Ender sent his last email eight months ago. It's been longer than that since I stopped responding to him.

Ender and I met when we were thirteen and I use the term met loosely. We connected in an online community for aspiring writers who shared short stories and poems and, I don't know, just clicked. We started reading and commenting on each other's posts. Soon it turned to emailing back and forth once we discovered we were the same age. For the first year we talked, we didn't share any personal details because, well, *stranger danger*. We quickly realized we were both more honest with each other than anyone else in our lives. We decided not to share details that would lead to finding out who we were, in the real world. In the world outside the one we'd created together through our emails. We agreed not to search for each other on social media or google. I stuck to the promise, even after I stopped responding to his emails.

I don't even know his last name or where he lives. For all I know, I could have been talking to a middle-aged creep this whole time. Still, I know deep in my gut that isn't the case. The email conversations were always age appropriate and never made me feel uncomfortable. Our writing even aged with both of us. Going from silly rantings of tweens to deeper conversations of teens. I knew I was safe with Ender.

We told each other our deepest fears and darkest secrets and didn't want to risk losing our anonymous confidant. We've been emailing back and forth for the past five years. Sometimes just once a day. Sometimes every other day. More often than not, it was back-and-forth conversations all day long. That is, until last summer; when Ender made a confession, and I stopped responding to his emails altogether.

I must have dozed off eventually because I woke up to the bus driver announcing that we'd arrived at the Easton station.

I'm here. I've made it.

My new life can start and I can leave people like Ender—along with the drama and heartache of it all—in the past. I can develop new relationships and move on. I can heal my broken heart, the one I broke all on my own. People will see me for what I want them to see, without the scars of my past so prominently on display.

Everyone is shuffling around the bus, gathering their things, and making their way to the front. I pull my backpack onto my lap and dig out my phone. No new text messages and no missed calls. I'm not surprised. It's not as-if I expected Mom to check in on me. Who knows if she even remembers that I was supposed to be leaving for college today? Or if she even remembers I got into college.

Standing, I pull down the single black suitcase I've brought with me from the overhead storage. It's a good-sized suitcase, but it's scratched to hell. It contains almost my entire life. A few dozen items of clothing, a set of new bed sheets I splurged on, my only other pair of shoes, and a small bag of cheap drugstore toiletries and makeup.

I make my way off the bus, step into the warm sun and, oh my god, the *humidity.* The thin t-shirt I'm wearing, which was already damp with sweat, clings to me instantly. It's like standing in a sauna after running a 5k. Humidity like this didn't exist back home on the coast of California. If the weather is going to be unbearable, I need to find a second-hand store. I only own one pair of shorts.

I wipe sweat from my neck and move onto the last part of my journey to my new life—finding the local bus stop. Conveniently, it's right out in front of the main bus station. I find a spot on a low rock wall to sit under the shade of a tree. It's only a few degrees cooler in the shade, but I'll take it over baking in the sun. I've got about an hour of waiting before the next bus that's stopping at the college arrives. The school is only a few miles away, but I don't feel like walking down the road with my suitcase in this heat. Waiting for another bus, it is.

Luckily, I convinced my advisor to let me start classes during the summer quarter. It meant explaining my living situation and the Mom situation, but thankfully the advisor didn't ask too many questions once she had the Cliff Notes version. Having a bed and a place to call, mostly my own, will be worth spending the summer in class. Plus, I'm hoping arriving now, in June instead of August with all the other incoming freshmen, means a better selection of jobs available. In a town like Easton, with a population of less than five thousand, made up of mostly college students—I can't imagine there are a lot of options to begin with. A job is at the top of my priorities list. The scholarship I received doesn't quite cover everything I'll need to survive and definitely doesn't cover any luxuries or fun.

I take in my surroundings for the first time as I cool off. This whole town is straight out of a Gilmore Girls episode. None of the shops or restaurants appear to be chains, and there are more people jogging and riding bikes than driving cars. All the businesses appear to be locally owned and I don't recognize any of the names. Across the street is a sports shop, a clothing store where everything looks out of my budget, a bakery, and a drugstore which clearly isn't a typical CVS or Rite Aide. The sign above it actually just reads "Drugstore". The busiest place on the block is a diner. My stomach growls, admonishing me for not having eaten since four this morning.

There must be some snacks in my backpack somewhere. A half-empty bag of hot chips sits at the bottom of my bag that I fish out and start devouring. Before I know it, my mouth is on fire and when I go to chug from my water bottle, it's empty. A vague memory of passing a water fountain walking over here comes to mind. Needing immediate relief for my burning mouth, I throw on my backpack, grab the empty water bottle, and start the hunt. When the shiny silver fountain comes into view, I rush over and start filling my bottle. After chugging half the first fill and filling it again, I cup one hand under the water to splash my face and ease the salty taste of sweat. If the fountain stream was bigger, I swear I'd dunk my entire head in it just to cool off.

I've been standing at this fountain too long. I turn around to head back to my shade and my suitcase. Except... there is no longer a suitcase in the shade of the tree.

Oh. My. God.

How could I have been so stupid? I never leave my belongings unattended. I know better.

Great, the heat is frying my brain.

I rush to the tree, looking around. My suitcase is definitely gone. There's no one else waiting at the bus stop. My heart sinks as I drop to the grass and tears start streaming down my face, completely out of my control. Practically everything I own is in my suitcase. There wasn't much in there, but it's all I have. I think of the new bed sheets. I've been dreaming of crawling into those new sheets for weeks. All of my savings won't even be enough to replace everything. Between the hiccups I now have from trying to control my sobs, I try to remind myself that I still have my backpack. And in my backpack is my cell phone, laptop, and jewelry box. I was at least smart enough to keep my most valuable items in my backpack and keep a better eye on it.

"Um, are you okay?"

Pulling my face from my hands, I look up to where the deep voice came from. I find the most incredible hazel eyes looking down at me from a tall, toned, and stupidly gorgeous guy who looks to be about my age. Instantly embarrassed, I wipe the tears from my face. The stranger is standing perfectly in front of the sun, so it's casting a halo of light around him. He looks like an angel. A sun-tanned, dark-haired, chiseled angel.

"I'm fine," I say, trying to wipe the last of the tears from my face. "I'm just an idiot."

"And why are you an idiot?"

"I left my luggage here while I filled up my water bottle and now it's gone."

"Oh! That was yours? I saw Jesse take it."

"Jesse? Who's Jesse!?" I say.

I'm practically shouting at him with excitement and a bit of anger at whomever this Jesse character is who stole my bag.

He lets out a small chuckle. In response to my anger, my excitement, or my hysterics, I'm not quite sure which. His laugh is deep, throaty, and incredibly sexy.

"Come with me," he says.

The stranger moves toward the main greyhound bus area I came from. I jump up and follow behind him eagerly, not caring I'm a hot sweaty mess—no, a *crying* hot sweaty mess. I find myself staring at his ass. His jeans are just tight enough to show the curves of it. Moving my gaze up, I take in his sculpted shoulders and toned arms that completely fill his shirt sleeves. There's a hint of a tattoo peeking out at the bottom of his rolled-up shirt sleeve on his left bicep. The tall, handsome stranger leads me back toward the ticket booth and starts talking to the guy behind the window.

"Hey Jesse, I found the owner of that luggage you grabbed from out front."

The ticket taker, a guy who also looks about my age with short curly brown hair and intensely broad shoulders, responds, but I can't hear what he says. He disappears only to reappear seconds later through a side door, pulling my beat-up suitcase behind him. This Jesse guy doesn't just have broad shoulders, he's huge all over. He's well over six feet tall and must be more than twice my weight, but he still looks very fit somehow. If I had to guess, he's an athlete of some sort, maybe a wrestler or football player. He's nowhere near as handsome as the guy who brought me over here, but he's cute. His face has a boyish quality in contrast to his very manly body.

I squeal in delight at seeing my possessions again.

"Oh, Thank God! You, Jesse, are my new hero," I say.

"Awe don't thank me. I just held it back here for you. Henry was the true hero finding you."

Jesse hands off my suitcase and gives Henry a fist bump–then disappears behind the door again, into his booth. I grip my luggage firmly and bring it extra close to my body. I am not letting it out of my sight again.

"Thank you, Henry, was it?" I ask, turning to the handsome stranger. Who, I guess, isn't quite a stranger anymore now that I know his name.

"Yeah, that's me... and you are..."

Henry smiles and sticks out his hand. I put my hand into his outstretched one. His hand is warm and envelops mine completely. My whole body responds to his touch. It's almost as if my skin has been waiting for this specific person's skin to make contact with it. I know my cheeks are red, and I can't blame the sun. After too long, I pull myself together to respond to him.

"Madison. Thank you again, so much! I don't know what I would do if this suitcase was gone forever."

He pulls his hand away like I've burned him and now I'm self-conscious my hands are sweaty, or I held his for too long. Great, now he thinks I'm a freak.

"Yeah, I'm sure having to buy all new clothes for vacation would suck," he says, not quite looking me in the eye.

"Oh, I'm not on vacation. I'm moving here. This is basically everything I own," I respond, giving my suitcase a small spin. "I start classes at Pinehurst next week."

The end of my last sentence is hurried because I'm worried I'm sharing too much information, too quickly, with someone I don't even know. Maybe I'm just being paranoid, but I feel like he's suddenly looking at me differently.

Henry clears his throat and runs one hand across his chiseled jaw, which has a healthy five o'clock shadow. A desire to know what that stubble would feel like against the delicate skin of my inner thighs comes out of nowhere. Whoa... where did these thoughts come from? I never lust after guys like this, especially not guys I just met. It must be the heat. I clear my throat and wipe sweat from the back of my neck. It feels like it just got five degrees hotter, and I didn't think it was possible.

Henry pushes his hands in his front pockets, making his toned arms look even more muscular, and breaks the silence.

"Oh cool. I go there too. Umm, maybe I'll see you around campus."

Okay, am I imagining things or is he disappointed I'm not just a tourist? Or did he notice me practically drooling over him and has a girlfriend lurking around somewhere? It seems like he's trying to end this conversation and get away from me.

"Yeah, maybe. Well, thanks again so much for helping me track down my suitcase."

I give him a small wave and start heading toward my spot on the rock wall to wait for the bus. The conversation and interaction got awkward, so I made my exit quickly. Glancing at my phone, I see I still have forty minutes left until the bus arrives, even after the excitement. I try to get as comfortable as possible in the heat. I pop my headphones back on and turn up my music, trying to calm my racing heart.

CHAPTER TWO

HENDERSON

Madison! Madison? Why did the gorgeous girl with golden eyes and beautiful brown hair have to be named Madison? She's not my Madison, my Mads, she couldn't be. Why, when I've been trying hard not to think about everything I've fucked up in the past year, does the mysterious, beautiful stranger have to be named Madison?

I've been good. I've been going to work and football practice, getting ready for classes. I haven't emailed her in months, so I've only thought about her half the time I used to. But now–now my thoughts are consumed by her. Rather than creepily standing here and continuing to watch her walk away, I turn around and head for the ticket booth.

Jesse is sitting behind the plexiglass window feverishly typing away on his phone with a concerned look on his face. I tap my knuckles on the window to get his attention.

"What's up?" he says, not looking up.

"Dude, what if I was a customer?"

"You're not. What's going on?"

Jesse has been my best friend since third grade when he moved here from Virginia. One day, halfway through the year, he showed up in Ms. Beverley's class. There was an empty desk next to me, so that's where the teacher had him sit. He was shy, and I wasn't. As soon as he sat down, I practically shouted.

"Hi, I'm Henderson, but my friends call me Henry!"

There was a hole in one of his shoes, and the jeans he wore were dirty and tattered. It was cold enough outside to snow, and he didn't have a jacket. When it was time for recess, I left my jacket inside so he wouldn't be the only one without one. A few other kids and I played kickball, and I invited him to join us. He joined us but didn't crack jokes or horse around with the rest of us. Back then, he was painfully shy. Sometimes I miss that shyness because it's definitely gone now.

When he didn't show up with a jacket for the rest of that week, I brought an extra one from home on Monday. Mom dropped me at school early so I could place it on his chair. That way, the other kids would think maybe he'd left it there over the weekend. She said this way it wouldn't draw attention to him or embarrass him. Third-grade me didn't understand how he'd be embarrassed, but I did as she said. Mom says I've always been sensitive and cared about making sure other people felt seen, loved, and included.

When he arrived at school, he didn't say anything, but he put the jacket on before heading out to recess. We've been best friends ever since, but we still haven't talked about the jacket.

Turns out Jesse moved here to live with his grandma because his mom was sick, but his grandma wasn't exactly the best guardian. We were much older when I learned when he said his mom was sick, he meant she was struggling with mental illness and not accepting treatment. Things eventually got so bad at his mom's house child services stepped in and placed him with his grandma. However, they failed to ensure his grandma was capable of giving him everything he needed.

My mom, our friend's parents, and his girlfriend Taylor's parents all supported Jesse in any way they could over the years. He never complained about living with his grandma or the hand he was dealt. Even if her house did smell because she had something like ten cats who all pissed anywhere they wanted. Let's just say sleepovers were never at Jesse's growing up.

His grandma passed away a few years ago. We thought he would have to move away again. Jesse knew he had an aunt he'd met only once somewhere in Illinois. Thankfully, our friend Emmett's parents worked some magic, aka threw around some money and became his guardians.

Emmett, our other best friend, can come off as a bit of a dick when you first meet him. Especially being the son of one of the richest men in town. Really, he's a big teddy bear but ask a girl he's hooked up with and you'll get a different answer. He got even softer when his parents had his little sister, Emily. She's eight now and Emmett spoils her more than their parents do. No one is looking forward to when she's old enough to date. Emmett will definitely go full big brother mode on any punk kid who dares look at her.

"Are you breaking your fingers texting Taylor?" I ask.

"Yeah. She's moving into her dorm today. She wants to celebrate tonight before classes start on Monday. You down?"

"Definitely. Just let me know the plan and I'll pick you guys up."

"You gonna invite the pretty brunette?" he asks, his attention still mostly on his phone

"Madison?"

"Oh, Maaaaaadison is it?" he sings "Yeah, her."

Jesse doesn't have the same gut-punch reaction to her name the way I did. Jesse doesn't know a thing about my Mads. No one does. I thought about telling Taylor, but I didn't want to ask her to keep it from Jesse. It's not that I'm embarrassed, I'm not. It's just my relationship with Mads is special and has an almost magical quality to it because it only exists in my email inbox. Bringing it out into my real life, telling my friends... I was so afraid it would be tainted somehow by the harsh realities of life. Somehow, I still managed to let my real life ruin the life I had with Mads.

"No way man. The last thing I need right now is to get mixed up with someone new before they even start hearing the rumors. I'm out of here. My shift just finished, and I gotta beat Mom home and do the dishes."

"Later," he says with a half-assed wave, still not looking up from his phone.

Shaking my head at him, even though he doesn't see me, I back away from the window, heading to my truck in the employee parking lot. I don't work at the bus station with Jesse. I work across the street at the local sports store. All the employees of the shops around here get to use the bus station's employee parking lot since none of them have their own. Mr. Grissom, the owner of Grissom's Sports, was one of the few people in town who'd even entertained the idea of hiring me when I started looking for a job at the beginning of the year. No one else wanted the attention of hiring the troublemaker.

Mr. Grissom didn't care though, but Mr. Grissom is an asshole and doesn't care about much. He especially doesn't care about the town gossip. When the rumors died down and more of the real story came out, I probably could have found a better job, but decided to stay loyal to the sports store. It's easy work and the hours and pay are decent, plus Mr. Grissom works with my school and football schedule.

As I go to pull out of the parking lot, I see Madison sitting on the rock wall under a tree with her suitcase clenched between her legs. Against my better judgment, I make a snap decision to pull over in front of her and honk.

She looks up curiously and pulls her headphones off her ears, staring at me.

"Are you waiting for the bus?" I ask, leaning over the bench seat to shout at her through the open window.

"Yeah." She nods, yelling back, "The one headed for campus is supposed to be here soon."

"Do you want a ride? It's really no problem, I'll pass the school on my way home. If the bus schedule says the next bus is supposed to be here in half an hour, don't expect it for at least an hour. There's only one local bus here and the bus driver, Shannon, talks a LOT at every stop. Plus, I know she doesn't look like it, but my truck has excellent air conditioning."

Okay, dude, you're rambling and sound a little creepy. You're coming off as way too eager to get her in your car. Dial it back just a little and remember... you don't want any new relationships and this girl is not a replacement for Mads.

But somehow, with that last bit about the air conditioning, I've got her attention. She bites her bottom lip and looks like she's trying to decide if I'm an ax murderer or not. Holy hell, why did she have to do that? Does she even know how incredibly sexy she looks when she has her lip tucked into her mouth like that? After a few more seconds, she stands and starts dragging her suitcase toward my car. I jump out and walk around my truck to help her put it in the back. She hesitates before handing the luggage over to me, a nervous look on her face.

"I promise not to let anyone steal it from my truck," I say.

She laughs and passes me the suitcase. Her laugh is beautiful and I want to make her do it again. I place her luggage in the truck bed, then open the passenger door for her. She looks at me curiously as I stand with the door open, but she gets in and puts her backpack on the floorboard. When she's safely tucked inside, I shut the door.

Should I not have opened the door? Was it too much? It's not like we're on a date. I'm just giving her a ride. I push the confusion out of my mind and make my way around the car, sliding into the driver's side. Madison is leaning forward, her face practically pushed against the air conditioning vent, her eyes closed. I let out a short laugh and turn the air to a cooler setting. She sits back and exhales loudly as I pull away from the curb.

"So, you'll be living in the dorms?" I ask, trying to keep the conversation light. Trying and failing to keep my eyes on the road and not on her.

"Yup."

Her focus is on the town as we drive down Main Street. I take advantage of the red light ahead and look at her.

Her soft brown hair is no longer piled on top of her head and drops a few inches below her shoulders. She must have pulled it down when she got into the car. It's not a dark brown, it's more the color of an acorn. When the sun hits it, some strands appear golden. They look natural, not the way a girl's hair looks after she's been to the salon. I noticed earlier she's kind of tall for a girl. If I had to guess, I would say she's about five-eight or five-nine. The perfect height that she could easily lay her head on my shoulder if we hugged. It's a nice thought.

Although I think my favorite feature of hers has to be her lips. When I saw her chewing on her bottom lip earlier, I was so incredibly turned on. Her lips are plump but not that big, and they look velvety soft. Like if I ran my thumb across them, they'd feel like icing on a cupcake. I wonder if they taste like icing, maybe strawberry or vanilla? She doesn't appear to be wearing any lipstick. They're just naturally a rosy color. Plump, pink, cupcake icing lips. I can't take my eyes off them and imagine how they'd feel wrapped around–.

"Do you live in the dorms, too?"

Startled by her sudden talking again, I flinch just a little.

I hope she didn't notice me staring at her lips. I am an asshole. She'd think I was too if she knew what I was just imagining. I turn on my blinker to make a right turn toward campus and answer her, shaking my head and the thoughts of her soft lips out of it.

"No, I still live at home with my mom. It's cheaper and my mom needs me."

I don't know why I shared that last part with her.

"Oh," is all she says, but she's looking at me now. I can see her out of the corner of my eye.

Campus is only a few blocks away now. We talk easily for the few minutes it takes to get there, sharing our majors and classes. I'm disappointed when I realize we won't have any classes together. She's an English major which makes me even more uneasy because I think that's the path my Mads would have taken. My Mads always avoided the subject of college. I'm not even sure if she decided she wanted to go to college. Maybe she's moving into the dorms at *her* college right now, exploring the campus and finding all the best places to sit and write in the afternoons. My day-dreaming takes a dark turn when I think of the possibility of her meeting a guy, just like the Madison in my car, met me. The idea of her meeting some random college guy and falling in love has me white-knuckling the steering wheel. I try to rein in my thoughts and be present in the car.

The Madison in my car is a good distraction from the Mads I shouldn't be thinking about. As much as I keep repeating in my head—*right now is not the time for dating*—I can't help but notice how comfortable I feel around her. How much I'm dreading this car ride ending.

I pull up as close to the dorms as I can and put the truck in park. I don't make a move to get out because I don't want this to be over. We continue chatting even after I park. Madison is telling me about a documentary she watched on the bus ride here and a documentary has never sounded more appealing to me than it does being described by the beautiful girl sitting next to me. She's just finished telling me the last details of the film and we're just goofily smiling at each other in the silence now.

Madison looks around and her eyes go wide.

"Oh my gosh, how long have we been parked at the school? I am so sorry, I just kept talking," she says, reaching for the truck's door handle.

"Only a few minutes," I lie.

It's been nearly twenty, but I didn't want her to ever stop talking. We both get out of my truck and I walk around it, getting her suitcase out of the back. It's only summer quarter, but there are still quite a few students on campus moving into the dorms early. I place her suitcase wheels on the ground and start pushing it toward her. Our fingers brush and my body heats the same way it did when we shook hands. I look up and see zero reaction from her. Good, she must not have even noticed our fingers touched. This is all just in *my* head.

We're both now standing on the sidewalk awkwardly. Her clutching her suitcase as if someone could snatch it again at any moment and me with my hands pushed into my front pockets and staring down at my shoes.

"Well, I'm sure you want to find your dorm room and get settled in," I say, breaking the silence.

"Yeah, I probably should."

Madison looks up at the dorm buildings. She looks nervous and I find myself wanting to wrap my arms around her and tell her everything is going to be amazing.

"Thank you so much for the ride," she says.

"No problem. I'll uh, see you around maybe?"

"Yeah maybe. Thanks again for the ride. Bye Henry," she says as she starts walking away.

I briefly considered asking for her number but remember I shouldn't be involving anyone else in my mess of a life and she doesn't seem like the type of girl you could date casually. She seems like the type of girl you fall madly in love with. The type of girl who, if you get just one taste, you're addicted. Besides, she's already at the building, pulling the doors open and disappearing.

I jump back into my truck and push my face toward the air vent just how Madison did, except I'm used to the humidity in Easton. I'm sweating for entirely different reasons.

CHAPTER THREE

MADISON

After checking in and getting my dorm room key, it only takes me a few minutes to track down my room.

Fourth floor, sixth door from the stairs.

There are no elevators and having only one suitcase is currently a blessing. Pinehurst is a small campus and dorms are limited to incoming freshmen only. Which means I'll have to move into off-campus housing next year and live with even more people. But, that's next year's problem and right now I just have to worry about sharing the dorm room with one other person.

I push open the door to my new home. The space is bigger than I expected. I'd looked up photos online and may have even stalked a few previous students on social media. Thank you internet for giving me the ability to know what my surroundings will be like before I'm thrust into a new situation. The anxieties I get occasionally, thank you as well.

Standing in the doorway, I'm able to scan the entire place. There are two twin beds on opposite sides of the room. Wooden bed frames raise the beds high enough that they've tucked desks underneath each of them. The built-in ladder at the foot of the bed is needed to get to the actual bed part. Beneath a large window, two nightstand style dressers with four drawers each separate the beds. I notice there's only one real closet in the corner of the room, but it's huge.

By the look of things, my roommate has already been here. Half the closet is filled with clothes and shoes, and the bed on the left is already made with pink bedding. No sight of the roommate herself yet. Kitchens and bathrooms are communal by each dorm building floor, so maybe she's off exploring them. There are still a few boxes she has left to unpack. She must be coming back at some point. I take advantage of having the room to myself and peek around a bit. Her clothes hanging in the closet consist of dresses, florals, and pastels. Her style is much cuter than my own. The shoe collection in the closet is more ballet flats and colored converse than any other style of shoe. A girly girl for sure, but practical, not a single pair of heels in sight.

I'm not fashion challenged, but my wardrobe is incredibly basic. Anything my mom bought me before she became less than motherly, I've outgrown. I couldn't afford the newest styles and trends with my meager after-school job paychecks, let alone the designer brands that girls back at my high school all wore. Jeans and basic T-shirts are what I usually go for. Otherwise, it's simple black leggings or short flowy dresses. If you wear the basics, you don't have to worry about other girls questioning what designer you are or aren't wearing. Hopefully, the clothing brand judgment is something everyone left back in high school.

I was supposed to have the room to myself until the start of the year, but I got notified a week ago I'd have a summer roommate after all. It was so last minute that even though I had my new roommates contact info—I didn't have time to email her. She sent me an email a few days ago that made it seem like she's genuinely excited to meet me and be roommates. I hope her expectations aren't too high, because I don't have a lot of experience with friendships.

To: madisoncartwright11@gmail.com
From: taylornottinaturner@gmail.com
Date: June 5th 12:31
Subject: Your New Roomie

Hi Madison, I'm Taylor!

I'm your new roommate at Pinehurst and I can't wait to meet you! I'll be moving in on Friday. When will you be moving in?

I'm a local in Easton, but moved here when I was 13. I've lived all over. Montana was probably my favorite state to live in before I landed in Easton. But Easton definitely feels more like home than anywhere else. I'm only moving into the dorms because I am dying to get some independence and the dorms were the cheapest option! Sorry, I'm rambling.

Move-in-weekend and the first day of classes are right around the corner, so I totally get it if you don't have time to write back before then!

Just know I'm super excited to meet you!

Taylor

I pull my suitcase over to my side of the room, lay it down on the floor, and unzip it. I put away my few outfits in the nightstand drawers first. Then I throw my new bedding up onto the bed. I'll worry about that later. If I put it on now, I'll be too tempted to climb in and nap. At the bottom of my backpack is a wooden jewelry box. It's one of the most important things in my bag. It has the few very personal items I own. A silver necklace that was Dad's grandmother's. A torn and tattered photo of Dad holding me when I was about two years old. And a few other things that have become precious to me. Stacked neatly at the bottom of the box are my favorite emails from Ender. I tuck the box into the bottom drawer of the nightstand under my pajamas.

Hiding the jewelry box is done out of habit more than anything. Originally, its purpose was solely for storing those printed emails. At home, I'd even pried up one of the wooden floorboards to hide it. Mom had made it a habit of going through my room when I wasn't home, and I didn't want her to find them. Toward the end of living with her, I worried she'd find the necklace and take it–that was added to the box too.

I put my laptop on the desk, plug it in to charge and climb up to my bed to put on the new sheets. The door opens as I struggle to put the last corner in place. In walks a tiny blonde in a short floral summer dress, pink converse high tops, bright blue eyes and an even brighter smile. She's carrying a stack of books that's so tall she has to crane her neck to see around them. Our eyes meet.

"Hi! You must be Madison! I'm Taylor!" she says while unloading the stack of books onto her desk.

Should I climb down and shake her hand? Give her a hug? What is a proper greeting for someone you just moved in with? I decide to stay where I am, offering a small wave and a smile.

"Yup, that's me!"

"I hope you don't mind that I chose a side of the room before you got here. This side looks like it will get more of the early morning sun, so I took it, hoping you'd appreciate the other side of the room. Plus, in all the horror movies, the bed that's closest to the door is always the first victim and so I gave you the bed furthest from the door—"

Taylor's talking fast and animated, waving her hands around now that she's put her books down. Unintentionally, I've halfway tuned her out as she goes on about her favorite horror movies. She's small, like 5 feet tall at most. She's talking a mile a minute, but her voice is kind of soothing, with its pitch raising and lowering with her excitement.

I realize she's stopped talking and is staring at me. Shit. I think she asked me a question.

"I'm sorry. What was that?" I ask. Here's to hoping I haven't already offended my new roommate.

"Oh, I just asked if you needed help bringing in any more stuff."

Suddenly, I feel a little self-conscious about having so few things.

"Um, no, this is it. Wanted to travel light since it was so far," I lie.

"Totally get it! I moved around a ton when I was younger, it wasn't until I moved here, and we knew we wouldn't have to keep moving, that I finally started feeling like I could collect things. Didn't have to worry about having to fit my stuff into only a few boxes anymore, ya know?"

Man, this girl can talk, but it's oddly refreshing to have so much friendly chatter. I've spent so much time alone the past few years that I think I'll enjoy having a roommate. Having someone constant in my life. I hope her eagerness to get along and be friends is genuine.

"So, what's your major? Mine's psychology. I think I want to be a counselor of some sort but haven't fully decided. That's what the next four years are for right, figuring out who we want to be? That and having a lot of fun. I mean, I can only have as much fun as someone who's basically married can have–" She laughs.

I raise my eyebrows at her in curiosity. "Married?"

"That's what our friends joke, at least. I met my boyfriend the first week after I moved here, and we've basically been inseparable since. I promise, we still know how to have fun. You'll probably get to meet him soon. He was planning on stopping by."

I'm liking this girl more and more as she continues talking. She makes me feel calm, which is strange. Her energy is a lot more intense than I'm used to. Plus, she's pocket-sized with a smile that's practically permanent, which makes her even easier to adore.

"My major is English. Writing is pretty much the only thing I've ever loved. Well, almost the only thing."

Thankfully, she doesn't press me to explain what I mean. Something starts chirping in her pocket, and she pulls out her cell phone and answers it with a smile.

"Hey babe."

Must be her boyfriend on the phone. I don't want to look like I'm eavesdropping, so I continue arranging the sheets and comforter on my bed. In our small dorm room, I can't help but hear her side of the conversation.

"Oh yay, perfect! We'll meet you there at eight then, and don't worry about coming over to help me unpack, I'm actually almost done. I was too excited, so I got an early start."

Taylor's silent, but she has her phone tucked between her shoulder and her ear as she breaks down some of the empty boxes.

"Yes, 'we', my new roomie, remember! She's new in town, so I doubt she knows anyone else to hang out with tonight, and I think you guys are gonna love her!"

My ears prick as I wonder what plans my new roommate is volunteering me for and how I'm going to get out of them. How am I supposed to say no to a girl like her? She's all bubble gum and rainbows and with a smile that bright, I have a feeling her sad and disappointed faces are debilitating.

The phone she was talking on gets set on her desk and she turns her attention back to me as I'm climbing down from my bed.

"So, some friends and I are meeting up at the barn to celebrate before classes start Monday and you're coming with!"

It's a statement, not a question.

"The barn?" I ask, curious but cautious.

I knew having a roommate would mean I would have to dodge a few invites to parties when my social battery was low. I'm not sure this was an invitation. It sounded more like a demand, but in the sweetest way possible. I want to make friends and I can already tell I want to be Taylor's friend, but today was already such a long day.

"Yea, our friend Emmett's dad, is like the richest man in Easton. He owns this barn just a few miles away. We've been using it as a hangout for a while. I guess Emmett's dad figures it keeps us from trying to get into the bars and it's got a finished loft bedroom, so Emmett usually crashes there half the time. It will be fun but low key, I promise. You have to come!"

I don't want to piss her off on the first day, but I don't feel up to a party and definitely not one that sounds like it will only be a few people. I can't blend in with a small party of close friends. They for sure would ask me a ton of questions, and I haven't decided how to answer all the typical new girl questions. There's been a war going on in my mind for weeks now. Trying to debate what information I share with the people I meet here and what information I keep buried deep down inside me forever.

"Ya know, I really want to get settled in and it was such a long day today. But I promise I'll come to the next one."

Taylor has a pouty look but concedes.

"Alright, I understand, but you'll love my friends, so you definitely need to meet them soon. I know they'll love you too!"

Taylor unpacks for a little while longer. I excuse myself to go to the bookstore before it closes. It's almost sunset but the heat and humidity are still lingering. Thank God our dorm rooms have air conditioning.

I make my way across the campus courtyard toward the bookstore. The campus isn't too big, but the courtyard is beautiful. There are tons of open grass areas and lots of big white oak trees. They give the perfect shady areas that I can't wait to spend afternoons under—writing and studying when the weather gets nicer.

When I find the library, I almost gasp. It's a beautiful two-story brick building with huge floor-to-ceiling windows that let in the perfect amount of the evening sun. There are big tables for studying and rows of computers on the first floor. The second floor, open and visible from the first, has small lounge sets tucked into the rows and rows of books. They look as if they'd make the perfect little reading nooks to curl up in. I inhale deeply, sighing at the comforting scent of the books. I'm tempted to drop into one of the plush brown leather chairs and start writing, but I know the place closes soon and I still need to find a few books for my classes.

Luckily, the books I need are all available in the re-sell section, so I grab them and head up to the register. What I assume is a student is behind the desk, a large circular area in the middle of the first floor. I place my stack of books on the counter and smile at him. The name tag on his shirt says Adam. He's tall but not as tall as Henry, with dirty blonde hair, deep blue eyes like the Pacific Ocean and a clean-shaven face. Cute, I think to myself, but ordinary. I'm not sure why I'm even comparing him to Henry or why I can't seem to get Henry out of my thoughts.

The guy behind the counter—Adam—smiles back at me, but there's something unsettling about the way he's staring at me. So intently, unnecessarily leaning over to grab each book before he scans it. I take out my student account card and pay for the books, doing the mental math on how much will be left for other supplies.

"Do you know if the school has a jobs board of any kind?" I ask him as he's scanning my card, trying to break the awkward silence of him staring at me.

"Yeah, it's on the school's website, but all the summer jobs are probably taken. Your best bet is to walk down Main Street looking for help-wanted signs. If you want to give me your number, I can let you know if I hear of any new ones."

He leans on the counter and I realize he has the perfect view right down my shirt. I'm not sure if I should take him seriously or not, but I give him a half smile, only raising one corner of my mouth.

"Thanks, that's sweet, but I'm sure I'll manage," I say and grab my books as he hands me my receipt.

Before he can press the suggestion further, I turn and leave.

When I get back to the dorm room with my books, I'm relieved that Taylor's already left. I don't know if I would have won out against her sweetness and sad eyes if she started asking me to go to the barn again. I put my books on my desk and leave again to track down something to eat. I'm just now realizing I've eaten nothing but a few chips since before I got on the bus and I'm starving.

I end up grabbing a sandwich and a salad from the dining hall, and sit down to eat them at one of the indoor tables. No way am I going back out into that heat when there's air conditioning inside. Going back to my dorm room to eat doesn't feel quite right because we never discussed food in the room rules.

I pull my headphones up over my ears and turn my music on from my phone. There are only a few people lingering around the dining hall, but putting on headphones seems like a good way to keep to myself. Small talk with strangers isn't something I have the capacity for right now. There's been enough of that for one day.

I scroll social media on my phone, but after a few minutes, without even thinking much about it, I open my old email account and scroll all the way to last summer and start reading an email at random.

To: madisrad@gmail.com

From: ravensfan4lyfe@gmail.com
Date: June 02 10:21 PM
Subject: Re: Summer Plans

I don't really have any summer plans. This is probably my last summer of freedom. Hopefully, by next summer I'll be training with a college football team.

Mostly I plan on hanging with my friends, working a summer job to make some extra cash, and of course... emailing you.

What are your plans? Besides emailing your favorite person in the world, me.

I'm actually at a party right now at my friend's place. It's the first one of the summer. There must be like 100 kids here. Everyone from our high school's upper class is here pounding cheap beer, playing beer pong, and making out with the same people they've been making out with for years.

To clarify, I am making out with no one. That girl I told you about still get's extra flirty around me, but tonight for some reason she's decided I'm not worth the trouble and has been all over one of my best friends.

But Mads, I would much rather be sitting in a coffee shop reading or writing or even better listening to you read me poems. Don't get me wrong, I love my friends. I am lucky to have the group of friends I do, but... lately I'm over it all. Lately, I cannot wait to get out of this tiny town. Does that make me a cliche?

Your Best Friend,
Ender

I remember when Ender started signing his emails, *your best friend*. We were both fifteen, and I admitted I'd never had a best friend. I explained it's not that I didn't have any friends, I just never had best friends.

When I was younger, I had a hard time fitting in. There was more than one run-in with the mean girls. As I got older, there were other obstacles. Best friends wanted to do things like have sleepovers. That was something I couldn't do, not with my mom. Ender knew not to push after that explanation and instead let me know he was now my best friend. He never let me forget it, and from then on, signed off every email, *your best friend*. I started signing off on all my emails, *your BFF*, shortly after, and I meant it.

Ender was my best friend, and I hoped I was truly his.

Having a best friend you'd never met in real life was strange sometimes. A friend whose voice you'd never heard, laugh you'd never heard. Touch you'd never felt and hugs you'd never experienced. I didn't even know much about what he looked like. Still, there were certain things about our unique relationship I wouldn't trade for anything. Being able to be so honest and vulnerable with him being top of the list.

After I finish my sandwich and throw away my trash, I head toward the dorms. It's only eight p.m. but I'm exhausted. I put on some pajamas and crawl up into my bed, planning to read one of my newly acquired textbooks until I fall asleep. I want to be up bright and early to start my job hunting.

Chapter Four

Henderson

"Potatoooooo!" I yell, coming into the house and turning off the alarm. Before I can even get the last number punched in, my sweet eight-year-old corgi is standing at my feet excitedly shaking her stump of a tail and pawing at my ankles. I crouch down and give her ears a good rub as she tries to give me kisses.

I've got about forty-five minutes to get the dishes done before Mom gets home. I turn on some music and get to work. As the last plate is going in the dishwasher, I hear the front door unlock. I wipe my hands on a dish towel and go to greet my mom.

She looks happier than she did this time last year, despite working all day at the hospital. I take the grocery bags from her hands and give her a kiss on the cheek.

"How was work?" I ask.

"Oh, the usual. How was Grissoms?"

I contemplate telling her about meeting Madison and giving her a ride to campus. I don't because Mom will just ask a million questions. The questions will lead to her worrying. I can hear her now–*Henderson, is now a good time for girls? It may jeopardize your future. And honey, you have such a bright future.*

"Slow. I was gonna shower and then hang out at the barn."

"Do you want dinner first? I bought stuff to make spaghetti!"

"Yum, yes, please!"

"Okay, you get cleaned up and I'll get it started," and before I can even make it out of the kitchen, I hear her add, "But promise me you will not drink tonight, not even one beer."

"Mom," I groan.

"Henderson, I mean it, you're on probation and that means no getting into trouble."

She doesn't say it to scold me or in a harsh way. She says it with concern and worry in her eyes. I hold on to my mom's shoulders gently, making sure she's looking me in the eye. She knows I wouldn't risk it. She knows I don't drink or do drugs. I wouldn't do anything to put us back in the spotlight.

"Mom, I know. I promise." I kiss her cheek and head upstairs to shower.

When I get out of the shower, I pull on a clean pair of underwear, and lay on my bed on top of the blankets. I grab my phone off the nightstand and start scrolling through sports news. My phone vibrates in my hand as a text comes in.

Jesse: You inviting the hot chick from the bus stop tonight?
Me: No
Jesse: Boring. So can you pick up me and Tay in an hour?
Jesse: We're at my place.
Me: Yup. I'll be there.
Jesse: Bitchin.

Jesse says the weirdest shit. He doesn't care about what slang is popular. He's always using and coming up with the funniest words. It makes me realize, sometimes I care too much. I've always cared about being what others expect of me. It started when I was young. Dad would tell me I was going to be an NFL quarterback one day. Playing for the Ravens has been our shared dream for as long as I can remember. Or, at least, it used to be. He built up these dreams for me. I tried to take the path that made sense for someone who could achieve those dreams.

It's probably why I have never once shared my passion for writing with anyone besides Mads. I miss that a lot. Having someone I could share those hidden parts of me with. I've barely written anything that wasn't a school assignment since she stopped responding to me. It's not that I was writing for her, but she gave me the confidence to write.

Getting up, I rummage through the basket of clean clothes at the end of my bed and pull out a pair of dark jeans and a gray henley. I put on the clothes and slip on my shoes. One of the best parts about Easton is, no matter how hot and humid it is during the day, the nights are cool and dry.

When I make it down to the kitchen, it smells incredible. Mom is just pulling a loaf of garlic bread out of the oven and there are already two plates filled with pasta on the kitchen counter. I take a seat and start digging in. We only ever eat in the kitchen at the breakfast bar or in the living room in front of the TV. Never in the dining room. At least since it's been just the two of us.

Mom has been cooking more often and it makes me incredibly happy. Not only because she's an amazing cook, but because I know she enjoys it. And seeing her do anything she enjoys these days is progress and proof that I did the right thing. It reinforces my knowledge that the consequences I'm suffering now are worth it. The best part is, if she doesn't want to cook, she doesn't. She does it only when the mood strikes her.

I finish dinner and rinse my plate before putting it in the sink. After saying goodbye to Mom and scratching between Potato's ears, I head out to my truck.

I only live a few blocks from campus, which was one of the many reasons I decided to keep living at home instead of in the dorms or with friends. Being there for my mom was the biggest reason. Since my dad left, I've been both more and less worried about her in different ways. She seems to be doing so much better over the past few months. She's smiling more, wearing makeup occasionally, and has even gone out to lunch with Emmett's mom a few times. Something she hadn't–no, couldn't–do over the past few years. Still, I just think it's best I stick around a little longer. It's the least I can do.

Jesse lives in the apartments across the street from campus. When I get there to pick him up, the parking lot is packed. I pull up to the curb on the street and fire off a text to him, letting him know where I'm at. I check the passenger floorboard to make sure there's no trash or water bottles in the way for when they get in. That's when I notice a folded up piece of paper. I reach over and grab it, not recognizing what it is. I open it and start reading and WHAT THE ACTUAL FUCK?

What is this? Why is it printed? Who printed it? Why is it in my car?

It's a copy of an email I sent to Mads. But it's not just any email. It's the email I fired off from my phone while I sat in the cold and empty room at the police station. Where I sat with blood on my hands and my shirt. It's the email I sent where I poured my whole damn heart out to her.

Beads of sweat collect on my forehead, my heart is pounding and my ears are ringing. My truck's passenger door opens and I jump. I quickly fold the paper back up and shove it in my front pocket as Taylor slides into the truck. She scoots to the middle of the bench seat. Jesse squeezes in after her with a six-pack of beer and a small bottle of vodka.

"Are you okay?" Taylor asks me with obvious concern in her eyes.

I've known Taylor for years and in those years she's never been one who could hide her emotions or keep herself from speaking exactly what's on her mind. It's one of my favorite qualities about her. Right now though, it's a problem.

I must have a screwed up look on my face for her to ask me that. I quickly plaster on the biggest smile I can manage and demand my heart to stop trying to jump out of my chest. I'm almost worried they can hear my heart pounding and my heavy breathing.

"All good, you just startled me," I tell her.

"Were you daydreaming about that sweet thing you gave a ride home? Don't think I didn't see you, Henry," Jesse chimes in.

Taylor looks at me and then at Jesse, eyes wide.

"What? A girl? Who is she? Do I know her?"

"It's nobody," I interrupt Taylor before she can make it all the way to twenty-one questions.

My head is still spinning from what I just found. I can't sit here and answer questions about giving Madison a ride when I know the printed out email was left behind by her. I'm still trying to figure out what the hell this all means.

"Just a girl who's new at Pinehurst and was waiting for the local bus to take her there from the Greyhound drop off. You know how the buses run, so I gave her a ride. Not a big deal. Now, mind putting on your seat belt so we can go?"

Taylor slumps in the seat, lets out a huff and puts her seatbelt on. Then dramatically crosses her arms across her chest like a toddler throwing a tantrum.

"Awe Babe, I'm sorry I didn't tell you sooner. I tried to get him to invite her tonight, and it was a no-go," Jesse assures her.

I don't know why Taylor has become so obsessed with my love life. Ever since the decision was made that I would be staying in town and going to Pinehurst, she freaks out if I even look at a girl. She's tried to set me up on more than one date I've had to decline. If she doesn't give it a rest soon, my declines will no longer be so polite.

"Well," Taylor says, patting my arm, "We're gonna have a blast tonight, regardless! To the barn!" She squeals.

We all laugh at her enthusiasm.

The barn is a huge white building that Emmett's dad let him take over a few years ago as a hang-out spot. It's not very rustic for a barn, and is likely one of the biggest ones in the country, if I were to guess. I pull the truck right into the barn through the large open doors and cut the engine. Half of it is used for us to park our cars and for Emmett to store his four wheelers. The other half has a few couches and chairs around a TV and gaming setup. There's a ping-pong table that's never been used for ping-pong since it's been here and a small kitchenette. A set of stairs leads up to a loft style bedroom where Emmett crashes from time to time and a full sized bathroom with a shower and everything. I don't think this barn has ever even had an animal in it. Emmett's mom hired decorators so everything from the rugs in front of the furniture to the hand towels in the bathroom have a bit of a *too nice for a barn* look to them.

It looks like Emmett is the only one here so far. He's lounging on the couch, playing Call of Duty and yelling at what is probably a bunch of ten-year-olds through his head set. Jesse jumps over the back of the couch and half lands on Emmett, pulling more than a few curse words out of him. Taylor walks by Emmett, ruffling his shaggy blonde hair before she takes up her usual spot in one of the oversized arm chairs. It truly could fit four or five Taylors on it. I playfully slap Emmett on the back of the head, then make my way up the stairs to the bathroom. The paper I found in my car is burning a hole in my pocket.

Once I'm safely inside the bathroom, I pull the now crumpled paper out. I carefully smooth it out on my leg, noticing just how worn and fragile it is. This time I manage to keep my heart beat at an almost normal rate and take the time to look deliberately at it. The paper looks like it was printed just a few days after it was emailed. And as I suspected, it was definitely printed from Mads email account. An email from Ender to Mads.

I chose not to use Henderson or Henry when I posted my short stories in the groups where Madison and I met. Ender seemed like a good enough pen name. When Mads and I started emailing back and forth, I never told her my real name or the nickname my friends use.

One time my dad caught me writing a fantasy story about a dragon who fell in love with a princess. I was like ten and it was a stupid concept, but he laughed at me and said writing dumb stories wasn't going to get me to the NFL.

I only ever wrote in secret after that, so I guess keeping my name as Ender was a way of protecting that part of me. It was a way of protecting the person I was with Madison. Eventually, Ender started to feel like my alter ego. He was the man I wanted to be, but wasn't quite brave enough to actually be. I guess it wouldn't take a rocket scientist to see Ender could be a nickname for Henderson, but almost everyone calls me Henry. That's how Madison met me today, as Henry.

I know what having this email printed in my hands must mean, but it doesn't mean I'm not struggling to reconcile it. My brain just doesn't want to make sense of it.

It means the girl in my truck today wasn't just a Madison, but was my Mads. I carefully fold the paper and push it back into my pocket and sit on the closed toilet seat, leaning forward and putting my head between my legs. I think I might pass out.

How is this possible? How is she here? And holy shit, she's even more gorgeous than I've been picturing her all these years. As the reality of the situation sets in, the more logical and practical questions come to mind. Like, did she know who I was? There's no way, right? It was all too coincidental running into her at the bus station. I'm relieved to know she's alive and seems to be doing well despite her break down at losing her luggage.

Over the past ten months, I've had a million scenarios in my head. Some of which were outlandish and purely to make me feel better about the obvious rejection I'd received. But here we are. In the same state, same town, going to the same damn college. I guess her presence here and the fact she appears healthy means she truly did just have a visceral reaction to that email. The email she printed.

I gather myself and wash my hands before I make my way down to the rest of the group. If I'm up here any longer, someone will start making crude jokes at my expense. When I make it downstairs, Emmett and Jesse have already cracked open beers and Taylor has a red cup in her hands. If I know Taylor, the red cup is filled with a lot of vodka and very little orange juice. Taylor likes to have fun and I don't fault her for that. She grew up with strict parents. It makes sense she likes to let loose when she can.

I settle down into one of the other oversized armchairs and try to pay attention to the conversation. Emmett's droning on about some girl he had over the night before. Instead of Jesse egging him on and asking the questions, it's Taylor as usual. I swear that girl lives vicariously through everyone else's sex and love lives. She and Jesse have been together so long, they've only been with each other. I don't doubt they love each other or would ever want to be with anyone else, but Taylor reads too many romance novels and thinks everyone else's lives should be like the books she reads.

"Did you let this one stay the night or did you hit it and quit it? Did you call the Uber before she could even get her clothes back on?"

Emmett, who looks and sounds like he drank a whole six-pack to himself before we even showed up, winks at Taylor and says, "A gentleman doesn't kiss and tell."

"Well, Emmett, good thing you've never been a gentleman," Taylor retorts.

The conversation of his latest conquest goes on for another five minutes. Taylor asking questions and trying to pull details out of Emmett and Emmett responding with what sounds like a lot of half truths. Jesse's just listening and smiling over at Taylor like a love sick puppy dog.

Jesse and Emmett spend the next few hours taking turns playing video games. When Jesse plays, he lets Taylor wear the headset so she can do the shit talking. For a five-foot-nothing blonde who looks like she should have birds dressing her in the morning, she's got a mouth on her when she drinks.

I try to keep myself in the moment, but my thoughts keep drifting back to the printed email in my pocket and the girl who was in my truck just a few hours ago. Analyzing every word I said, every word she said. Thinking back to every time I touched her or she looked at me. I can't believe after five years I was actually sitting in the same car as Mads. I talked to her face to face and even shook her hand.

My thoughts are interrupted by the sound of a car pulling into the building. I turn around in my chair to see who's here, not realizing anyone else was invited. I don't recognize the car. It's a dark lifted truck that's giving off very much—*bro energy*. My question of who could be in the car is quickly answered and I wince, sinking lower into my chair.

A loud "What's up bitches?" comes from the direction of the truck, followed by the clicking of heels headed our way.

"Hey Jackie, who's your friend?" Emmett asks, puffing out his chest and tilting the beer bottle in his hand toward the clearly spends too much time in the gym driver of the bro truck.

I can see just by slightly tilting my head that Jackie walks over to her new friend and wraps her arms around his waist while he unceremoniously grabs her ass.

Although she's answering Emmett's question, her eyes are on me.

"This is Caleb. He's new in town. He's gonna be playing football for Pinehurst," she smirks with the last bit of information.

Great, not only do I have to put up with this douchebag following Jackie around like a puppy dog, but I also have to deal with him on the field.

Emmett, who gets way too much pleasure out of stirring the pot, gives me a wide drunken smile.

"You hear that Henry? Caleb here is gonna be joining us on the football field next week!"

He can hardly contain his laughter as he informs me of what Jackie just made abundantly clear.

Jackie and our new friend Caleb take up residence on the loveseat. With how close they're sitting, you could fit half the football team on the loveseat still.

"So Henry, where's your new friend I heard about?" Jackie asks, taking a sip of the hard seltzer she just pulled out of her purse. She says this all while doing an absolutely horrible job of hiding the disgust and jealousy she obviously has of even the thought of me with someone else.

Jackie and I dated for a few months in high school senior year. I knew she had a crush on me since we were kids, but I didn't just avoid dating her. I didn't date anyone. I was busy focusing on football and school. I had one goal; get recruited to a power 5 program where I could be the starting quarterback within two years. And I did it. I made that goal happen. By the end of junior year, I knew I was going to be recruited by Virginia Tech. Of course, it all came crashing down when they got news of my arrest. So, senior year, I had no more fucks to give. I asked Jackie to winter formal, and she ran with it. Not unexpectedly, she led everyone to believe we were a full on couple after that and I didn't stop her. We had fun for six months until I got my head out of my ass this past spring and stopped leading her on. I knew I would never want anything serious with her. I knew she was just a distraction from everything I screwed up and everything I lost, including Mads.

Wait, is she asking why Mads isn't here? How does she even know I met a girl today?

I glare at Jesse.

"Sorry dude," Jesse whispers.

"He didn't bring anyone with him, Jackie," Taylor interjects while trying and failing to hold back her giggles. "But now we know why Caleb is here." She hiccups and is full-on laughing now.

Well, Taylor's definitely tipsy. Taylor's always been a lightweight, but she's never sloppy. If anything, she's even more sweet but with a lot of extra sass. She doesn't hold back what's on her mind even more when she drinks, if that's possible. I roll my eyes. My friends have no concept of keeping their mouths shut.

Jackie is staring daggers at Taylor, but quickly turns her attention to her new lap dog. Literally, this dude is practically in her lap. Are there not any hot girls where he comes from? Jackie starts petting–actually petting–Caleb's hair. I feel nothing other than a desire to just get home and go to bed. I need a good night's sleep so I can figure out what the hell I'm going to do about the fact Mads is in my town, going to my college.

I'm for sure going to end up running into her, and then what? Do I tell her who I am?

I stand up, deciding it's time to get out of here.

"I think it's time for me to call it a night. Taylor, Jesse, you guys want a ride home?"

"Oh, but the fun is just getting started," Taylor giggles.

Jesse nods at me when I look over at him. He walks over to Taylor and crouches down in front of her.

"Let's go darling, your place or mine?" he asks.

Taylor stands up on the chair and hops onto Jesse's back.

"Ohhh mine! Let's christen my new dorm room!" she squeals as Jesse bounces her around on his back.

With Taylor secured on Jesse's back, we all start walking toward my truck. I feel a sudden pang of jealousy watching them. This is a new feeling and I can't help but wonder if today's events brought it on. Meeting Mads, without even realizing it at the time, has me longing for everything I wanted with her. Everything I still want with her.

Chapter Five

Madison

I was having another nightmare about sleeping in an alcove of the mall parking lot when I'm startled awake by noises. I don't move, but crack open my eyes, terrified of who might be there. Quickly remembering I'm in my new dorm room–I realize it's Taylor's giggling I'm hearing and a man's voice shushing her and ushering her toward her bed.

"Shhh. Babe. You have a roommate, remember?" he says.

Not being quiet at all, Taylor says, "Oh, yeah! She seems awesome. I can't wait for you to meet her!"

"Well, she won't think we're awesome if you wake her up on your first night as roommates!"

They both climb up into her bed and settle down. Guests in the dorm room wasn't part of a conversation we got to have earlier. Honestly, I don't care if Taylor brings her boyfriend back here. Not much can sour the comfort I'm enjoying in this bed, with my new sheets.

I start to drift off to sleep again, but hear something. Am I hearing–Oh my God. I am. It's Taylor moaning. I'm laying facing her side of the room. Being careful not to move too much, I slowly open my eyes. The room is dark, but just enough moonlight is creeping through the blinds I can make out the shapes of Taylor and her boyfriend in the bed next to me. It is very clear her boyfriend is under the blanket, while Taylor is not. My imagination runs wild instantly, and I can't help but imagine his face is buried between her legs by the way her breathing and moans are getting louder.

He shushes her and his hand comes out from under the blankets and goes to cover her mouth. Taylor wraps one hand over his and uses her other to push what I assume is his head back down. I shouldn't be watching this. I should close my eyes and go back to sleep, but I can't seem to make myself. And, yup, I am definitely getting turned on.

Taylor arches her back and I can see her hands are now clenching the blankets and I can hear her moans reaching a peak just as she does. The boyfriend comes crawling out from under the covers and slides in behind her just as she turns toward me, and I snap my eyes shut.

I hear Taylor whisper, "Amazing. I owe you in the morning."

She's clearly had a few drinks, and she's snoring before her boyfriend can even respond. The boyfriend giggles and I can hear him getting settled and soon he's snoring, too.

What just happened still has me stunned. Is this going to be a regular occurrence? Do I care if it is? I'm not a prude and it's not the first time I've been in a room where people are getting it on without a care in the world about who sees or hears.

Silently, I turn over to face the wall and let thoughts of what I just saw and heard consume me. Soon I'm imagining it's me with a guy between my legs making me moan. I didn't see Taylor's boyfriend's face, so he isn't who I'm imagining. The helpful guy who gave me a ride home easily creeps into my mind. Henry's face becomes clear, and I imagine him licking up my thighs and nibbling at them as he makes his way up. An imaginary warm breath rolling over me, before he slides his hand up to rub the most sensitive part of me.

As the fantasy plays out, I find myself slipping my hand slowly and quietly into my pajama shorts and finding the part of me that's hardly been touched by anyone else. I roll my clit between two fingers, slowly at first, but pick up my pace as the fantasy evolves in my mind. The mind movie has Henry dipping his tongue between my legs and running it from the very top of my folds down until he pushes his face up against me and his tongue into me as far as he can.

Soon I'm breathing harder and forcing myself to be as quiet as possible. My free hand pinches and pulls at my nipple and that does it. The release I was after crashes over me in a tremendous wave and I bite my lip to keep myself from audibly moaning, holding my breath to trap the sounds of my orgasm in my throat.

As the waves of pleasure slow and I come down from the high, I realize just how long it's been since I'd done that and just how badly I needed release. I fall asleep in seconds and have nothing but pleasant dreams for the rest of the night. Dreams filled with a sweet guy with hazel-colored eyes who helps desperate girls find lost luggage and give them rides so they don't have to wait in the heat for the bus.

My alarm is sounding next to me and I quickly shut it off, unsure if my roommate and her boyfriend are still sleeping. It feels like I just fell asleep, but I promised myself I'd get up early and start the job hunt. I look across the room to find Taylor and her boyfriend still sound asleep–him pushed up against the wall and her cuddling to his back. Slowly, I creep down from my bed, careful not to wake them. I grab my backpack and shove my nicest pair of black leggings, a white button-up shirt, and my toiletry bag into it. Gently throwing it over my shoulder, I hook my fingers through my sandals and slip out of the room, heading toward the bathrooms to shower.

It's early enough on a Saturday morning, the whole place is empty. Pulling my shirt out of my backpack, I drape it over one of the shower stalls, hoping the steam from my shower will get most of the wrinkles out. I take a quick shower and apply a little mascara, concealer, and lipstick after brushing my teeth. Most of the wrinkles are out of my shirt now. I put it on, then shove all my things into my backpack.

One advantage I have when job hunting is how many places I've worked. Over the past few years I've waitressed, answered phones at a veterinary office and worked retail. It wasn't easy keeping a job while still focusing on school and being back and forth between Mom's house and wherever else I could find to sleep when she was on a bender.

Mom wasn't always such a mess. It started with one too many glasses of wine at night after Dad passed. Then progressed to going out to the bars most nights by the time I was fifteen. At least by then I was able to ride the bus on my own. Before I knew it, she was bringing home strange men. And those strange men were bringing in the drugs.

I wasn't even mad at first. I felt sorry for her. She got pregnant with me when she was seventeen years old and her parents kicked her out. My dad was around and stepped up even with only being eighteen himself when I was born. But he died in a freak accident at work when I was twelve. By the time he passed away, they'd both been working steadily and had their lives together. They'd saved and bought a small house in a friendly neighborhood the year before Dad died. Mom got some money as a death benefit from Dad's accident, but I'm sure it's long gone now. The last time I was at her house I noticed collection notices, and a lot of them. I guess drugs are expensive and they are even more expensive when you're buying them for whatever piece of crap boyfriend you're housing that month.

By the time I was sixteen, I couldn't take it anymore. So I started crashing on friends' couches, really anywhere else I could, most of the time. When things got diabolical, or the guy she was on a bender with was a little too friendly, I got desperate and spent a few nights sleeping on the streets. I knew if I could hold out and make it through high school, I'd be able to move away and start over at college.

I remember from the ride over to campus from the bus stop that it's only about two miles to downtown. I'll have the most luck finding a job there, so instead of waiting for the local bus, I decide to just walk. I make it to Main Street quicker than I expected. Most shops are just starting to open. I make my way into every store, asking if they're hiring and if I could have an application. After almost twenty places, I've only managed to get one application. There's the diner up ahead and my stomach reacts audibly to the scents of bacon and coffee wafting out of it. I shouldn't be spending money, especially when I have a free meal plan at school, but I won't last any longer on the job hunt if I don't eat something.

A flurry of chimes sound when I open the door to the diner and I smile at the 1950s-style decor. The place has black-and-white checkered floors, red and white vinyl booths, and a big jukebox on one wall playing Earth Angel by The Penguins. The walls are covered in framed photos of everyone from Marilyn Monroe to James Dean. Taking a closer look, I realize most of them are signed and some even have personal messages on them.

It's noisy, but I like it. People are chatting and laughing in their booths, forks and knives are clinking against plates. I love places like this where they lean into a theme and Dad loved 50s music. We used to have a daddy-daughter date night once a month at a local diner just like this. He would give me extra quarters to play all our favorite songs by Elvis and Patsy Cline on the jukebox. I have to suppress a squeal when I see the waitress behind the counter is wearing a vintage diner uniform, just like the ones where Dad and I went. I take an empty red barstool at the almost full breakfast bar and an older woman with a cheery smile hands me a menu.

"Coffee dear?" She questions, nodding at the waiting coffee mug.

"Yes, please. And I'll just have some pancakes with a side of the delicious smelling bacon, please."

"Coming right up, sweetie." And she's off to top off everyone's coffees.

I look around the diner some more and notice she seems to be the only waitress working and more than half the tables are full. I wonder if someone called out sick or if maybe they're hiring. I make a mental note to ask before I leave. My pancakes and bacon are placed in front of me a few minutes later, and I dig in. These have got to be some of the best pancakes I have ever eaten in my life, and I devour every bite.

When the waitress comes around with my bill, the diner has slowed down quite a bit. I take the opportunity to ask if they're hiring.

"Is it that obvious?" She giggles. "You know someone looking for a job?"

"Me," I say.

"Oh, we rarely get kids your age wanting to work here. Do you have any experience waitressing?"

"Tons."

She looks at me, pondering for a minute. "If you're up for the early morning and late-night shifts, the gig is yours."

"Absolutely! I'm a student over at Pinehurst and my classes are all midday, so it's perfect! When can I start?" I ask, trying and failing not to sound overly excited.

"How about you come in for the nine to midnight shift tonight and Bev can train you. I'm Joy, by the way. I own the place. It's been in my family since it was opened in 1956. What was your name, sweetheart?"

"Madison. Madison Cartwright," I say, leaning over and shaking her hand.

"Nice to meet you, Madison. Let me grab you a uniform before you go. And breakfast is on the house." She winks and heads to the back.

I can't believe it. I did it. I found a job on my first day looking. At a place where I can see myself enjoying my time. Maybe I wasn't fooling myself. Maybe this is where things turn around and I can find some peace and maybe even a little happiness.

I take my new uniform and head back to campus, stopping on the way home at the drugstore. I want to pick up some snacks for my room and a few toiletries. I don't usually wear a ton of makeup, but knowing I have a job now, I spend a little extra money on a new tube of mascara and blush to treat myself. At any rate, looking a little more put together wouldn't hurt.

I'm browsing the magazine aisle just to kill some time before the rest of my walk home when I hear a familiar voice, which is strange since I don't really know anyone in this town. I walk toward the end of the aisle and peek around the corner, curious, and that's when I see him. Henry is standing there all toned, suntanned, and gorgeous. Just like I remembered him from yesterday. He's at the register buying a bag of chips and a soda. The girl ringing up his items isn't even trying to hide her infatuation. I can't blame her. He is literally the definition of a total hunk.

He's wearing running shoes, joggers that leave very little to the imagination, and a tight white T-shirt. The sleeves on his T-shirt are higher than yesterday's shirt, revealing more of the tattoo on his arm. It looks like the tattoo is script but I'm way too far away to read it. I'm dying to know what it says. I want to run my hand up his bicep and push his shirt up to reveal the rest of the tattoo and then run my tongue along the words and... Oh my god what is wrong with me? I have never fantasized about someone this often; let alone someone I don't even know. The register girl is handing him his receipt and I duck back into the aisle before he can notice me.

Once I hear the door chime and know he's gone, I make my way to the checkout. I've gotta get out of here and get home before I say or do something stupid.

Music is on full blast when I walk into our dorm room. Taylor is dancing around the room, still in her pajamas, singing along loudly. She beams when she notices me and holds out her hairbrush microphone to me, still singing along. I drop my bag next to my desk and laugh at her incredibly infectious spirit. She turns the music down and plops down in her desk chair.

"You were out and about early this morning," she says.

"Yeah, I uh, went job hunting."

"Oh yeah, any luck?"

"Actually, yes. I start over at Main Street Diner tonight!"

"Oh, you're gonna love it there! Did you meet Joy? She's basically everyone in town's extra Mom or Grandma. Oh, and you have to try their onion rings, they are to die for!"

"Yeah, Joy is who hired me. I'm excited. I loved the vibe of the place and they seem like they're busy, so hopefully the tips will be good."

I rummage around in my drawers for a T-shirt, turning my back to Taylor to switch out my button-up for something more comfortable.

"So, did you have fun last night with your friends?" I ask, turning back around to her.

"Oh yeah, but I totally wish you would have come."

"Next time," I promise her. "I think I'm gonna get ahead on some of the reading for classes on Monday and then take a nap before my shift tonight at nine. I'll be there until close, but I promise I'll be quiet when I come home."

Taylor's cheeks blush.

"Oh my God. I forgot to apologize. Did we wake you last night? I had a few drinks and I know I was probably totally loud. I didn't even ask if bringing guys back to the room was okay. I feel awful, I am so -"

I cut her off laughing.

"It's okay Taylor, I promise. You weren't *that* loud," I say with a knowing grin.

"Oh Jesus," she says, hanging her head in her hands.

Now I do laugh. I'm not trying to make her feel bad, but it is kind of hilarious how embarrassed she is. I just hope she knows I'm only teasing and not making fun of her. And I hope she doesn't know what I did last night laying in my own bed.

"Seriously, Taylor, it's not a big deal, I promise. I'm only teasing you. And your boyfriend is welcome here any time."

"Thanks for being so cool. But, I promise it was a one-time thing. Jesse has his own room at his apartment, so there's no reason for us to put you in that position again. I was just drunk and, well... it sounded like fun being in a new place," she admits, her cheeks turning pink again. "Plus, Jesse is like five million feet tall and he won't be able to walk for a week after spending just one night in my tiny bed."

"Jesse?" I ask.

"Oh, yeah. My boyfriend. Wait, Did I never even tell you his name?"

I shake my head. Wondering silently if it could be the Jesse who works at the bus station. But that would be too strange, right?

"Well, I'm headed over to his place now. We're gonna spend the day together since neither of us has work and we'll probably be super busy next week for the first week of classes. But, since I have an eight a.m. class tomorrow, I'll be here when you get back from work. But, hey, why don't you give me your number, and maybe we should keep each other updated if we're not gonna be staying in the dorm room. That way, if you meet a hot guy and stay at his place, I don't think you've been kidnapped by an ax-wielding psycho who's going to chop you into pieces."

She's laughing, but man, this girl loves her true crime and horror. She passes me her phone, and I put my number in, texting myself so I have hers too. She grabs her purse and heads out as I pull out the syllabus for Monday's creative writing class. It looks like one of our first assignments is to write a three-thousand-word story about a character who overcomes adversity. Wondering if I should just write the story about my own life, I start doodling mindlessly. I'm not sure I've actually overcome anything. I feel like all I've been doing these past few years is surviving and shouldn't I be thriving to have overcome anything?

Surprisingly not feeling in the mood to write, I pull out the syllabus for my historical literature class and start reading the chapters the professor assigned for this week.

CHAPTER SIX

HENDERSON

I feel hungover and I didn't even drink last night. I slept like complete garbage. Tossing and turning all night, replaying every moment I was with Madison yesterday. Every time our hands touched. Every smile she aimed at me. The warm color of her golden eyes. The fullness of her lips. After all these years, I met Mads in real life and I didn't even know it was her. I want to go back. I want a do-over.

Madison is even more beautiful than I've been imagining her and a million times more sexy. She's tall with a lot of curves and has hair just dying to be wrapped up in my fingers and gently pulled on. Her laugh consumed me and I didn't even understand why. All the feelings I had seem validated now, knowing who she really is. Knowing the closeness I felt to her was because I have been close to her–*for years*. Close to her heart, her words, her mind.

The bell from the sports store door chimes, interrupting my daydreaming. A mom and her two boys are heading toward the counter.

"How can I help you?" I ask, pushing all thoughts of Mads away and being grateful I'm standing behind this counter because I'm pretty sure my pants are doing a horrible job of hiding the semi I have.

"Yes, I placed an order for new baseball cleats for the boys and got a call that they were ready," the woman tells me.

I find her order in a stack of boxes behind the counter and ring her up. This is the first customer that's walked through the door all day and I've been here for four hours. Sometimes I think Mr. Grissom has me open early on Saturdays and Sundays because he thinks it keeps me from partying. Little does he know I haven't drunk a single beer in over a year. Cheap beer isn't worth the risk when getting caught drinking would violate my probation terms, which I thankfully only have six months left of. But, today is my monthly check-in at the probation office. Mr. Grissom should be here any minute so my shift can end.

Right on time, the door chimes and he comes schlepping in. He throws a Sunday newspaper down on the counter and points his thumb at the door, letting me know I'm good to get out of here. Mr. Grissom's a man of very few words, but I appreciate that about him. I grab my gym bag from the back room and head to the parking lot. The probation office is on the other side of town, but I've got half an hour before my check-in time, so I take the scenic route. Patsy Cline's "Walkin After Midnight" starts playing through the speakers after I hit shuffle on my music.

Mads told me once she and her dad loved 50s music and Patsy Cline was one of her favorites. During one of our late night back and forth emailing sessions, she made me promise to download some songs. A few of the ones she suggested made it into permanent rotation on my playlists. Jesse and Emmett give me shit sometimes when they come on. I just lie and say I have them on there for my mom. I turn up the song and close my eyes at the red light and imagine Madison swaying in my arms to this song. Imagine running my hand through her soft brown hair and down her back. Our bodies pushed flush against each other, her head on my shoulder.

A horn from behind me pulls me out of my fantasy and I hit the gas to pull through the intersection. I can't keep fantasizing about her like this. Last night when I couldn't sleep, I made my decision. I'm not going to tell her who I am. Clearly, she wants nothing to do with me since she hasn't responded to my emails in almost a year. Sure, we now live in the same town and go to the same college, but I can at least try to avoid her. And if I run into her, I know how to be polite but keep my distance. Plus, what's the point of telling her who I am? She'll probably go so far as to transfer schools just to get away from me.

I pull into the probation office parking lot and find a space near the entrance. When I make it inside, I take a seat in a row of chairs against the wall and wait for my officer to call me back. By the looks of it, I'm the youngest person in here, and I'd be lying if I wasn't intimidated by some of the other people waiting in chairs next to me. Luckily, I only got stuck spending one night in a holding cell when everything happened and I was all alone because I was still a minor. The feeling of being caged in, not free to leave whenever I wanted, was still enough to make me want to pull my hair out. Plus, having to go to the bathroom out in the open was something I never want to experience again.

"Henderson Adler!" I hear from an office down the hall. I get up and make my way down there to see Officer Gatlin sitting behind his desk with a small plastic container held out to me. "Need a sample, Adler," he says without even looking up at me.

I take the container and head to the bathroom. Pissing in a plastic cup should be something I'm used to by now. I've been doing it once a month for the past six months.

After I fill the cup and drop the sample off, I head back into Officer Gatlin's office. I take my usual spot in one of the plastic chairs in front of his desk and lean back into it, getting comfortable. Sometimes these check-ins take five minutes, sometimes I'm here for half an hour. The longer visits aren't any different from the short ones. Gatlin usually just shuffles around papers and makes me sit in silence and then randomly excuses me. I wonder if it's some type of psychological tactic. That or he's just lonely and likes the company.

"So, Adler, are you staying out of trouble?" He asks with a hint of a smile.

He knows I am. Officer Gatlin is actually pretty cool and is half the reason I only have six months of probation left. He pleaded my case to the judge and got my probation term reduced from five years to just one.

I nod my head.

"Yup, just working, going to practice, and getting ready for classes that start this week."

"No unwanted visitors at home?"

He's wanting to know if my dad's tried to come back. He has not.

"Well, I'm sitting here and not in jail. That should tell you that no, my dad has not tried to come back home."

Officer Gatlin doesn't find this response as amusing as I do.

"Look, kid, you've got six months left. Just six months and this can all be behind you. We both know you got the short end of the shit stick. But when your dad grew up in this town and played college ball with Judge Thompson, well–people don't want to believe the people they know and trust are capable of the shit your dad was."

The shit my dad was capable of, was giving my mom a black eye and breaking two of her ribs. That's what has me sitting in front of Officer Gatlin.

Dad was never a warm and fuzzy father or husband. I have memories of him talking down to my mom since I was a kid. Little digs like insulting her cooking or making her second guess her outfit choices, but he never hit her. At least I didn't think he did. I just thought he was an asshole and my mom stayed with him for me.

As I got a little older, he took his anger out on both of us from time to time. Most of his anger toward me was when I wasn't doing well enough on the football field or wasn't getting the grades he wanted me to get. With Mom, his anger was because she didn't have dinner waiting for him when he got home, even though she herself was working ten-hour shifts at the hospital. Or he'd accuse her of flirting with one of his friends or spending too much money going shopping with Emmett's mom.

A few years ago, she stopped going out with her friends altogether and only worked four-hour shifts so she could be home enough to keep the house spotless and have dinner ready for him. It helped for a little while, but then I noticed he was finding new things to get angry at her for. She wasn't wearing enough makeup, or she was wearing too much. Dinner was too hot, or it was too cold. He'd grab her arm or throw things, but I never saw him hit her. Not until that night.

"I know, Officer Grissom. Promise, he hasn't shown up. Hasn't even called."

"Alright kid, well, get out of here. Practice is at three, right?"

"Yeah, I'm heading straight there after this."

Officer Grissom shakes my hand and I head out to my truck.

On my drive to practice, I'm white knuckling the steering wheel. Every time I go to one of these check-ins, Dad gets brought up and I hate it. And when Grissom brings up Dad, it brings up memories of that night. Memories of coming into the house and hearing the loud crack and thinking someone dropped something–only to find out it was the sound of my dad's fist connecting with my mom's face. When I turned the corner of the entryway into the living room, I was in complete shock. The first thing I saw was his fist going full force and full speed to her stomach. I didn't react right away because I was honestly just so *confused*. I thought I was dreaming or my eyes were playing tricks on me.

By the time he'd hit her again, she'd crumpled to the floor, and I'd already picked up the trophy.

Football practice today is freaking boring. The team has been on the field for an hour and spent half of that time just standing around. Jesse and Emmett used the past twenty minutes to argue about whether Xbox or PlayStation is the superior game console. I'm about to intervene and tell them they're both idiots.

Jesse is my oldest friend. I would trust him with my life, but Emmett and I have a different kind of friendship. He's a tight end on the team, which means *my safety* is often in his hands. There's a trust I have to bestow on him unlike anyone else. He's also shown up for me off the field in ways no one else has. I should tell him how grateful I am for him, but he'll probably just tell me I'm messing with his bad boy persona. He's got a reputation to protect and all that shit.

Coach eventually sees nothing else is going to get accomplished today and releases us for the day. We all start gathering our bags from the sidelines and head to the parking lot. The school just received a donation to remodel the locker rooms and they won't be ready for another 2 weeks. I can't say for sure, but I'm almost certain the *anonymous* donation came from Caleb's parents. Pretty sure the guy thinks he can buy his way into a starting position.

"Hey, need a ride?" I ask Jesse when I'm almost to my truck.

"Nah, Emmett's gonna drop me off."

"Alright, later." I bump Jesse's fist and give a small wave to Emmett as they get into Emmett's car.

Emmett's parents tried to buy Jesse a car as a graduation gift, but Jesse refused. He was grateful for the gesture but said he wanted to prove to himself he could save up and buy a car on his own. Last we talked about it, he was only a few months off from being able to afford one. He keeps making jokes about buying a Mini Cooper. Jesse is six foot four, and over two hundred and fifty pounds. I stopped giving him shit about it because at this point I hope he does buy the tiny car because it will be hilarious.

Mom and Dad gave me my truck for my sixteenth birthday. It was actually my grandpa's before it was mine. A pale blue, beautifully maintained and updated, 1963 Chevy. I didn't know this until recently, but Mom used to drive the truck when she first met my dad. One of the first things he did after they got married was buy her a Lexus. Apparently, it was a gift from Dad after one of their more tumultuous fights. The truck was never driven again and sat covered in storage until she convinced my dad to let me have it.

It makes me pissed off, but mostly sad, to know they were fighting and Dad was manipulating her for that long. Over the past year, Mom has shared some of her secrets with me. Some she had no choice but to share when they came out in court, others have come out in our monthly family therapy sessions, and a few get slipped into random dinner conversations. She doesn't say these things to make me angry or sad, or to make me hate my father even more. Then again, I don't think it's even possible to hate that man more. She tells me because she feels guilty, I think. I suspect it's her way of trying to help heal our relationship.

She feels guilt and shame for not speaking up sooner. She feels guilt and shame for not pressing charges against him, even when it could have helped my case. I'm not angry at her. I couldn't be because I have no clue what it was like for her. To hide her reality from everyone; her friends and even her own son. I know she thought she was just protecting me all these years.

At least Mom and I have both stopped waiting on apologies from a man who thinks he's done no wrong. A man who is such a coward, he left town and never looked back. Dad packed two suitcases of shit, jumped in his car and hightailed it to Florida. One of his old college buddies lives there.

Mom probably did the right thing, not telling me. Because who knows, maybe if I would have found out about the abuse earlier, I wouldn't have had enough self-control to stop before actually killing him. Or maybe if I found out about it when I was too young, I wouldn't have had the physical strength to almost kill him. Neither of those scenarios sits right with me. Nothing about this situation sits right with me. But it happened–and it's my reality, my past. I'm working to overcome it. I just hope I overcome it before it overcomes me.

CHAPTER SEVEN

MADISON

My shift is dragging on, and it's been a slow day. Thanks to a few regulars, the tips are still great. I've been working at the diner now for a little over three weeks. It's been just as great as I suspected it would be. Joy is an incredible boss, always willing to work with my class schedule. She even checks in with me to make sure I'm getting enough time to study and do homework. I think she can sense I don't exactly have any type of parent figure looking out for me, even though I haven't shared any details with her about my situation. She's careful not to ask too many questions about life back home. I appreciate her keen sense of awareness.

I'm also pretty certain Joy is overpaying me, but I'm not complaining. If I could save up just a little more money, I can finally afford my first car. Having a car in this town isn't a necessity, but having the security of something that's mine would be nice. If I'd had a car when I was in high school it would have saved me from some of the hard choices I had to make when I couldn't stay at home.

The bell at the door chimes and I shout over my shoulder, "I'll be right with you," as I finish hanging another customer's order up for Chuck in the kitchen.

"Take your time, hot stuff," a familiar voice giggles.

Taylor.

Excited to see my roommate, I turn around with a huge smile on my face, hoping she can add some excitement to this boring shift. When I turn around, I'm surprised to see the guy from the bus station ticket booth holding her hand. But also, not surprised at all. This town is freakishly small.

"Hey. Lost luggage girl!" Jesse beams and holds his hand up for a high five.

I slap his hand, shaking my head at his nickname. Even from the brief interaction I had with him at the bus station, I knew I liked Jesse. He comes across as a guy who is always in a good mood. The type who can usually find a way to make even the most mundane things fun. These two dating isn't shocking at all.

"I am still so embarrassed," I admit.

Taylor's looking back and forth at us like we each just grew an extra head.

"Wait! You two know each other already?"

"Yeah Babe, this is who Henry gave a ride to on move-in day."

I'm surprised, and a little confused. Why would Jesse explain me that way to her and not as the girl whose luggage he basically stole?

"Oh my gosh, that was YOU!" Taylor screeches.

I'm unsure why she seems so... elated about this revelation. I choose to ignore it.

"So, are you guys here for dinner? Do you want a booth?"

"Yes to dinner. No to the booth," Taylor says. "We'll just sit at the counter so we can bug you."

They sit down at two of the counter stools and I bring them water and menus. An older couple is waiting for me at the register. I excuse myself to go help them. When I get back behind the counter, Jesse and Taylor have turned toward each other and are sharing quick kisses and giggling.

They are almost sickeningly sweet. Now I understand the jokes about being married. They stop and turn back toward me as I come to rest in front of them.

"So, Madison," Jesse starts. "How are you liking Easton?"

"Honestly, it's great. I love my job here, even if today is hellishly slow. I don't care for the humidity, but I'm excited to experience a real fall soon. We basically only have summer and winter back home. Plus, my classes have been fun."

"Well, you'll love fall even more when you find out how freaking awesome it's going to be watching me smash some dudes on the football field."

He takes one hand, balls it into a fist and smashes it into his other hand while he says this. Taylor and I both laugh at his little demonstration. He feigns being hurt by our laughter but is chuckling a little himself–glad to know he doesn't take himself too seriously. Those are the type of people I like to surround myself with. Ones who can crack jokes about themselves and find humor in being silly.

I take their order; Taylor gets a burger and onion rings. Jesse orders spaghetti and meatballs with a glass of milk.

I try to keep myself busy bussing a few tables and refilling the ketchup bottles. Soon, Taylor and Jesse are the only customers. After I drop off their food, I head to the far end of the counter where I have one of my textbooks open. Joy already gave me permission to do homework when it's slow, but I try not to take advantage of the privilege. I'm reading through the textbook for my creative writing class and it's talking about confessional writing. About how this style of writing is usually directly related to divulging shameful matters. It reminds me of something Ender and I used to do in our emails.

I can't remember how or why it started, but we would send each other emails with the subject line being *Confession* and then confess something.

Sometimes it was completely stupid and trivial, like *Confession: I just ate an entire pizza in one sitting*, but other times it was deeper and more raw, like *Confession: I just dumped all of my mom's wine down the drain.*

The unspoken rule was we didn't ever judge each other for our confessions, we didn't ask questions and we didn't try to fix the problem immediately if there was one. We just replied with, *I hear you.* I miss that. I miss being able to pour my heart out and have my worries and fears and disappointments in myself acknowledged in such a simple way. It was like it was our way of holding each other when we couldn't actually hold each other. I break my promise to myself for the millionth time and pull out my phone. Search "confession" in my email account and start mindlessly scrolling through some of his confessions, skipping the most recent email in my inbox.

Confession: I sometimes don't even care about football.

Confession: I lied to my friends tonight and said I had homework. I don't have any homework. I just want to work on my new short story and email back and forth with you.

Confession: I actually love broccoli.

Confession: I now know every word to at least three Patsy Cline songs.

Reading through these makes me smile and laugh, but they also make me sad. Selfishly sad, because I lost the one person I could tell almost anything to. It was cathartic to share the confessions, and although I still share them in drafts, it's not the same. Unsent emails don't get responses. There's no *I hear you* to ease my burdens.

"Hey Madison! Do you work tomorrow?" Taylor calls to me from the other end of the counter, breaking me out of my day dreaming.

I shove my phone back into my uniform pocket and walk down to her and Jesse.

"Nope. I get the whole day off. I don't even have any classes because my professor canceled the one class I have for tomorrow."

I plan on sleeping in, being lazy and maybe getting some homework done. I feel like I haven't had any down time since I got here. I've felt the pressure to not waste a minute of my time.

"Want to go with Jesse and me to the carnival they have over in West-point? It's the next town over, only about a forty-five-minute drive. My sister is letting me borrow her car. It will be funnnn." She sings.

Sister? How did I not know Taylor had a sister? I guess we've both been so busy we haven't gotten to know each other as well as I thought. Taylor is practically impossible to say no to, and as much as I wanted to be lazy, it would be nice to spend more time with her.

"Yeah," Jesse says, "I'm gonna see how many times I can go on the Gravitron before I puke."

Taylor gives Jesse a playful slap on his chest and I laugh.

"Okay fine. But only if you promise they'll have funnel cake!"

Taylor excitedly claps her hands and turns her attention back to her burger. Jesse is shoveling his spaghetti into his mouth sloppily, slurping the ends of the noodles into his mouth. I shake my head, giggle, and walk away to help the girl who just walked in. For such a big and manly guy, Jesse is essentially a toddler. I think I'm going to adore him.

"Hi," I say, greeting the new customer.

"I called in an order for Aubrey," she says.

I notice her faded overalls and pale pink long sleeve shirt first, but her gorgeous fiery red-orange hair is what catches my attention.

"Oh, yeah. The onion rings. Let me grab those for you."

What is with the people in this town and their addiction to these damn onion rings?

The carnival turns out to be a dozen rides and a few food stalls. Not exactly impressive, but in small towns, I guess people are easily impressed. We ride all the rides twice before taking a break to grab something to eat. To my complete disappointment, no funnel cake. I settled for a corn dog and deep-fried Oreos.

I remember once Mom and Dad took me to a carnival when I was about eight, but it was a lot bigger. We spent all afternoon riding the rides, playing carnival games, and eating a ton of junk food. When it got dark and all the lights on the rides came on, Dad and I went on the Ferris wheel. Just the two of us.

The ride stopped when we were at the top. You could almost see our house, we were so high up. Dad pulled me in close and whispered a story in my ear about him and Mom.

When your mom and I were young, we rode a Ferris wheel just like this. When it stopped at the top, I kissed her for the very first time!

When his story was over, he tickled me and kissed me on the top of my head and the Ferris wheel started to move again. I miss Dad so much.

My parent's relationship wasn't perfect, not by a long shot. As I got older, they argued a lot and there was constant tension. I think they both felt they got together and stayed together because of their circumstances. When Dad died, Mom was completely devastated. The drinking started because she was depressed. Lately, I've wondered if she was depressed because she missed my dad or because she was a single mother overnight.

Before Dad died, Mom was the picture-perfect, uber-involved, class room-mom type. She lived for school carnivals, taking me to ballet class, screaming from the sidelines at my soccer games. After he died, all of it stopped within a year. I stopped all the extra activities and sports, too. Some, just because I was tired of trying to get rides from other kids on the team. Others, I realized I only ever did because they made Mom happy. When they no longer gave her any joy, there was no use making myself miserable in pointe shoes.

We're sitting at a picnic table eating our food when someone starts talking from behind me.

"Hey, Taylor. Jesse."

I turn to see who it is, only to find the guy from the library. The one who hit on me the day I arrived in Easton.

"Hi, Adam!" Taylor responds.

Jesse gives him a curt nod, but says nothing and shoves more of his pizza into his mouth. I could totally be imagining things, but I don't think Jesse likes Adam very much. Taylor, oblivious to Jesse's change in mood, introduces us.

"This is Madison, my roommate. Madison, this is Adam. We work together in the library."

"We've met, actually," I say, even though I doubt he remembers me.

"Oh yeah. Totally, I remember."

I'm almost positive he's lying by the confused look on his face, but I take the high road and don't call him out.

Taylor and Adam talk about work and school for a while. He doesn't address me or Jesse again, he doesn't even say bye to either of us when he leaves.

"So, you met Adam?" Taylor asks when he's out of earshot.

"Yeah. When I bought my textbooks. He, uh, looked down my shirt and asked for my number."

Jesse scoffs, "Sounds about right."

Taylor purses her lips together but keeps quiet. I think my earlier assumptions of Jesse not liking Adam, weren't just in my head. He definitely doesn't care for the guy.

We opt out of a third go on the rides and decide to head home after finishing our food. The ride home is quiet and the air in the car is thick with tension. When we drop Jesse off at his apartment, he leans over and gives Taylor a kiss goodbye and tells her he loves her. He says it slowly, looking into her eyes the whole time, and I feel like I shouldn't be watching. I get out of the car to take Jesse's place in the front seat. I kind of wish I could stay in the back because the front seems a little dangerous right now.

When we pull away, I can't help myself and ask Taylor if she's alright.

"Oh, I'm fine. Sorry about all that. Jesse thinks Adam has a thing for me. It's been a bit of an issue since I started working at the library. I tried explaining he's a flirt with everyone, but he still doesn't trust him."

I have very little experience with real relationships and real relationship problems, so I don't have any advice for her. The closest things I had to real relationships were using a guy for a place to crash and Ender. The latter of which I destroyed before it could even be anything. She doesn't seem worried though and changes the subject, telling me about the thriller book she's currently reading and how I absolutely *must* read it when she's finished.

Chapter Eight

Henderson

Easton is the kind of town that likes to make a big deal out of the most minor things. Today, we're celebrating the opening of a new coffee shop right across the street from the diner. As if people won't still just go to the diner for coffee because they'll say the new place is too fancy. The whole town is still celebrating though, because–any excuse. We're not talking about some small ribbon-cutting ceremony and balloons outside the door. No, that's not enough. Main Street is blocked off to traffic, the middle school marching band is here–in their uniforms, puff ball hats and all–and the Mayor is standing behind a podium giving a speech.

I'm only irritated because it means I had to park six blocks away for work today. I almost would have been better off walking. My shift ended at the height of the festivities. People are filling the street, all holding mini to-go cups with the new shop's logo. Someone's passing out pastries and kids are running around screaming and yelling.

This isn't half as nuts though as the annual events they put on. The fall festival would make some people feel like they were in an alternate reality. It's a week-long festival with pony rides, a chili cook-off, pie baking contests and every other small town cliché event they can shove into it. The entire month of December is packed with caroling, more than one tree lighting ceremony and mandatory decorations for the whole of Main Street. I can't wait to hear what Mr. Grissom thinks of it all when the next major festivity rolls around. I can almost hear his grumbling and cursing under his breath now.

I've only made it a block toward my car when a dog gets loose from its owner, and comes racing in front of me, leash dragging behind it. The dog crashes into a girl and she falls into me. I catch her around the waist before she can hit the ground.

"Jesus. Fuck," The girl exclaims as I help her upright.

I look up to say sarcastically *you're welcome*, but my voice catches in my throat when I realize the girl is Madison. My body reacts to holding her and my skin heats. Dammit, she is so gorgeous.

"Oh. You," she says, eyes wide.

"Me," I say, finding my voice.

"Sorry, that dog came out of nowhere."

"No worries, this place is a little out of control."

She brushes at her clothes and adjusts her top, switching the bag from the drugstore she's holding to her other hand. It opens the space between us and I take a small step closer to her without even thinking.

"You're making it a habit of rescuing me."

I smile, not sure how to respond. If she only knew how easily I would be her knight in shining armor. Hell, I'd even don some silly costume if she asked. Madison doesn't have a clue how completely wrapped around her finger I truly am.

"Well," she says, continuing her walk down the sidewalk. "Thanks again. I better get going."

"You're welcome." I say.

I start walking behind her, because of course we're heading in the same direction—this isn't awkward at all. After a few steps, she looks back and smiles at me.

"Are you following me?"

"What? No! I had to park on the street because of the–"

"Henry, I'm kidding. Look, we're obviously walking in the same direction and I could use the company. Today was a long day at work."

She doesn't have to tell me twice. I take several large, hurried steps to catch up with her. We're walking side by side now. The crowd has thinned, so we're not competing for sidewalk space with anyone else. I still walk as close to her as I can without making it too obvious how badly I want to be near her.

"You got a job?" I ask.

"I did. At the diner. A few shifts a week."

"Awesome. My mom and I eat there all the time. Maybe we'll come in on a night you're working."

She seems to mull this idea over, changing her glance from me to the path ahead several times before continuing the conversation.

"Yeah, maybe you can come in with Taylor and Jesse sometime," she says.

Well, that wasn't what I expected.

"You've met Taylor?" I ask.

"Actually, Taylor and I are roommates. I only found out her boyfriend is your friend Jesse recently, though."

Of course, in this thumbtack sized town, she would be roommates with one of my best friends. I laugh out loud at the revelation.

"Well, we should all hang out sometime together."

Madison's eyes widen. Shit. Did I just ask her out on a date? When she doesn't immediately answer, I change the subject and luckily the conversation picks back up. She's telling me about working at the diner now while I shamelessly admire her.

She's wearing a pair of denim shorts and a plain white t-shirt that dips in the front, just barely showing off the top curve of her breasts. She has one of the most beautiful bodies I've ever seen. I'm not delusional to the fact I would have this same sentiment no matter what her body looked like. All her physical features are heightened to my vain senses because I am so enamored with all of her non-physical features.

Like, right now, she's asking me about my classes and the way she looks at me as I tell her about my boring as shit classes–she's actually paying attention. Showing real interest, asking questions, and her eyes sparkle with genuine curiosity. Or the way she waited at the curb a few beats longer for an older woman to catch up to us so we could all walk across the street together. She does things for others and doesn't want praise for it. She may not even realize she's doing these things, it's just her natural, caring, personality.

She doesn't know, of course, I know what a good person she is. She doesn't know that I, Henry, know about the time when she was in eighth grade and she left anonymous notes in a girl's locker who was being picked on. They said things like, *you matter, your scrunchie is really cute* and *you did great on your book report*. She doesn't know I know these things because she told them to Ender, not Henry. Madison may not have had a lot of *best friends* in her life, but she was a great friend to many people who didn't even know it. She was an excellent best friend to me.

We've long passed where I parked my car and are almost at the college campus. I wanted to get as much time with her as I could and I don't have any plans today, so I don't interrupt the conversation and just keep walking with her. Walking with her, talking with her, about nothing–has been a gift. Hearing her voice, her laughter, noticing her little and big facial expressions, I take in as much of her presence as I can get.

We get to her dorm building and she stops outside the door abruptly.

"Oh my gosh, I totally walked here on autopilot. Where is your car parked? Not far, I hope," she says, looking around for my truck in the parking lot behind us.

"It's um—a few blocks back," I admit.

"Henry! Why didn't you stop me? I've been rambling this whole time."

"I wanted more time with you."

I'm surprised at my own admission and she seems to be too, judging by the way her mouth drops open a little and her cheeks blush. She is so incredibly sexy in ways I never imagined I'd find a girl sexy. Just the tiny movements of her lips or the pink hue of her cheeks turn me on.

"Well, I've actually got a study group I'm going to be late for. But thank you for walking with me, Henry."

She catches me off guard and throws her arms around my neck, giving me a hurried hug. My arms just briefly come up to her waist to hug her back before she's pulling away and ducking inside the building. I stand there staring at her through the glass doors, trying to remember the feel of her curves. She stops a few steps up the stairs and looks back at me, a shy smile on her face. I give a little half wave like an idiot, a big goofy grin on my face. Her smile broadens the faintest bit, and she continues up the stairs.

Now I know what the girls are always saying about a panty-dropping smile, because—damn.

So much for keeping my distance from her. As I start the walk back to my truck, I realize something. Once again, I did not ask for her number, I did not ask to see her again, I did not pass go, I will not be collecting $200.

Writing used to be something I really enjoyed. It was cathartic and helped me escape the pressure of always having to be perfect. The pressure of having to be the star football player, class president, homecoming king–all the things expected of me by my dad and the kids at school. Jesse was the class clown, Emmett was the class playboy, and I was the perfect one.

We all had our roles to play, but I don't think their roles came with a dad at home who called them a loser or a pussy when they didn't meet those expectations. It wasn't until after he left that I realized how verbally abusive he always was. The outbursts and anger from him were so far and few between, I overlooked them. I never saw the patterns of his behavior. It was too easy for me to forget one insult by the time the next one landed.

I was around Emmett's dad all the time and never once saw him raise his voice to his kids. Sure, he would get on them about doing chores or scold them when they brought home a bad grade, but it was different. That's obvious now that I can look back with clearer eyes. He never yelled, he never belittled them. I don't know how I didn't notice the difference between a real father, a real man, and whatever the hell my dad was.

I'm laying on my bed, lazily tossing a football into the air with nothing to do when I make the offhand decision to pull out one of my old writing journals. It takes a while because they're hidden in a box at the bottom of my closet, clothes and old football gear stacked on top of it. These probably don't have to be hidden away anymore with Dad gone. Mom and I have never talked about my writing, but I don't think she'd reject my love for it the way my dad did.

The notebook is an unassuming black one with a layer of dust on it now. Wiping it off, I open it to a blank page and start writing. I always loved writing by hand more than typing my stories out on the computer. I only ever typed them when I wanted to share them with Madison. I wonder if I'm feeling this urgency to write because of the time I spent with her today. The words flow out of my mind and on to the paper easily, even now, after all this time. A feeling of pride and a little disbelief at just how easy it feels consumes me.

The story begins with a young boy whose destiny is to become the next King. But the boy fears he doesn't agree with how the current King, his father, is ruling their land. The people are cast into divisive groups by the King, based simply on how he views their strengths and weaknesses. Those with brute physical strengths are regarded as higher class, while those with strengths related to the arts are lower class, useless in the King's eye. The young boy must make a decision, follow in his father's footsteps or forge his own path and give the people equality.

I write for hours, getting lost in the story. Lost in the way I'm able to release some of my own demons onto the paper. When I finally finish the short story, it's dark outside. This story is one of my favorites I've ever written. My heart aches at the longing I have to type it out and email it to Mads.

Mom should be home from work soon. I'm feeling renewed and lighter after being able to do something I've missed so much. I head down to the kitchen and decide I'm going to make dinner for Mom and me before she gets home. I only know how to cook a few things, and I'm not sure grilling burgers and throwing frozen french fries in the oven counts as cooking, but it's the thought that counts right?

Mom gets home just as I've finished cutting up the vegetables for the burgers and am pulling the fries out of the oven.

"In here, Mom," I yell.

She comes into the kitchen, looking tired, but her face lights up when she sees me.

"You made us dinner? Oh, Henderson, thank you sweetie. I was going to suggest ordering pizza because I'm exhausted, but this is so much better."

I notice her eyes are glassy as she looks at me and I have to turn away from her before she makes my emotions come to a head as well. I've always been sensitive, but my dad always did anything he could to squash that side of me. With him gone, and with the help of a pretty kick ass therapist, I'm trying to embrace that side of me a little more. Crying because your mom's happy you made dinner though—that's maybe a little too sensitive.

I make us both plates and we sit at the kitchen counter sharing the details of our days. I leave out the part about walking Madison to campus. We're nearly finished eating when I finally find the courage I've been searching for all through dinner.

"Mom, can I—can I share a story I wrote with you?" I ask her, staring at the remaining french fries on my plate.

She's not answering and there's a tightness in my chest. Was I wrong to bring this up to her? Is she going to react the way my dad used to?

"It's okay, forget it—"

"No, Henderson. I would love to read one of your stories."

I look at her. Her expression is soft and her eyes are brimming with unshed tears. She smiles at me and places a hand on my arm.

"I've been waiting a really long time for you to ask me that, sweetie."

I sigh, relieved, and push the handwritten story over to her, watching intently as she begins reading. I've had to stop myself several times from taking it back and ripping it up. My nerves and my shame are still bubbling under the surface. The damage my father did is still battling the work I've been doing to heal it.

When she finishes about twenty minutes later and sets the papers down on the counter, she doesn't say anything for a few minutes. But then she wipes at a few fallen tears, turns to me and embraces me in a hug like I haven't felt since I was a crying kid who had a scraped knee. I stop worrying about what is, or isn't, too sensitive and let my own tears fall now.

Chapter Nine

Madison

Life has been an endless stream of work, classes and studying. The books in my arms are trying to escape my grasp as I rush to class. My backpack was nowhere to be found, so I just grabbed my books and ran out of my room. I'm going to be late for class, but the quicker I can get there, the less of a scene I'll make. Said backpack is likely hiding under the laundry I've been letting pile up since I skipped doing it to go to the carnival with Taylor and Jesse. It's easier to go without doing laundry now that my meager wardrobe has grown a little. Totally worth letting a few things pile up, because I ended up having a blast at the carnival.

I still laugh when I think about how Jesse tried winning Taylor a stuffed animal on one of the games. He spent forty dollars on darts trying to pop the multi-colored balloons before finally making a deal with the guy running the game and just buying the stuffed animal outright. I tried saving him and explaining the game was rigged, but Jesse's confidence wasn't hearing me. He ended up paying eighty dollars for a stuffed animal that would probably cost ten at the store.

Taylor still gave him a doe eyed look and kissed him like they were the only two at that carnival when he handed her the pink stuffed cat. That cat now lives on her bed and she cuddles up to it every night. Despite their obvious issues over Adam, Jesse and Taylor are *that* couple. They'd make me sick if I wasn't so jealous.

The door to my class is just around the next corner, but I'm standing frozen. Glued to the spot on the ground by the world's strongest super glue. The tall and handsome guy I can't get out of my head is standing between me and the class I'm late for. As if I come with my own personal homing beacon that only he can hear, Henry lifts his eyes away from the conversation he's having with another student and meets mine. His face brightens, and he blesses me with one of his wide smiles that makes his singular dimple prominent. The speed walking I was doing to get to class isn't an excuse that would hold up in court for the current flush of my cheeks that are heating as he pats the guy he was talking to on the shoulder and walks toward me.

I'm still embarrassed about practically mauling him after he walked me home yesterday. I don't know what came over me. My body took over and I just lunged in for a hug. Now he's almost made it over to me.

I have not moved an inch–class be damned.

"Hi," he says, when the gap between us is down to just inches.

Even though I'm tall, Henry is taller and I have to look up through my lashes at him and he has to tilt his head to look down at me.

"Hi," I say, my voice coming out laced with something unexpected.

The grin that lit up his face is still there. That singular dimple is still strikingly on display.

"Are you coming or going to class?" he asks, nodding at the books I have clenched against my chest with both arms.

"Going."

"Oh, well, don't let me keep you," he says, as he moves to the side and makes a show of clearing my path.

"It's okay, we're not doing anything important today."

Lie. We are indeed doing very important things, just like we do every week in this class. Right now though, I would happily spend more time later making up for missing the class because that dimple and that smirk on his face are so close. Henry is so close I can smell the shampoo he uses—a fresh scent that reminds me of lazy afternoons spent lying on the sand at my favorite beach.

"Well—in that case—if you're up for skipping, I've got the rest of the day off. Would you like to come somewhere with me?"

"Where?" I ask, attempting to sound vaguely interested when in reality I'm about to explode with nervous energy.

"It's a surprise. But it's not far and I can have you back here in a few hours, promise," he says, holding up one hand and laying the other across his chest.

"Okay," I say, without even giving it much thought.

I follow him out to his truck and he once again opens the door for me, just as he did on that first day I arrived in Easton. I give him an appreciative smile and jump in. He closes the door behind me and jogs around the front to get in on his side.

"So now will you tell me where you're taking me, or are you planning on taking me into the woods to murder me?" I joke.

Henry's eyes go wide and he looks panicked.

"Henry, I'm joking. I trust you."

I realize I do—I trust him. In truth, I hardly know him, but the familiarity I feel every time I'm around him keeps me coming back. Making me want to get to know him more.

He lets out an awkward laugh. "You'll just have to see when we get there."

Is he nervous?

We drive for only a few minutes before he turns down a small and winding two lane road. There are large trees on either side of us, creating a canopy of shade. I roll down my window and breathe in the scent of pine.

It reminds me of camping in the mountains during the fall with my dad. Back before my mom was an addict, back when my dad was still alive. We would pitch a tent and roast marshmallows for smores and spend all day hiking or playing in the water of the creek. Those were simpler times, happier times.

The daydream fades when I realize we've stopped moving. We're parked in a small dirt turn off, nothing notable in sight.

"Oh my gosh, you are taking me into the woods to murder me."

"Only if you misbehave," he says with a flirtatious smile.

My stomach is instantly on fire with butterflies.

Henry laughs and unbuckles his seatbelt, climbing out of the truck. Once I've composed myself and am certain I will not have an orgasm just from that devilish smile alone–I follow his lead and get out of the truck.

We walk down a trail that isn't quite visible unless you know what you're looking for. It isn't a hard path to follow, but I'm grateful I'm wearing my tennis shoes today and not sandals. When we come out of the path blocked by tall trees and the blue sky is visible again, we're standing in a field of tall grass. Trees surround the field on every side, hiding this little clearing, sheltering it.

Henry drops and sits in the grass, leaning back on his arms, his legs outstretched in front of him. I do the same.

"Can I tell you something?" Henry says.

"Of course."

"I've never brought anyone here before," he says, looking up at the sky as he talks.

There's more he wants to say, I can sense it. So I stay quiet. Patiently waiting as he gathers his thoughts.

"I found this place by accident a while back. Well—actually my dog did," he laughs at the memory. "I had to pull over to let her do her business, and she pulled free of her leash. I ended up chasing her all the way here. Now I come here whenever I need to think, or just get away."

His admissions tug at my heart and the weight of knowing he's shared this place only with me has me conflicted.

Every time I'm breathing the same air as Henry, I want to be closer to him—in more ways than one. Those desires are terrifying. Those desires of wanting to let someone into my life and my heart are the same desires I ran from with Ender. How is it fair to let myself fall for Henry—a guy I met just over a month ago—when I cut Ender—a guy who was my best friend for years—out of my life entirely? The dichotomy is too much to think about and I push it from my mind, forcing myself to be present. Enjoy the here and now, in this peaceful, hidden field—with Henry.

This is the second time in as many days I've been alone with Henry. Each time has been filled with charged moments of intense feelings and a strange familiarity I can't quite pinpoint. Almost as if an invisible string is connecting me to him and every time I'm near him, the string gets shorter and shorter. Soon I'll be faced with a decision—let the string pull me to Henry intrinsically, or cut the connection altogether.

Chapter Ten

Henderson

Bringing Madison here was a calculated risk. One I would repeat a thousand times just to continue seeing the sun shine on her face turned up to the sky. Her neck extended and her eyes closed, a faint smile on her lips. Out here in this space is the most content I've seen her since she's arrived in Easton. I'm happy to have helped her find a few minutes of peace, grateful the usual look of nervousness and anxiety is washed from her skin.

"If you could only eat one food for the rest of your life, what would it be?" she asks.

We've been going back and forth like this for the past half hour. It reminds me of the confession game we played in our emails. I choose all of my questions and answers carefully, though. I'm not ready to tell her who I am. It's selfish and maybe deceitful, but I'm not ready to give up these moments. That's my fear–that I'll tell her I'm Ender and she'll abandon me the way she did him. Thankfully, most of the questions she's asked have been light like this one.

"The onion rings from the diner," I say.

"Seriously? Why is everyone so obsessed with those things?"

"Have you not tried them?"

I turn my head to stare at her in disbelief. She turns her head to look at me. I'm not sure when we transitioned from sitting to lying on our backs. Looking at her now, I realize how close we are. A small shift would have our sides pressed against each other. The tank top she's wearing leaves her arms bare and I long to run my fingers across her smooth, sun-kissed skin.

"I have," she says, "and I've had better."

"Easton doesn't exactly have a lot of options, so we try not to be too picky here."

The conversation dies out. It's my turn to ask her a question, but I'm finding it difficult to string words together to make a sentence. I'm transfixed by the gold flecks in her eyes, the curve of her lips that are slightly parted, her chest rising and falling with her breaths.

Madison pushes her lips together and swallows, then relaxes her lips to inhale deeply. Her breathing has gotten more pronounced. Exhales causing her to form a tight circle with her lips as she works to control it. I want more than anything to let my lips cross the short distance to hers and taste her, but I can't. Not like this—not when she doesn't know who I really am.

Her eyes fall closed, her head is still turned in my direction. It would be so easy to just tilt my head forward and capture her lips in mine.

Kicking myself, I clear my throat.

"I should probably get you back to campus," I say.

The moment is gone. The opportunity breaks into a million pieces and floats in the wind, scattering among the trees that surround us.

She opens her eyes slowly and nods. The walk back to my truck is silent, punctuated only by the rustling of the pine needles on the trees and chirping of birds.

"What's the best thing you've read in the past few years?" I ask her, breaking the silence on our drive back to campus.

She doesn't look at me, but I can see the crinkle around her eyes and the corner of her lips turn up as she ponders the question.

"An email from a friend," she says. "It was the most beautiful email I've ever read."

I don't dare ask her to elaborate, but she grants me answers to my curiosity.

"His words were brave and honest. Something I haven't been able to be."

My breath catches in my throat and my knuckles turn white with the force of my grip on the steering wheel.

I want to scream the truth. Shout from the top of my lungs that it's me. I wrote those words. Mostly, I want her to tell me why she never responded. I'm a coward and don't say anything. The silence settles between us again.

"Thank you for the adventure, Henry," she says as I put my truck in park along the curb near the dorm rooms.

"You're welcome Madison."

Then she's gone. The inside of my truck feels like a void without her presence. I drive home ruminating on her words about the email I'd sent her. I knew from finding the printed out copy that the words and confessions I made meant something to her, but hearing her say out loud how she feels about them—it makes me hopeful that she has feelings for me buried somewhere. At least, feelings for Ender.

Sometimes I have trouble piecing out the parts of me that are Henry–football star, loyal friend, son–and the parts that are Ender–writer, best friend to Madison, sensitive. My only hope is to show Madison both of those parts now, so when I get the courage to tell her the secret I've been keeping–the consequences might not be so severe.

My phone rings, startling me out of my deep thoughts. When I answer, Coach is on the other end wondering where the hell I am.

Fuck. I'm supposed to be at practice right now.

"I'll be there in five," I tell him and turn around, heading back to campus.

I don't even bother going to the locker room. My bag is in the back of the truck and I quickly change into my practice gear in the parking lot. Someone whistles when I pull my shirt over my head and start putting on my shoulder pads. I ignore them and start jogging onto the field.

"Sorry Coach–I uh, got hung up," I say, slightly out of breath.

"Just get your ass on the field," he says, blowing his whistle to get the team's attention.

"Dude, where the fuck were you?" Jesse asks.

Not being at practice on time is completely out of character for me, so I'm not surprised at Jesse's curiosity. Before I put my helmet on, I give him a loaded grin and wink.

"Oh, hell yes. About time," he says, laughing and putting on his own helmet before taking his place in the O line.

Okay, maybe alluding what I did to Jesse was wrong–but I'm just tired of him and Taylor being up my ass about dating. If he thinks I'm getting some, then maybe they'll both leave me alone for a little while. Yes, I'm probably the only person on this football field that isn't currently having sex. Hell, even Coach has a sex life. His wife just announced last week they're expecting baby number two. I have my reasons for being celibate. Or I have a reason–a beautiful girl with full lips, golden brown eyes and long legs.

By the time practice is over, I'm spent. Emmett wasn't here today and his back up just didn't give it his all. No one is allowed to actually tackle me during practice–too much of an injury risk. But that doesn't mean I don't have to run a shit ton more when my tight end is basically a kid in a sandbox. No point in chewing out this guy. I'll save my ass chewing for Emmett, who should have been here today.

"Where the hell was Emmett?" I ask Jesse as we walk out to my car.

"No clue, man. Called him the other day to see if he wanted to go grab food, but he didn't answer and never called back."

I'm worried about him, but I'm sure he's just balls deep in some new girl. I pull out my phone and fire off an angry text, anyway.

Me: Got my ass handed to me at practice today. Where the hell are you?
Emmett: Sorry, had an appointment. Will be there tomorrow.
Me: What? Was the appointment with a blonde or a brunette?
Emmett: Both ;)

What an ass. I throw my gear bag in the back of my truck and my phone on the dashboard.

"Do you want a ride home?" I ask Jesse.

"Nah, I'll walk," he says, and heads toward his apartment.

I don't mind giving Jesse a ride after practice. It's less than a mile from the practice field to his apartment, but I know how dead a long practice can make you feel. Today, I'm grateful he wants to walk because I need the alone time. I'm still replaying the afternoon I spent with Mads over and over in my mind. I don't need Jesse asking me anymore questions if he notices I can't get out of my own head.

Chapter Eleven

Madison

I've taken refuge in the library trying to get some studying done. Someone on our floor decided today was a good day to have a rave in their room. Our R.A. is out of town and they're taking advantage of it, I guess. The repetitive music and thumping of my walls was giving me a migraine. When I'd attempted to read the same chapter for the fourth time without even understanding anything I read, I gave up and came here. The big comfy chair I found in a dim corner on the second floor has become my new temporary study lounge. For a Wednesday afternoon right before midterms, it's unexpectedly quiet. There have only been a few students making their way through the rows of books in the hour I've been here, and no one else is studying on this floor.

The first six weeks of classes flew by. Summer quarter has been busier than I expected. Between taking the max amount of credits I could and working at the diner four days a week, I rarely find time for anything else. I've only seen Taylor a few times since the carnival. We're on different sleep schedules, mostly. She has early morning classes and is in bed by nine most weeknights while I got stuck with midday classes and work either the 6 p.m. to midnight shift or the 6 a.m. to noon shift.

We managed to have lunch together a few times between classes, but not much else. She's working today in the library so I stopped and said hi to her on my way in. Working in the library must be a dream and I am seriously jealous. Not that I haven't loved working at the diner. The tips are great and Bev and Joy are wonderful to work with. Chuck, the main cook, has yet to warm up to me, but Joy says he's just a *grumpy old geezer* and to not take it personally. I'm determined to make him adore me.

But working on campus would mean no two-mile walk to work, and working in the library would mean being surrounded by books all day. I also know working a campus job comes with perks like getting on the good side of professors and getting first dibs on the used books. Since I picked up my course books so close to classes starting, most of them have torn pages and penises drawn on them. Apparently, being in college doesn't equal maturity. There were also more than a few mystery stains that I had to take sanitizer wipes to.

Taylor's behind the check-out desk in the center of the library with Adam. I can see them from where I'm hiding out and they seem–*close*. I know she said Jesse has nothing to worry about, and it's none of my business, but I can't help but get an icky feeling.

Whatever is or isn't going on over there fizzles out as Taylor leaves the desk to shelve books and I turn my attention back to studying. I'm working on a writing assignment where we have to re-write an already published article. There were a dozen sources to choose from and I chose an article by Christiane Amanpour, where she wrote about women in war. Go big or go home, right? If I wasn't majoring in English, Journalism would definitely be my second choice. Traveling the world and reporting on things that matter would be the thrill of a lifetime. But I'm not brave enough.

I've made it about half way through the assignment when I'm startled by what sounds like books falling to the ground an aisle over. I look up but can't see who's responsible for the noise. Henry comes peeking around the corner with an embarrassed smile on his lips, putting an end to my curiosity. My heart beat instantly doubles and my palms go so sweaty I have to drop the pen in my hand and rub them on my jeans.

"Hey," he says, breaking the silence.

"Hi," I squeak back.

"Sorry about that. I, um, didn't mean to disturb you."

Henry hasn't moved from being half hidden behind the row of books. A war inside me is raging where one side wants him to stay where he is and the other wants to be straddling him.

"No worries," I tell him. "Not like I own the place."

Chuckling, he moves toward me and declares one side of the war victor, but I steel myself and don't make any attempts to straddle him. At least not yet.

He's wearing a pair of joggers again, and dammit if my eyes didn't fall straight down to his dick. I don't make it a habit of checking out guys' junk, but from what I can see through the tight material, he has a lot of something in there. He sits casually in the big leather armchair next to me, leaning into one corner and facing me. I do the same, leaning into the opposite corner of my chair so I'm turned more toward him. He clears his throat, and I didn't know a sound most people find repulsive could turn me on.

"So, how are your classes? I hope you didn't have any problems missing that class."

"No problems," I say. It indeed was a small problem. I've been having to study more the past two weeks just to make up for it. "Classes are great. Some are a little harder than I expected."

"What is it you're working on? Can I see?" He asks, nodding his head toward my notebook.

A warm sensation brushes across my cheeks as embarrassment settles in. Shaking my head and pulling myself out of the internal monologue I was in, I drop my eyes to my notebook. I wasn't actually working on my assignment in the notebook. It's just my latest word dump and poem attempts. Suddenly embarrassed, I pull the notebook closer to me. I haven't shared my poetry with anyone I know, except Ender. That was different because we shared everything. *Almost everything.* I never told Ender how bad things got with my mom. It's not like he would have judged me or even been able to do anything to help. I just didn't want him to see me as weak. Shame can wreak havoc on relationships.

Sure, Ender would have worried about me sleeping at a different place every other night, and he would have been fuming if he knew I spent a few nights sleeping outside. Henry must sense my hesitation because he offers me an out.

"If it's private, then I get it. I'm sorry, I shouldn't have asked."

The sheepish look he has on his face is pretty adorable and makes my heart warm. I trust him, I realize. I hardly know him, but I've always been pretty good at reading people and something is telling me I can trust him.

"No. I mean, yes, it's kind of private, but it's also kind of embarrassing. It's just a lot of brain dump and some pieces of poems."

"If you don't want to share, it's okay. But I doubt it's embarrassing, especially if it's your thoughts."

I hesitate again, chewing on my lip. I do it when I get nervous or anxious and don't even realize it, but when I look back at Henry, I can see him staring at my lips. His eyelids are heavy and his lips are parted. When I release my lip from my teeth's grip with a pop, he exhales and sticks his own tongue out, slowly running it across his top lip. My eyes never leave his lips, and it feels like it takes hours for his tongue to make it across them. Instinctively, my legs press tight together.

Without any more thought, I hand the notebook over to him. My arousal apparently fueling an unexpected moment of courage.

"Go ahead, you can read it. But only this page, please."

If anything, it gives me an opportunity to stare at him while he's distracted, and he won't be able to notice the drool about to come out of my mouth. His hair is styled today, I've only ever seen it natural. It's not very long but untamed by product, it can look a little wild. Today he looks polished, put together. When it's messy, it's cute, but like this, it's sexy and makes him look a little older. I don't know how old he even is, I realize, but he must be about my age because he mentioned he's only in his first year here. He has the same stubble across his chin and jaw I've seen him with before.

While he looks over my notebook, his lips are pursed together and his jaw is slightly clenched. He parts his lips just the tiniest bit occasionally and sucks in air through his teeth. There's something incredibly sexy about it, and I want him to do it again.

"How old are you?" I ask him.

He only briefly looks up at me before turning his attention back to my notebook.

"Forty-seven," he jokes. "How old are you?"

"Not forty-seven."

His eyes meet mine and he holds my gaze this time.

"I'm eighteen."

"Oh, me too," I say.

Once again, his attention goes back to my notebook.

I wish I could see inside his mind and know what he's thinking as he reads over my words. I want to know what's causing the subtle changes in his expressions. Why his eyes are closing lazily sometimes and widening with curiosity at others. I'm about to ask him to say something, anything, because the not-knowing is killing me and he's been looking over the notebook for what feels like decades.

Henry finally closes my notebook and hands it back to me. He doesn't say anything for a long time. I'm about to just shove all my books into my backpack and leave out of total embarrassment when he stands up and starts walking toward the book shelves. My notebook is a little messy, and there were some pretty raw emotions on the page I let him read, but his reaction still wasn't what I was expecting. Is he serious? Who just up and walks away from someone after they've let you into one of their most private spaces? Now I'm getting kind of pissed off and I'm about to call after him when he turns around.

"Are you coming?"

He wants me to follow him? Then why the hell didn't he say so? The huge smile that spreads across my lips is completely out of my control. My body seems to react of its own volition around Henry frequently. I get up, brush off my pride, and follow him.

We land in the poetry section and he scans the shelves. Still a little irritated, and a lot confused, I stand there with my arms crossed, waiting. Henry pulls a book out of the shelves and walks over to me, our toes practically touching as he hands it to me. I look at the book in my hands and back up at him for an explanation. His hands are tucked in his front pockets, but he doesn't move to give me any space.

"It's a collection of modern poets, all women. I found it the first week of classes and I think you're gonna love it. It's not what you'd probably expect someone like me to be checking out from the library, but let's just say I've needed to do some soul searching and knew reading women's words was a good place to start."

I'm stunned, and a little impressed. Henry doesn't seem the type. This is refreshing.

"Definitely didn't have you pegged for the poetry type, I can admit that. And really not the type who consciously gravitates toward women's words. That's actually kind of beautiful."

We're standing here now, just staring at each other, the book in my hands fitting between us by the narrowest of margins. Without thinking,

I suck my bottom lip in, chewing on it lightly. Henry's breathing gets raspier, more shallow. His eyes light up with emotion and I think I see desire in them.

Henry leans forward first, but I close the gap and our lips meet. At first, they're just pressed against each other perfectly still. Neither of us moving a muscle for several earth shatteringly long seconds. But slowly he begins to part his lips and uses his tongue to part mine. Running his tongue gently between my lips, from one edge to the other. The movement reminds me of the fantasy I played out in my mind while I got myself off in my bed. A warmth is growing deep in my stomach and traveling lower. I'm still holding the book with both hands between us, but his hand comes up to cradle my jaw, his fingertips in my hair. The faintest moan escapes me when his tongue meets mine.

Then, as fast as it began, it's over. Henry's pulled away and has put several feet of space between us. He runs his hand over his face as I stare at him. I'm dizzy from the feel of his hand on me and the taste of him in my mouth.

"I am so sorry," he says, and rushes past me out of the row of books we were hidden between.

Chapter Twelve

Henderson

I don't know what a panic attack feels like, but I think I'm having one. Really, it's just shame and embarrassment because I am a complete dick.

I'm sitting in my truck, my head on the steering wheel, trying to process what happened. I can still taste her on my lips, a warm taste with a hint of vanilla. The feel of her soft hair is still making my fingertips tingle. Gripping the steering wheel, I let out my frustrations and emotions with an audible groan.

She is most likely so pissed off and confused right now, but honestly, so am I. Getting lost in her scent, her touch and her taste for those brief moments was one of the best feelings I've ever experienced. I didn't *want* to stop. I wanted to deepen the kiss, to run my hand through her hair to the back of her head and pull her into me. Let our bodies touch as much as they possibly could.

As much as I wanted that, as soon as I got the first taste of her, I knew it was wrong. I knew I couldn't let her kiss me as Henry when she didn't know I was Ender. Kissing her felt familiar in the best way, but she can't have any of the same emotional ties to my touch. There has to be a way I can come clean and tell her who I am with no repercussions. If I don't tell her in the right way or wait too long to tell her, she'll never trust me again.

Even if she stopped talking to me, stopped talking to Ender, I know she trusts him. I know she trusts me.

Reading her journal, seeing her handwriting for the first time, made me think back to all the poems she shared with me. All the beautiful words she'd typed over the years. All the secrets we would share with each other, letting all of our vulnerabilities be on full display for each other in the words we typed. But, there in that little book, I could see her words in a new way. I noticed the soft curves of some words like *life* and *promise*, the ending letters swooping up and around the page into doodles. There were other words that were sunken into the pages where she felt more passion, or maybe anger, and pressed her pen harder to the paper. It was so much of what I adored about her right in front of me.

All these years I've felt like I could see her when I read her emails, especially her poems. I couldn't see her physically, but I could see her for who she really was. Who she was in her deepest and darkest parts alongside her brightest and most heartwarming. Touching the words she wrote in that journal with her own hand gave me chills. When we were standing so close, hidden between the rows of books, I could smell her unique scent and it was overwhelming.

My heart rate is finally slowing down. I'm supposed to be on the football field warming up for practice in twenty minutes. I'm parked in the lot by the field, so it's a short walk and I don't have to worry about running into her if she's leaving the library. She probably left right after I did. Most likely she's in the main parking lot looking for my car so she can key it. No, the Mads I know isn't vindictive, and she definitely doesn't handle any kind of confrontation well.

She once told me about a time when she was young, maybe in fourth or fifth grade, when all the *cool girls* made fun of her because she brought a stuffed animal to a sleepover. They teased her about it and ignored her for the rest of the night. She called her mom and faked a stomachache so she could get picked up early. She didn't tell her mom the truth, that the girls were little bitches. And when the girls acted as if nothing happened at school on Monday, she wasn't mean to them. She didn't even ask them why they were mean to her. She kept playing with them at recess like nothing ever happened. When she told me that story, it made me want to go back in time and hug that poor girl. The girl who just wanted to fit in and have friends. It also made me want to kick sand at those mean girls.

Fifteen minutes until I need to be on the field. The weight of my gym bag slung over my shoulder as I walk to the field is nothing compared to the weight of the mistake I just made.

The entire team is pretty much here already. I should be one of the first people on the field for practices since I'm the quarterback, but I've found it hard to care that much. It's not like the coaches will kick me off the team. Hell, I could not show up to practice and still start every game. When you're a team whose best record in the past ten years is going 2 and 12, you don't pass on a quarterback who once had his pick of D1 schools.

Emmett and Jesse being on the team is one of the few reasons I even agreed to play for Pinehurst. That and I'm still weighing my options of trying for the pros when I graduate and if I don't play for the next four years, there's no way I'd stay in shape.

Jesse never really took football seriously, but he says it's fun, so he still plays. Emmett could have played for a better school and I have my suspicions he turned down a few offers. Lately, Emmett's been acting weirder than normal. I brought it up once, that I thought he was wasting his talent here. He almost bit my head off. I've since avoided the subject. He's been missing a lot of practice lately, but he's here today. Nobody seems to know where he goes when he's not here.

Practice seems to drag on for longer than normal. We don't have any games until fall, but a lot of these guys are in shit shape. The coaches are all in crappy moods and make us run drills until half the team is puking in trash cans. There should seriously be some kind of scoring advantage to being a team who practices in the heat and humidity we have to deal with. When we finally get released, I don't follow the team into the recently finished locker rooms. I just head home to change and shower.

Mom won't be home until late. She's been picking up extra shifts at the hospital. Without Dad's income, money is tight. Even though school is paid for, I still try to work as many shifts at Grissom's as I can. That way, I don't have to ask her for money. If she got her way, I wouldn't work at all and focus solely on school and football, but she lost that argument when I told her I'd drop football if it meant I couldn't work and help pay some bills. I don't need much, so my paycheck mostly sits in my bank account. I've started slipping twenty-dollar bills into Mom's wallet occasionally. Deceitful? Maybe. Anyway, I think she knows I'm doing it.

My relationship dynamic with Mom instantly changed after last summer. When your kid beats the shit out of your husband because he was beating the shit out of you... it's hard to have a normal mother-son relationship after that. Therapy has helped, so has learning to be completely honest with each other, as much as we can. That's a work in progress for both of us.

I've also had to do a lot of learning, re-learning and unlearning. I realized I let the shit my dad would say to my mom slide for all those years but didn't react until I saw him physically hurting her. That's part of why I read the book of poems I showed Mads. I slipped up and told my therapist about one of Mads poems once and she suggested the book.

I've been meaning to tell Mom about Madison—I think it's only right. Mads has been such a huge part of my life for so long and with the new developments of her being right here in Easton, I think it's time. Her first Mom reaction will be to lecture me about Internet safety and how I shouldn't have been talking to strangers online at thirteen. She would follow it up with solid advice honestly. Her own love life may have been complete shit, but she somehow gives good relationship advice. She's a big reason I finally broke things off with Jackie. She's one of the ones that helped me realize I was using her.

I don't know if I'm ready to share Mads with anyone just yet. There's still a strong desire in my gut to keep that part of my life protected a little while longer. I'm not ready to face facts, not ready to reconcile the relationship I had online with Mads with the relationship I've done nothing but screw up with Madison in real life. Talking about Mads out loud will lead me to confronting the fact that maybe she stopped responding to my emails for a valid reason. Her being here now, in Easton, complicates everything.

After I shower and get dressed, I try to focus on some homework. I'm only taking two classes over the summer and I'm only taking them so I can have the minimum number of classes in fall to remain eligible for football. I did what was expected of me and chose a path to a Health Science degree. Even though I have very little interest in anything to do with it and the classes are boring as shit. I also can't think of any career it could lead me to that wouldn't make me want to stab myself in the face with a pair of scissors.

I can't concentrate. My stomach lets out a growl, louder than the music I'm listening to. I've been so in my own head I haven't eaten since breakfast this morning. I decide to text Emmett.

Me: hey. Wanna go grab food at the diner?
Emmett: Yeah. Pick me up. I'm at the barn.
Me: Be there in 10

Shoving my phone in my pocket, I head downstairs to grab my keys and put on my shoes.

Emmett's waiting outside when I pull onto the gravel drive at the barn.

"Dude. You look like shit," I tell him when he gets in.

He's at least showered since practice, but his hair is a mess. He's got bags under his eyes I didn't notice before, and his skin looks gray. I knew most of the guys were out of shape, but I've never seen Emmett look so beat up after a practice before.

"Practice was a bitch today," He snaps. "You were on that field, you know."

"Okay, geeze. Sorry."

I pull back out onto the road and head for the diner. I know she probably doesn't want to see me and I still can't decide if I'm heading to the diner hoping she's working or hoping she's not. If she is, I don't even know what I'll say or if I'll have the balls to say anything at all. Plus, if she is there and I say something to her, I'll have to explain everything to Emmett. He's already in a bad mood, so I don't want his opinion right now—so I just keep driving.

I park in the bus station's employee parking lot because street parking is full and no one will bat an eye at my truck being there. We walk down the street toward the diner and the knots in my stomach twist tighter the closer we get. When we make it inside the diner, I scan the place for Madison. I see Joy and Bev are both behind the long counter. If they're both here, I doubt Madison is working. I catch Joy's eye and give her a little wave. She nods her head toward the back of the restaurant, letting me know it's okay for us to take our usual booth.

The knots in my stomach slowly start untwisting and I relax into the vinyl booth bench. I guess it's a good thing she isn't working. Coming in here after what I did to her in the library and not even having a plan for what to say was kind of a dick move. I think about trying to look her up in the school directory and emailing her, but that seems a bit stalkerish and like a step backward. I think about sending her an email from my Ender email account, but that will only complicate things more. Would she even respond to it? I've gotta come up with a plan. I don't want that kiss to be our last.

CHAPTER THIRTEEN

MADISON

I'm still reeling from the kiss in the library as I walk to work. Who knew a kiss that brief could still be felt days later. I can still taste him and I've brushed my teeth multiple times since then. I find myself gently touching my lips with my fingertips as I walk. As amazing as that kiss was, I'm also confused, and a little pissed off. I can't believe he would just run off. I've been going over every likely scenario of why he would apologize and leave the way he did.

Does he have a girlfriend? Did my breath taste or smell bad? These reasons keep rolling around in my mind. None of them seem to fit, or maybe all of them do. I eventually give up, resigning to the fact that I may never know. It doesn't stop me from still feeling that kiss, remembering it. I did not know a kiss, even one so brief, could feel that way.

I kissed Liam more than I've kissed anyone else. He's the guy I was sort of kinda, sort of not dating senior year. Really, I was just using him for a place to stay every once in a while. He was a few years older than me and had an apartment with a couple of roommates. But he "wasn't into labels" and wanted to "keep things kush" so it was never that serious. Which was fine by me because he smoked more pot than he could afford at his minimum wage job.

When I was kissing him, my thoughts usually wandered to things on my to-do list or how his mouth tasted like Doritos constantly. I don't ever even remember seeing him eat Doritos. It made no sense.

When I kissed Henry, my mind went completely blank at first. All my senses took over, my sense of touch, taste, and smell going into overdrive. I can remember every tiny sensation. Every gentle brushing of our skin. Trying to make it through work today is going to be brutal. My mind is filled with memories that make me tingle all over.

I'm working with Bev this morning, which means my shift will be fun and go by fast. Bev likes to make sure the jukebox is always on so she can dance around while we work. I've even let her pull me into her dance breaks occasionally. The diner is busy with its usual morning rush of people grabbing food before heading off to school or work. There are the regulars that sit at the counter while they drink their coffee and read the newspaper. A few of them even have laptops open, getting a head start on the day's work.

I pause for a minute and think about how lucky I am. Lucky to have gotten this job. To have ended up in this town where I'm feeling at peace. Like I belong. Taylor has been the perfect roommate and the closer we get, the more I know she's someone I'll be friends with for the rest of my life. I tease her regularly about not sticking me in a hideous dress when I'm a bridesmaid at her and Jesse's wedding one day. I don't think I've ever had a friend I could talk to about plans so far in the future.

All of my friends have been the kind that I only see at school or work, never making a genuine connection with any of them. In the last few years of highschool, friends were a necessary evil. A means to an end. Someone I was close enough to I could ask to crash on their couch for a night or two. Yet, not close enough to have to explain why I needed a place to crash. They were friends that didn't ask questions.

Sometimes I think I'll share more of my past with Taylor—it's not as if she hasn't asked me about my life before coming to Easton. I am just the queen of diverting the conversation and dodging the hard questions. She never presses me when I do it, and that makes me love her even more. It's a happy balance between her seeming to be genuinely interested in me and my life, but still recognizing when there are things I don't want to talk about.

The door to the diner chimes and a young couple is walking in, holding hands.

"Hi," I greet them, "Booth or table?"

"Booth, please," one of the young women says.

I lead them over to a booth and they slide into it, sitting on the same side, never releasing their hands from each other. I sigh as I walk away to get them drinks. As I'm filling their cups with soda, I think to myself—I wouldn't mind having someone to hold hands with all the time and be so in love that we do corny things. Things like sit on the same side of a booth in a diner.

Bev must see my day dreaming.

"What's the look on your face, sweetheart?"

Bev is in her fifties, with short brown hair and fake boobs. This isn't something I'm guessing about—she told me they're fake. She always has a full face of makeup on, *always*.

Her and Joy are best friends and she's worked here at the diner off and on since she was a young mother in her twenties. The story is, she started working again five years ago when her husband passed away from a heart attack. They had a life insurance policy for him, so she doesn't need the money. She enjoys staying busy.

Bev is always trying to give me advice and frequently asks about my essentially non-existent love life. She offers at least once a week to set me up with one of the guys from her church. She's sweet and she means well, but I can barely handle the guy that's already in my life. The one who likes to kiss the life out of me and run away. Not to mention Ender, the guy online I abandoned who I can't seem to forget, no matter how good kissing Henry felt.

I brush Bev's question off and get back to work. The couple in the booth continues to make love sick puppy dog eyes at each other and I feel something I'm not used to–jealousy. I remember over the years getting pangs of jealousy when Ender would talk about girls. I never admitted that to him. But it was there, just under the surface. One time I caught Liam flirting with a barista, I felt nothing. Not an ounce of jealousy. The thought of seeing Henry flirt with someone–that sets my skin on fire and makes me feel a rage I didn't know I was capable of.

What has that boy and that kiss done to me?

"Get changed. We're going to go watch the idiots hit each other."

I've just walked into our dorm room after my shift, and Taylor is shoving snacks and drinks into a bag. She hasn't even turned to look at me.

"Um, I'm sorry, we're doing what?"

"We're gonna go watch the football practice. I promised Jesse I would, they've been practicing for almost a month and I haven't made it to one yet. So, today's the day!" she says, as she drops a book into her bag.

"And you're bringing a book?" I question her, raising my eyebrows at her.

She turns to face me finally.

"Yup. Football is boring as shit, and football practice is even more bor-ing. Jesse and I have come to an agreement. I can read during practices, but not during games."

I think about this for a minute before asking, "So... why even go to the practice then?"

"Because Jesse likes it when I do, and I like making Jesse happy," she says, with a soft expression.

She says this so easily, as if doing things you might loathe for the chance to see someone else smile is the easiest thing in the world. I wish I could have this trait, but my track record shows I usually run from anything that makes me even the slightest bit nervous or uncomfortable. Case in point; my complete silence and refusal to respond to Ender's emails rather than confront my own feelings.

I have nothing else to do the rest of the day, so I change into some cut-offs and a loose fitting band tee and go with her.

We make it to the football practice field and Taylor spreads out a blanket under a tree on a hill for us to sit on. We're about a hundred yards away from the action–if you can call it that–but still close enough we can hear Jesse when he cat calls to Taylor and yells, *"Hey baby."*

He follows up his greeting with a few goofy dance moves. Taylor waves a hand at him and pulls out her book to start reading.

I didn't think to bring a book for myself, so instead I lean back on my arms and actually watch the team practice. The team is close enough I can see their faces if I squint, but really they look like nothing more than a sea of muscles and sweat. I spot Jesse talking to a guy whose back is turned to me in a cut off shirt. I notice many of the guys are sporting similar looks. Ripped and cut up shirts and tank tops over their shoulder pads with the tight, ass hugging pants I'm used to seeing football players wear on television.

They've all been standing around talking to each other and goofing off, not actually practicing anything, it seems. An older man in a polo shirt, tan shorts and a baseball cap with the school logo on it, blows a whistle. He must be the coach. The football players all take different positions on the field. The guy Jesse was talking to moves to the center and Jesse is a few people over from him. I hear a lot of quick yelling I don't understand and the guy in the center catches the football that's tossed to him. After that, what I can only see as chaos ensues.

Guys are running in different directions, players that were crouched down across from each other start pushing and shoving. The cracks of their hard uniforms hitting is loud and I can hear lots of grunting and yelling. I'm transfixed. I don't understand what exactly is going on, but Taylor was wrong. This isn't boring at all, it's kind of fiercely hot. The grunting and yelling, the sweating, and the tight pants. This must be why some girls love football.

The guy in the center just threw the football to the other end of the field. Someone catches it and takes off running in the same direction the ball was traveling. When he makes it to the end of the field, he drops the ball on the ground and starts dancing around. The ball thrower watched the whole thing play out, but he isn't celebrating like everyone else. Was that not supposed to happen? Now the guy who threw the ball is walking toward the coach, his head hanging, staring at the grass as he walks. That's when I realize the guy is Henry. Strange, he never mentioned he's on the football team.

I can confidently say I have never watched a football game in its entirety. I've seen football games on television when someone else was watching them and I happened to be in the room, but I will never claim to know the rules of the sport. I am, however, nearly certain that Henry's position is called the Quarterback and that what just happened was a good thing for him and his team. Ender played football and my limited knowledge is mostly from his emails. Ender was apparently good, and he was supposed to be going to college on a full scholarship to play. He never updated me on what school he chose before we stopped emailing. I'm realizing now I don't even remember if he told me what position he played. I haven't been re-reading his old emails as much; I've been so busy between classes, homework, working at the diner and spending some time with Taylor when I can.

If I'm right, and what just happened on the field was a good thing for Henry, why does he look so sad? And why, with him looking so sad, am I still so turned on by him right now? He has washboard abs that are prominently on display because of his ripped half shirt, and the muscles in his arms flex strongly as he wrings his hands while talking to the coach. He twists and turns, stretching and arching his back, making the muscles in his butt look more defined. I didn't even know someone could have muscles in their ass like that.

I watch the practice intently for the next half hour, following Henry as he runs around in small circles while the other players try to stop him from being able to throw the ball. He never once shows the same enthusiasm as the other guys on the team, and the despondent look never leaves his face. The coach blows his whistle several times in quick succession and the players all start making their way off the field. I think football may have just become my new favorite sport.

"Hey Taylor, I think it's over," I say, looking over at her.

She's lying on her back, her book on her chest, fast asleep.

Chapter Fourteen

Henderson

We're almost on the edge of town now, and I have no idea where we're going. Emmett texted me and said he needed my help with something. He picked me up twenty minutes ago. He won't tell me where the hell we're going or what we're doing, even though I've asked. Multiple times. It doesn't stop me from trying again.

"Dude. Where the fuck are we going?"

Silence.

"I swear, Emmett, if you're taking me on some wild drug deal or some shit–you know I can't get in trouble."

"Fuck Henry, seriously. First, you know I don't do drugs. Second, fuck you for thinking I would ever put you in a situation like that."

I shut up. Not because I'm not still worried about whatever exploit we're on, but because I know he's telling the truth.

He finally pulls off the main road onto a dirt one and heads south. The road is bumpy and we're creating a dust storm behind us because Emmett only knows how to drive one speed, fast. I have to hang onto my seat more than once before he finally slows down. Even though it's pitch dark outside, I recognize where we are. Knowing where we are doesn't give me a clue to what the hell we're doing.

"Emmett, there's nothing even out here except the water tower."

He looks at me and grins. Shit.

He pulls right off the dirt road into the overgrown weeds and grass, parking the car a few yards from the water tower. Emmett shuts off the car, unbuckles his seatbelt, and gets out of the car without saying another word. I sigh and reluctantly follow him as he walks to the base of the water tower. When I finally catch up to him, he's just standing there looking up at it, not talking.

The water tower has been here at the edge of town my entire life. I look up at the structure looming over us. It's old, but the town spends the money to maintain it because it's become such a fixture. It's the first thing you see when you're driving into town from the next biggest city.

"Let's go," Emmett says, and starts climbing the ladder.

"Are you serious right now?"

He pauses on the ladder and looks at me.

"We've been talking about climbing this behemoth since we were kids and still haven't. Now start climbing."

By the time I give up and follow him, he's almost at the top. When I make it to the top myself, he's sitting with his legs dangling over the edge, arms resting on the rail in front of him. I sit down next to him and do the same.

"Holy shit," I whisper, taking in the view.

From where we're sitting, you can see the entire town of Easton. There are dots of light everywhere. You can even see where the college is because it's just a little brighter than everywhere else. We sit in silence for a long time, just staring out at the vast darkness in contrast to the town and its dancing lights.

I wonder in that moment which light is the light Madison is standing under. I wonder what she's doing now and if she's thinking about me. If she's at work or if she's in her dorm room studying. I actively try not to think of the possibility of her hanging out with another guy. I *do* think of the possibility of her in the shower, standing under a hot stream of water and running soapy hands across her skin.

Fuck. I am so damn horny and this is not the time or place.

Emmett interrupts my thoughts.

"Do you ever wonder what it would be like to live somewhere else?" he asks, not looking at me, still just looking straight out into the night.

"Yeah, sometimes. I mean, I'm not even supposed to be living here right now, so I guess I've definitely thought about it."

I have indeed thought about it. Sometimes it's all I think about. How I'm not supposed to be in this town. How I'm supposed to be exploring a new place and a new life. Then I think about the fact that if I'd left the way I planned–I never would have noticed a beautiful girl with golden eyes crying in front of the bus stop.

"I don't think I've experienced even a fraction of what life is supposed to be. I've never had a girlfriend. I've never lived anywhere but here. Hell, I've never even had a real job."

Hearing Emmett be so poignant is a little jarring, and I struggle to find the words to respond to him. He continues before I can piece anything together.

"I want us all to go on a trip together. Somewhere warm but not as humid as here. Somewhere we can get into bars legally and just spend entire days laying on warm sand and drinking beers."

"Well, there's always Mexico, but I don't know how any of us will find the time with football and classes and work."

He sighs and looks at me.

"We need to find the time, Henderson."

He never calls me Henderson. Before I can question him, he's up on his feet and heading back down the ladder. I follow him, wondering what in the hell is going on. I'm a shitty friend. I should be more concerned, but Emmett's always been in his own world. Maybe the realities of finally being in college are getting to him. Or maybe his parents are making him get a job soon and he just wants to blow off steam before it happens.

On the drive home, he goes back to the Emmett I'm used to. Cracking jokes, talking about football, sharing graphic details of one of the cheerleaders he hooked up with a few weeks ago. It's as if the water tower and his words of longing for a different life never even happened. It was just a figment of my imagination.

I haven't had sex in over six months. Not that I've had a lot of sex in my life, but I imagine it's similar to drugs. You want more once you get a taste. You'll go back to it over and over. I've never done drugs, though. I've smoked pot a few times, but I don't think it would qualify me for any bad boy awards. I just sat on the couch in the basement and played video games for hours and demolished an entire pizza. Thrilling shit.

I realize it's been too long since I've had sex because I'm staring at the pie my mom left on the counter and thinking that idiot from the 90s movie maybe wasn't such an idiot after all. I've been sitting at the kitchen counter for an hour trying to get a paper done for my last summer final. It's due at midnight and I put it off. Now I'm annoyed because it's taking me longer than usual. I just can't get myself to be interested in the ins and outs of nutrition. It's boring.

If I wanted to, I could be having sex. With someone, maybe Jackie, or pretty much any girl who goes after the football team. That's not my style, though, and there's only one person I want to have sex with. Of course, I can't because that would be fifty shades of fucked up. Having sex with someone when you're holding power over them with such a big secret as—*we've actually been emailing since we were kids and I know this, but you don't*—doesn't seem like something I'd be very proud of.

Somewhere between thinking salacious thoughts about a pie and thinking about having sex with Madison, my pants got way too tight. I could just go upstairs and take care of it, but I promised Jesse I'd give him a ride to work since it's a million degrees outside. I read more of my boring as shit textbook and it does the trick to calm me down. I clean up all my school stuff and leave to go pick up Jesse.

I haven't heard from Emmett since our adventure of climbing the water tower a few nights ago. I'm tempted to ask Jesse if he's noticed anything different about him, but think better of it and keep my mouth shut. I've been waiting outside Jesse's apartment for almost fifteen minutes. I've texted him twice and called once, no response and no answer. I'm just about to leave when I see him and Taylor rushing down the stairs from his upstairs unit. Taylor's hair is a mess, and Jesse is buttoning the last buttons on his shirt. He pulls open the front door of the car and asks if I can drop Taylor off at her parents' house.

"Sure, but she might want to look in a mirror before I do," I tell him with a laugh.

He's got a proud grin on his face, but moves out of the way to let Taylor sit in the front seat. She slides in and buckles her seatbelt before pulling down the visor mirror to get to work fixing her hair.

"Thanks for the ride, man. It's hotter than a monkey's ass outside today and I was not looking forward to walking to work."

I shake my head at his analogy.

"So, Henry," Taylor starts, "are you going to Caleb's party tomorrow tonight?"

I groan. Caleb has been talking about this damn party for weeks. Caleb is a decent football player and wouldn't be so much of a douche if he didn't try so damn hard to get everyone to love him—his inability to be a team player and his need to be a show off aside. He's already got half the team up his ass because he flaunts Daddy's money. There's nothing a bunch of college kids love more than free booze and a rich kid who supplies it, so of course he's throwing a rager while his parents are out of town.

I ended up chewing his ass out on the field the other day because I was so sick of hearing about it. The guy acts as if he's a freshman in high school, not college.

"Yeah, what else am I gonna do? I'm turning in my last final today and don't have any new assignments yet."

I can think of a million things I would rather do than go to the party, but Quarterback Henry won't admit any of them. Play the part, keep up the facade, go to the shitty party.

I drop off Jesse and head to the other side of town to drop off Taylor. Taylor's parents live in one of the newer subdivisions, one of the few the town has allowed in decades. Her dad's retired from the military and her mom is a retired school teacher. Taylor mentioned they've been thinking about selling their house and traveling. I know Taylor loves her family, but I also know she feels she barely knows her dad, because he was always gone too much over-seas while she was growing up. It makes sense she moved out of the house and into the dorms. I also know her dad did not approve of her being in such a committed relationship with Jesse for so long, even though her mom absolutely adores Jesse.

"Henry, are you going to at least try to have fun at this party? You've been in a sour mood for months and I can't even imagine what you've been dealing with the past year, but—I just want to see you happy."

Taylor is always looking out for everyone else, always worried about her friends. It makes her a great friend but also sometimes an annoying one. I push my annoyance aside and remind myself she means well.

"I promise to try," I say, trying to meet her halfway.

"That's all I ask."

Taylor leans back in her seat with a smug smile on her face, satisfied by my answer. I'm sure she feels like she's won, but I'm still not even a little excited about this party.

CHAPTER FIFTEEN

MADISON

I work most weekends, but Joy gave me tomorrow off. I just have to make it through today's Saturday morning rush. My plan is to spend the afternoon getting all my laundry done. Then I'll have all day Sunday to do whatever I want. Napping and exploring the library are boldly on my to-do list. I haven't been able to find much time to write just for myself either. Sure, I've done a ton of writing for some of my classes, but it's not the same as just writing what I want and writing for the pure joy of it. I turned in all my finals for my summer classes at the beginning of the week. Now I have the next few weeks to plan for fall quarter and the influx of students when the school year officially starts.

My shift goes by pretty fast and I may have even gotten a hint of a smile out of Chuck when I started singing orders to him every time I came up to the window. I think it was my attempt at opera that finally did him in. After I change out of my work clothes and wave bye to Joy, I start my walk home. I'm not a fan of how much time the walk to and from work takes, but I have learned to enjoy the walk. Easton is a beautiful town. Every street is perfectly manicured and the whole town has the same charming details like decorative iron street lights and tons of trees everywhere. I can't wait until fall when all the trees start to change color.

I've almost saved up for a car. A few more weeks of stashing away my tips and I think I can make it happen. Easton will start getting snow before it's even officially winter and walking two miles each way in the snow to work doesn't sound fun. I'll also need to invest in snow boots and a warm jacket just to get around campus. I've managed to add to my savings over the past few weeks and I've now got three grand put away. There would be more in my savings account, but I needed some summer clothes and a new pair of shoes. Easton doesn't have much in the way of second hand options. Thankfully, they have a Target one town over. I bought everything I needed there except the shoes. I splurged and ordered a new pair of Converse online. Just a pair of simple black high tops, but I haven't had new sneakers in years and I'm glad to have a pair that the soles aren't wafer thin on.

I make it back to my dorm room and it's empty. Taylor must be hanging out with Jesse. I'm exhausted, but I begin the arduous task of sorting my laundry. Get it done now and you'll have all day tomorrow to relax, I tell myself. I've been working on it for a few minutes when the door opens and Taylor comes bursting in.

"We're going to a party tonight!" Taylor says, with even more enthusiasm than she normally has about everything in life.

Shit. I promised her I wouldn't bail the next time she invited me to a party and I don't have work or classes as an excuse. I've somehow made it the entire summer quarter without getting roped into an actual party. The kind with lots of other people from school and booze–and most likely Henry. It's not that I don't want to socialize and I adore Taylor and Jesse, so I'm sure I'll love their other friends. I just don't know if I even know how to have fun anymore at parties. By the time I was old enough that my friends were having parties–my life at home was falling apart. I've only ever been to a few and I've only ever been drunk once. I'm not gonna lie and say I didn't have a blast while I was drinking, but I hated the hangover. It made me wonder how the hell my mom drank so much and so often.

"Well hello to you," I say, tossing a pair of leggings into the darks pile.

"Someone Jesse knows on the football team is throwing a party to celebrate the end of classes. You've dodged me all summer. It will be so much fun and you promised you'd come, eventually. I know you don't have work tomorrow so..."

I cringe. There's no way I'm getting out of this.

"I did promise. Okay, where's this party? How are we getting there and what should I wear?" I ask, trying to at least match a little of her excitement.

Taylor jumps up and down and starts pulling clothes from her closet. A deep blue dress that looks like it won't even cover half my ass and a pair of black combat boots are dropped on my desk.

"You'll wear this. Trust me, it will look amazing on you," she says while heading back to her closet to pick out an outfit for herself. "The guy who's throwing the party is named Caleb. I met him once. Jesse says he can be a prick, but apparently his parents are out of town and his house is massive and he said he'd supply all the drinks. Emmett and Jesse are gonna pick us up at nine."

I eye the dress and then look at Taylor, who is grinning from ear to ear.

"Fine, but you're helping me with my laundry first," I tell her.

"Taylor. I'm almost seven inches taller than you. There's no way this dress is going to fit me."

"Oh, just put it on!" she says, grabbing the dress and pushing it toward me.

Taylor stands there with the dress held out in one hand, the other on her tiny hip. She looks serious, and it's a hilarious look for her. So out of place when I'm used to her near constant megawatt smile.

I groan, take the dress, and start attempting to put it on. She did as I asked and helped me get all my laundry done earlier so I'll humor her with this dress.

This dress definitely isn't something I would normally wear, but I appreciate that she wants to pair it with combat boots to give it a little more of an edgy look. Heels are something I've only worn once, to a dance in eighth grade, and I was miserable the whole time. Having someone to share clothes and get ready for parties with is more fun than I thought it would be. This is probably something every girl got to do in high school, but I didn't.

Shockingly, when I finish shimming into the dress, it fits. The hem comes several inches below my butt. I turn and look at myself in the mirror. Damn! Taylor was right. This dress looks fucking fantastic. I slowly look myself over in the mirror. The dress is simple, but it's the perfect length and just tight enough to show off my figure but not so tight I can't breathe.

"Taylor, how does this fit you *and* me?" I ask her as I admire myself in the mirror.

"It comes down to my knees," she says, laughing while she touches up her makeup at her desk.

I pull on the combat boots and it's perfect. I look good and I actually feel good. Maybe this night will be fun after all, and it's been way too long since I've had fun. I left my hair down, just adding some curl to the ends. I stick with my usual minimal makeup; mascara, a little blush and lipstick, against protests from Taylor, who wants to add more. We head out to the parking lot right at nine to get picked up by Taylor's friend Emmett.

A mid-sized SUV pulls into the parking lot and Taylor lets me know it's our ride. She'd mentioned that Emmett's family was rich, so I shouldn't be surprised at how nice his car is. I don't even recognize what brand it is, but I can tell it's expensive. The SUV pulls up to the curb and the front passenger door opens and out comes Jesse.

"Madison, you darling, can sit up front with Emmett so I can kiss on my girl in the back."

Taylor giggles and climbs into the back seat, Jesse patting her butt as she does. I lean over and look into the front seat and wave at Emmett as Jesse climbs in the back behind Taylor.

"Hi, I'm Madison! I guess I'm up here with you so those two can make out," I inform him, pointing my thumb at the back seat.

"Hey, Emmett," he says, extending his hand out to me. "Come on in, I don't bite."

I shake his hand, then take my place in the front seat. Emmett adjusts the rearview mirror so he can see Taylor and Jesse and says flatly, "You are NOT making out back there the whole drive to the party."

I turn in my seat a little and see Jesse play tackling Taylor and giving her big loud kisses all over her face as she giggles and pretends to push him off. Emmett shakes his head and readjusts the mirror before pulling away from the curb.

"So, Madison, what kind of music do you listen to?" Emmett asks, poking at the touch screen dash radio.

"Oh ya know, all the basic top 40 is good with me. But... and don't any of you dare laugh, 50s music is kinda my favorite."

"No freaking way," Jesse screeches from the back seat.

"Way." I say flatly.

"That's pretty interesting, actually," Emmett says. "We always catch our boy Henry listening to shit like Elvis and Patsy Cline. Says he has it on his playlist for when his mom and him are together, but he gets all bitchy if you try to skip the songs. Plus, he knows every word and sings them under his breath."

"Actually," Taylor says, "Madison and Henry already met. She's who he gave a ride to campus move-in weekend. Small world right, or I guess small town."

"So you're *that* Madison? Nice." Emmett says.

That Madison? Why does everyone seem to know about Henry giving me a ride and why the heck is it such a big freaking deal? It's as if everyone in the car knows the punchline to an inside joke except me. Great.

"Well sorry Madison, no 50s tonight. I need my party hype music to get me in the mood. Emmett, put it on the Pop station please," Taylor begs from the backseat.

I expect Emmett to protest, but he touches a few buttons and an Ariana Grande song is coming through the speakers now. Taylor starts dancing in her seat.

"Thank you!" she squeals.

Apparently, the party is on the other side of town in the more rural area so we've got about a twenty minute drive. Taylor, Jesse, and Emmett are all chatting over the music about how their finals went and the upcoming football season. Emmett asks me about my major and what classes I'm taking in the fall, where I moved from and all the usual first meeting get-to-know-you quick questions. I give the same repetitive answers I always give and ask him the same questions.

The conversation has died down a little when a Justin Bieber song comes on and Emmett and Jesse start singing along at the top of their lungs while Taylor loses it in a fit of laughter. Taylor and Jesse really are a match. They both have permanent smiles and infectious personalities. I never stop laughing around them.

Emmett, on the other hand, is nice enough but has that brooding, bad-boy vibe. I've already heard from Taylor and Jesse that he's a bit of a player. The fact that he's looked at my boobs and my exposed legs numerous times didn't go unnoticed. I know to keep my distance. Plus, he's best friends with Henry and I would never. A reputation that I date my way through friends isn't a reputation I need. Not that I even think Henry would care, because he doesn't seem to care about me in general.

My phone chimes in the small crossbody bag I borrowed from Taylor and I dig it out to see who is texting me. I hope it's not Joy wanting me to come into work tomorrow. I was already looking forward to a lazy Sunday. Now that I have no clue what time we'll be at this party until, I want the opportunity to sleep in tomorrow even more.

But the text isn't from Joy, it's from my mom. I stare at the screen for I don't know how long before I even open it. When I open it, my heart sinks. It's not just one text but several she clearly fired off back to back.

Mom: Hey Baby. It's Mom. Can you come by the house?
Mom: I've got some of your favorite ice cream in the freezer we can share
Mom: You can meet my new boyfriend, Gary, you'll really love him
Mom: Oh, and I could use $20 if you could spare it I promise I'll pay you back

Holy hell. Should I be more heartbroken by the fact she doesn't know I'm not even in the same state as her or that she clearly only reached out because she needs money? The text messages continue to stare at me from my phone screen. My fingers don't move to type a single letter in reply. When will I stop being surprised at my mother's lack of concern for me? Or her lack of interest in me? Sometime between losing my father and losing herself, I lost her too. Fuck that, I shouldn't be heartbroken, I should be pissed.

I hit the side button on my phone to turn the screen black and shove it back into my purse. Apparently, I shoved it in there a little too aggressively because Taylor leans forward and asks if I'm okay.

"Yeah, totally," I brush her off and change the subject. "So who's gonna tell me why it seems to be such a big deal that Henry gave me a ride to campus?"

Silence. No one is responding, but they're all looking at each other. Even Emmett seems to tighten his grip on the steering wheel. Okay, now I'm really interested in what the heck is going on.

"Seriously, you guys. Spill," I demand.

Taylor sighs.

"Okay, it's really not *that* big of a deal. It's just, objectively Henry is–"

"Yummy," Jesse says.

"Sex on a stick," Emmett adds.

"Hot," Taylor continues. "And well, he's never dated. Scratch that. He dated once, but it was Jackie, so it doesn't actually count."

"It was just a ride, you guys! But why doesn't Jackie count?" No one in this car knows about our walk home from town, our adventure to the meadow, or our kiss in the library. But I'm curious why they're all so invested in his love life and who the hell is Jackie? Is that jealousy I'm feeling? Yup, I'm feeling jealous of a girl I've never met over a boy I scarcely know. Who kissed me–and ran away.

Jesse speaks up first.

"Jackie doesn't count because she's been in love with Henry forever and he basically pity-dated her when he was in a shit place in his own life."

"Jesse. Don't," Emmett chimes in, looking back and giving him a death stare. Emmett grips the steering wheel tighter again and focuses back on the road.

"Jackie means well," Taylor adds "And seriously, she's been a good friend to all of us at one point or another but she's that friend that you keep at arm's length because, well, Jackie will always put herself first, ya know."

The car starts slowing down and we pull onto a gravel road as the conversation dies out. I want to ask a million questions, but I keep quiet. Up ahead are dozens of cars parked in the dirt off to the side of a huge house. It's not a new house, but it's a nice two story with a big wrap around front porch. It's painted a pale yellow with blue trim. There aren't a lot of new houses in Easton, I've discovered. You can tell who has money by how much land they have. It seems this guy's parents have a lot.

Emmett puts the car in park and we all start getting out. I'm suddenly very grateful to be wearing the combat boots Taylor lent me because the gravel is more dirt than anything else.

There are people hanging out on the front porch smoking cigarettes and drinking from red cups. The front doors are wide open and you can hear the loud music coming from inside. I can see a bonfire is raging around the back side of the house even from where I'm at out front. Indiscernible laughter and chatter comes from every direction. Butterflies swarm in my stomach. I pull at the hem of the dress I'm wearing, trying to cover up a little more. When I come around the car, Taylor loops her arm through mine.

"Come on, let's go find some drinks," she tells me and pulls me toward the house, Emmett and Jesse trailing behind us, whispering to each other.

I feel like the conversation in the car was taking a turn it wasn't supposed to. I don't know what the problem was, me asking about Henry or me asking about Jackie. And right now, I'm not sure I want to know.

Right now I want to find a drink and forget about the stupid texts I got on the way here.

Chapter Sixteen

Henderson

I got to the party before Emmett, Jesse, and Taylor. I should have just gone back to my car to wait for them when I realized they weren't here yet. But Jackie saw me and now I've been stuck in a corner of the kitchen while she tells me every excruciating detail about the summer internship she has. Before I stopped paying full attention to her, I learned that it's a few towns over for some indie fashion designer and although she's making it sound as if it's some super important role, if I had to guess, she spends most of her time getting her boss coffee.

Jackie takes a step closer every few minutes. I'm practically sitting on the kitchen counter at this point to avoid her pressing up against me. She smells like cheap beer and artificial coconut perfume. It's not the warm and inviting scent that Madison seems to always have. Suddenly she sounds like one of the adults on Peanuts and is touching my arm every five seconds. I nod when I think it's appropriate; mostly because I feel bad for using her last year. I didn't realize I was using her at first and when I did; I broke things off. I was in such a shit place last fall. I thought she'd be a good distraction from the reality of my life falling apart. With the help of my therapist and some hindsight, I realized I'd never even had a meaningful conversation with her. I knew I needed to break her heart.

For whatever reason, that hasn't stopped her from still flirting with me. Or trying to make me jealous by hanging on to any other guy whenever I'm around. Which is why I'm surprised she's even talking to me right now since this party is at Caleb's house and I thought he was her latest infatuation. I almost consider asking her why she isn't off with him, but I don't want her mistaking my question for jealousy.

I'm just about to lie and say I need to take a piss when I spot Emmett walking through the kitchen. He doesn't even see me and heads straight to the backyard. He's clearly on a mission to find someone. Some blonde with long legs is my guess.

"Jackie, I need to talk to Emmett, but I'll catch up with you later, okay?"

I gently put my hands on her arms to release myself from the corner she has me trapped in. Before I can get around her, Jesse and Taylor make their way into the kitchen, followed by Madison. Why didn't any of them mention she was coming?

I'm frozen in my spot. Taylor is giving me the evil eye, and Madison's expression isn't much better. She's definitely pissed about the way I completely abandoned her in the library. That's when I realize Jackie's hands are on my chest, and this looks like something it's not because my hands are still on her arms. I yank my hands down to my sides as if her arms are made of hot coals and move away from Jackie so her hands fall off my chest. But I don't do it fast enough. Madison's eyes lock with mine. Those big, beautiful golden eyes. Just as quickly as our eyes meet, Madison looks down at her feet. Then around the kitchen. Anywhere but at me.

I'm stuck where I am, not sure if I should walk toward them. Not sure what I'll say to Madison when I reach her. The decision's made for me when Taylor grabs Madison by the hand and pulls her toward the back yard. Shit. Why do I feel like I just fucked everything up? Again. Things were fucked up in the library, or maybe even before that. I move to follow them, but Jackie decides she's taking her attempts to get back with me up a notch and circles her arms around my waist. Jesse comes up next to us with a disappointed look on his face.

Taylor and Jesse have never been quiet about how they feel about me dating Jackie. We've all known Jackie for years and it's not that she's a bad person, she's just not always a genuine person. She can be shallow and vain and she can be a bully. She's also had her moments of being a good friend. When I broke up with her, she didn't make a big scene. She seemed to understand, even if she has delusions we can get back together.

"Hey man. Uh, what's going on?" Jesse asks, looking between me and Jackie.

Jackie takes it upon herself to speak first.

"Hey Jesse. Who's the new friend I saw Taylor with?"

She doesn't even try to hide her annoyance. Her words are laced with the kind of impending problem we've all come to know from Jackie. Jackie definitely noticed Madison and definitely noticed my reaction to her being here. Great, the last thing I need is her taking it upon herself to give Madison a hard time. I'm overcome with an urge to run to Madison and confess everything. Tell her it's me, Ender. Tell her I'm sorry for what I said in my email, sorry for running out on her in the library and just begging her to let things go back to the way they were. Begging her to go back to being my best friend. I just want to go back to being Ender and Mads.

I push the urge away. I know it's not fair to her to do that here, in this way. Plus, a huge part of me is still so worried that she'll bolt. That she'll run back to her dorm room and pack up her belongings in that beat up black suitcase and jump on the next bus out of here. So I'll take the route that might make me even more of an asshole and continue to try to be her friend as Henry. Maybe in time, I can tell her the truth without it blowing up in my face. But first, I've got to get away from Jackie.

"Is that Madison I saw with Taylor?" I ask Jesse, trying to sound nonchalant as I extract myself from Jackie's grip.

I don't want to give Jesse a chance to respond to Jackie's question. Jackie pouts but releases me. She does not, however, take the hint and remains standing right next to me.

"Yeah, she's Taylor's roommate. Isn't that wild? Small towns man," he says "I've known for weeks–"

"I uh–ran into her a few weeks ago and she told me, but wait–you've known all summer that Madison and your girlfriend were living togeth-er–and you didn't think to mention it?"

"I thought you didn't want to get involved with anyone?" Jesse says, squinting his eyes at me. "Plus, aren't you seeing someone?"

Shit. I forgot I let him think I was hooking up with someone when I didn't give him an excuse for being late to football practice that one time.

I shove my hands in my front pockets but don't answer him. The lies are piling up.

"Are you seeing someone new, Henry?" Jackie asks.

I forgot she was here.

"No," I spit out, gritting my teeth.

"I'm gonna head out back and make sure Taylor isn't doing shots. Are you coming?" Jesse asks, saving me from the string of questions I'm sure Jackie is about to fire off.

"Yeah, right behind you."

I don't wait for Jackie to protest and follow Jesse outside. I might as well ask him for a piggyback ride, I'm walking so close behind him. Eager to get away from Jackie. Longing to be near Madison.

We make it outside and the girls are sitting alone on lounge furniture by the pool. Red cups in their hands already and chatting about something. Taylor's cup is no doubt filled with vodka and fruit juice and I wonder what's in Madisons. I wonder if what she's drinking is making her full lips taste sweet.

Madison told me in our emails more than once that her mom started drinking a lot after her dad passed away. She'd told me about a handful of times she'd be at a party and have a beer or a hard seltzer. And the one time she got drunk, she said the hangover wasn't worth it. For all I know, there isn't actually any alcohol in her cup.

"Look who I found, ladies!" Jesse announces as we get closer.

"Hey Henry," Taylor says without even looking at me.

Taylor was always the most vocal and opinionated about me dating Jackie and how she'd prefer I *didn't* date Jackie. Does Taylor know about the kiss? Or about me running away mid-kiss like a jackass? Roommates share those kinds of stories, don't they?

"Madison, you remember our guy, Henry, right?" Jesse asks her, scooting into the seat behind Taylor, letting her sit between his open legs.

I turn my attention to Madison and she's looking up at me, biting her damn lip again. I nearly drop to my knees right there and my jeans instantly feel too tight. I smile at her. I wonder if she can hear my heart racing. It feels as if the entire offensive line is in my chest doing drills.

"Of course," she says. "Thanks again for the ride. It was very sweet of you."

She's smiling at first, but her smile fades after the words leave her lips. So, I'm guessing she *hasn't* told Taylor about the library, or any of the other times we've hung out. Are we pretending the kiss never happened? I want so badly to bring that smile she had a few moments ago back. Why does she look so—sad? Or maybe it's anger I'm seeing. Is she angry because of the library or Jackie? Or both?

I'm so nervous, I'm still trying to wrap my mind around the fact that this is my Mads sitting here right in front of me whose lips I've now tasted. The tight dress that shows just the right amount of skin isn't helping my nerves, either. I suddenly don't know how to talk to her or what to say, so I drone on with mundane small talk. I don't want anyone else to notice the tension between us. That stupid kiss–a moment of weakness–changed everything.

"It's pretty wild that you and Taylor are roommates," I say, playing along with her act.

"I guess this town is smaller than I thought it was."

She's just talking to me to be polite. I'm getting a vibe that she doesn't want me talking to her at all and she's itching to get away from me. Can I blame her? Her phone in her hand lights up and she looks down at it. The anger in her expression is more noticeable now, but the sadness is still there, too. I want to take her phone from her and tell whoever is making her face look that way to fuck off.

A group of guys from the football team are playing beer pong nearby. One of them calls me over before I can act on a crazy impulse. I want to ignore him. I want to keep talking to Madison. I want to do or say something to make her smile again. I excuse myself sheepishly and walk over to the guys, but Madison doesn't even look up from her phone. On the short walk over, I look back just once, only to see that Madison is now just staring down into her cup, her face somehow even sadder than it was just a moment before.

When I make it over to the guys, it turns out they just want to talk shit about practice and the coach. I stifle a groan but try to take part in the conversation. As quarterback, I'm supposed to be the heart of the team, and that means listening to these idiots complain. It's hard to be excited about football when I know I should be playing for a team whose games actually fill stadiums. Not to mention the fact that most days I question if I even want to play football anymore. I get confused about if it was ever really my dream, or just my dad's.

My back is to Madison, but I'm not so far away that I don't hear her voice when she starts talking. I tune out the guys and strain my ears to hear her better.

"Yeah, I just moved here this year, too. I'm an English major. What about you?"

A deep voice responds to her. There's something familiar about the voice and I can't take it any longer. I turn my head just enough to see who she's talking to. I instantly regret it.

My skin is on fire and my hand crushes the half empty water bottle I'm holding.

Fucking Caleb. She's talking to fucking Caleb.

He's sitting on the arm of the chair she's in and leaning in toward her. I can tell from here his gaze keeps falling to her chest and I know he has a perfect view of her tits from where he's sitting.

That prick.

He leans in and tucks a strand of hair behind her ear and whispers in it, and she laughs like he's a fucking professional comedian. That's it. I cannot take another minute of this.

CHAPTER SEVENTEEN

MADISON

There he was, standing in the kitchen, his back up against the counter with one of the most gorgeous girls I've ever seen pushed up against him. She's a little shorter than me, with golden blonde hair, perfectly styled in big bouncy curls down her back. Of course she has perfectly perky, not too big and not too small boobs and teeth so white they must be fake. Her makeup looks professionally done, but I'm sure she's just one of those girls who magically knows how to apply it all like she's a pro. Even her outfit is cool; a pair of tight black leather pants with a white corset and sky high heels.

My heart sinks all the way to my stomach. I should have known another girl was the reason he ran out of the library like the place was on fire. He has a girlfriend. I shouldn't be surprised and I have no claim to Henry. But why is there such a pit in my stomach seeing him so close to another girl? Why am I seething with jealousy right now?

I avert my eyes as quickly as I can manage, fearing he'll see the hurt in them. These feelings I'm having, they're not owed any merit. It was just one car ride, a walk through town, an afternoon laying in the grass, and one kiss. Only four tiny interactions—but one earth shattering kiss. In my mind they're huge though, cavernous and wide, with hidden tunnels full of treasures. To Henry, they're probably tiny blips. He doesn't owe me anything, and he's definitely free to date whoever he wants. Even if it makes me irrationally jealous.

I'm relieved when Taylor takes my hand and leads me outside. She takes us to a table filled with alcohol, mixers and cups. She pours vodka into two cups and tops them off with cranberry and orange juice before handing me one with a sympathetic smile.

"So, that would be Jackie," Taylor tells me as we find some chairs to sit in by the pool.

"Who?" I ask, staring out at the pool, pretending to be clueless about what she's talking about.

The pool is huge, with a diving board and a rock waterfall. A built in jacuzzi off to one side where I'm pretty sure people are currently having sex. I divert my attention back to my cup.

"Madison, we've been living together for months now. You're not fooling me. I saw the way your face fell when you saw Henry."

I sigh and look at her now, and she can definitely see the pain in my eyes. What she doesn't know is that it's not just about Henry. I'm still trying to process those texts from my mom.

"Awe Madison. I mean, I know Henry is hot as shit, but you had one interaction with him. What gives?"

"Taylor, I know. Trust me, I know this is crazy. Truly, I don't know why, but, I—there's just something about him. I can't explain it."

I don't tell Taylor about the times we've spent together or how I've been thinking about Henry nonstop since I met him. I've found myself looking for his hazel eyes in crowds on campus. I've done a double take when I see a guy with tattoos peeking out of their shirt sleeves. I even tried looking him up on social media, but he must be the only eighteen-year-old on the planet to not have a social media presence.

It's hard to describe, but from that first car ride, that first meeting, I feel like our souls knew each other. As if somehow, every action and every choice I made that day wasn't an accident, but was a step in a predetermined plan to put me in his path. Henry was so familiar from the first moment he laughed at my anger, from the first moment our hands touched. The afternoon we spent playing twenty-one questions, laying in the grass, only made those feelings stronger. When he ran off after our lips met in the library, it was as if a piece of my soul ran off with him.

I don't tell Taylor any of this. Even if I wanted to, there's no time because Jesse and Henry come walking up.

I know I'm talking to Henry, and he's talking back. But I feel like I'm under water or the conversation is happening in a sound proof bubble and I'm on the outside, not quite able to make out what we're saying. I just do my best to smile and hope I'm not making a fool out of myself.

How the hell does this one guy make me feel all this? I have never felt so insanely turned on just by looking at a man. His face is freshly shaved tonight and I notice that one singular dimple when he flashes his slightly crooked smile. I think about sticking my tongue in his dimple before trailing it over to his lips.

My phone buzzes in my hand, startling me, and I look down. She's just not giving up tonight, is she? She must be damn desperate because now her texts have turned mean.

Mom: Look, I'm your damn Mother. The least you can do is give me a lousy $20

Mom: Don't be such a selfish little bitch

I stare in disbelief. This isn't the first time she's asked me for money and, honestly, in the past she was more patient and more sly about it. Convincing me to come to the house before even asking for anything. If

I had it, I usually gave it to her because I'm pathetic and no matter how many times she's screwed up over the past few years... she's still my mom.

I flip my phone over in my lap, hell-bent on not responding, and look up only to realize Henry is gone. I give the backyard a quick glance and find him over by the beer pong table, chatting with a group of guys. He sure is good at running off.

Taylor and Jesse are now full on making out in the lounge chair across from me. I've only ever made out with 3 guys. My first official boyfriend, Carl, in eighth grade during an unsanctioned game of seven minutes in heaven. Alex, who was a dare at the summer carnival after freshman year. And Liam, the only guy I've had sex with–although, I'm not sure what we did could be considered sex. It was nothing like it is in the romance novels I read.

"And who might you be?"

I turn my head to see a very muscular blonde guy holding a bottle of whiskey staring at me.

"This is Madison, Taylor's roommate. She's new in town just like you, benchwarmer," Jesse says.

When did those two come up for air? Jesse's laughing at himself and his clever insult.

"No way in hell I'm on the bench after Coach finds out I'm the reason he's getting a nice raise this year."

The whiskey wielding guy turns his attention back to me, sitting on the arm of my chair. I scooch away just a little, but not so much it's obvious.

"Hi Madison, I'm Caleb. Are you enjoying my party?"

So this must be the guys' teammate Taylor told me about. I smile at him. He's kind of cute in a, "works out too much and is probably a little full of himself" kind of way. If Jesse says he's a prick, he probably is.

"I am. Your parents have a great house."

I smirk, wondering if he notices my subtle dig by making it clear I know this is all Mom and Dad's money and I'm not impressed. I can see Taylor suppressing a laugh out of the corner of my eye. Caleb doesn't seem to mind or notice.

He leans in and brushes a strand of my hair back and I freeze.

"And you haven't even seen the bedrooms yet," he whispers in my ear.

I consider pushing him away, but notice Henry staring at us over Caleb's shoulder. He looks seriously pissed, but he has no right to be. If he didn't want me talking to another guy, he should be over here talking to me instead. So I do the bitchy thing and put my hand on Caleb's bicep that's bigger than my head and giggle like a schoolgirl.

Mission accomplished. Henry is back to standing by us faster than I thought was possible.

"Hey Caleb, I see you've met Madison," he says through gritted teeth.

He clamps his hand down on Caleb's shoulder and not so subtly pulls him away from me.

"Yeah man, we were just getting to know each other. Weren't we babe?"

Caleb does not take the hint and looks right back at me and winks. This douche bag actually winks. I push down the bile rising in my throat. Let's hope this idiot doesn't get too attached while I use him.

"Yup. So Caleb, you play football? Are you, like, the quarterback?"

I try not to gag at my own repulsiveness as I bat my eyelashes at Caleb. I know damn well Caleb isn't the quarterback and Henry is. After watching their practice, I may have even done some research about football. Caleb, I'm almost positive, is a fill in player. No real role on the team, just an extra body.

Henry audibly groans and wipes a hand down his face. Jesse chokes on the beer he was drinking and Taylor buries her face in Jesse's chest, trying to cover her laugh.

Caleb looks pissed.

"No, benchwarmer isn't the quarterback. I am."

I look up at Henry and he's staring down at me with a fire in his eyes I didn't expect. I'm feeling a strange confidence I don't normally have, so I look Henry in the eyes, challenging him.

"Oh, and is your girlfriend a cheerleader?"

I know Taylor and Jesse said Jackie is his ex-girlfriend, but I can't help myself from making the comment. What I saw in the kitchen sure makes it look as if they may have gotten back together.

"I don't have a girlfriend," he practically spits through clenched teeth.

"Oh, I mean, the girl from the kitchen. Do you guys just not have a label on things?" I say, feigning ignorance.

Taylor clears her throat.

"Hey Madison, I've gotta find the little girl's room. Come with me?"

She's already standing and pulling me to my feet to follow her.

We weave our way through drunk college students. The house is a lot fuller than it was when we arrived an hour ago. She finds a hallway and pulls me down it, pushing open doors until she finds an empty room and pulls me in. We're in what must be a guest room. The furnishings are generic, but look expensive. There aren't any personal items I can see.

Taylor closes the door behind us, spins toward me and crosses her arms.

"Okay, what's up?"

"What do you mean?" I ask.

I'm playing dumb. The game I try to play doesn't work. She sees right through my innocence act.

"I know I don't know you all that well, but Caleb does *not* seem like your type. Like, at all."

I chew my lip, trying to decide how to answer her. A breath I didn't know I was holding comes out in an exaggerated huff and I sit on the bed in the corner of the room.

"I'm trying to make Henry jealous, okay? Is that what you want to hear?"

"I mean, at least it's honest. But why do you think you need to make Henry jealous?"

"Because for some reason I'm completely infatuated with him and he seems to not give a damn about me. And because he kissed me and he ran away."

Taylor sits down next to me on the bed.

"When did Caleb kiss you?"

"Not Caleb. Henry."

"No shit. When?!"

"A few weeks ago, in the library. I was studying for midterms. There was this poetry book and–"

I trail off, not sure I'm ready to share more details.

"Okay. Wow. Okay."

She's on her feet now, pacing in front of the bed. Looking back and forth between me and the floor.

"Here's the most I can tell you. Henry went through some shit last year. Like shit most people can't even imagine. The entire trajectory of his life changed. He's not even supposed to be in Easton still, but he is. He also probably has very little faith in love and relationships these days."

"Why, what happened?"

"That is so not my story to tell. But, Madison, he's one of my best friends and he is an incredible guy."

"So you think I should wait around for him?"

"I'm not saying that, and I'm not saying I don't think your fake flirting with Caleb isn't working–"

Taylor laughs and flops back down on the bed next to me, bumping her shoulder with mine.

"But I am saying, just be careful. The last thing you want is a guy like Caleb thinking he actually has a chance. Or a good guy like Henry thinking he doesn't."

"You're right. I get it. Thank you, Taylor, for being my friend."

"Anytime roomie, anytime. Now... let's get back out there before Henry and Caleb whip out their dicks and a ruler."

I laugh and let Taylor know I'm going to find a bathroom and meet her outside.

The bathroom has a line about five people deep, but I really need to pee, so I wait. I forgot alcohol can run straight through you. The door opens but before the next person can go in Jackie comes around the corner and cuts in the line. When she comes back out, she notices me and stops, hands on her hips.

"Madison, was it?" she says, looking at me with disgust.

What is this chick's deal? I haven't even met her. I wouldn't even know her name if it wasn't for Taylor. How and why does she know mine?

"Yeah, have we met?" I ask, pretending I don't know exactly who she is.

"No. But, I hear you're new. Welcome to Easton."

Her words seem like they should be sweet, nice even, but her body language screams bitch.

"Um, thanks."

The line for the bathroom moves and I move up.

"I'm Jackie, Henry's friend. I'm sure he's mentioned me. Maybe you and your boyfriend can double date with me and Henry sometime. We can show you around Easton."

"I don't have a boyfriend," I say.

"Oh, too bad. There's not a lot of guys worth anything in this town and, well, the good ones are taken."

Her voice pitches on the last word, making her point clear. I choose not to respond and just stare at her, moving up with the line again.

"Well, I'm sure we'll see each other around," she says.

The door to the bathroom opens, and I'm next. I duck inside, ending the conversation.

Wetting a hand towel I find in the drawer, I press it to my face and the back of my neck. Staring in the mirror, I try to pull myself together, give myself a quick pep talk. Jackie is a bitch, I decide. I wash my hands and head back out to the backyard to face whatever jock-off I started.

Before I make it outside, I notice Jackie's in the kitchen still. Her back is to me, but I can see large hands with a vice grip on her hips and her arms are raised up around the mystery person's neck. I guess she's not as concerned about getting back together with Henry as she tried to play. By the way she's moving her body, it must be a hell of a make-out session. If they don't move it to a bedroom soon–oh my fucking God.

It's Henry. She's lip locked with fucking Henry.

I run out of the kitchen and into the back yard as fast I can, making a beeline for Taylor and Jesse who are now alone. Internally demanding my own eyes not to betray me and start leaking all over my dress. I sit down with a little more indignation than I planned, the metal furniture making a loud scraping noise. Taylor and Jesse are both staring at me wide eyed.

"What, did the benchwarmer try to make a move? Do I need to kick his ass?"

Jesse is already on his feet, looking around the crowd for Caleb. I pull on his hand to get him to sit back down.

"No, no. It's not Caleb."

"Where's Henry?" Taylor asks knowingly.

"Inside, practically having sex with Jackie in the kitchen."

I almost choke on my words. Jackie's name comes out sharp and bitter and–jealous.

Jesse and Taylor look at each other. Then burst into laughter. Full-on hysterics. Bending at the waist, knee slapping and all.

I cross my arms in front of my chest.

"I really don't see what's so funny, guys."

Taylor wipes the tears from her eyes. Yes, she shed actual tears, she was laughing so hard.

"Mads, can I call you Mads?" Jesse asks while trying to catch his breath.

I groan out loud, double over, and hide my face in my hands. Jesse has no idea what he's just done.

"Okayyyyy, okay, sorry. No Mads."

"No," I assure him, sitting back up. "It's just…"

I pause, not knowing if I'm ready to share this part of my past with them. Taking a big breath and pressing my hands to my eyes, fixing the tears in place that are threatening to fall.

"It's just, I had this friend. A penpal. We met online. I've literally never even seen a picture of him. But he was my best friend, and we had a falling out last year. He was the only one who ever called me Mads."

"It's cool. Madison it is."

"No. Honestly, it's nice to hear someone call me Mads. I promise, if you guys wanna call me Mads I wouldn't mind."

Taylor reaches across the empty space and puts her hand on my knee.

"Mads. Babe. We're sorry for laughing, but I don't think you saw what you think you saw. Yes, Jackie and Henry dated, but he never had real feelings for her. She was just filling a void, and there is no way he would ever get back with her."

I want to believe her, but I know what I saw. Before I can argue, Caleb magically appears again.

"So, you gonna be my Beirut partner, Madison?"

I turn to look at him.

"I'm sorry, you're what?"

"Beirut, you have played it before, right?"

I stare at him, waiting for him to take the hint and explain what the hell he's talking about.

"Beirut," he says again, pointing to the beer pong table.

"You mean beer pong?"

Caleb laughs, it's loud and obnoxious. Nothing like Henry's throaty, sexy laugh.

"Where did you say you were from again?" Caleb asks.

I didn't, I think. You're just such an idiot you probably don't even realize you haven't asked me any personal questions.

"California." I say, my tone flat.

"Well Cali girl, would you want to be my *beer pong* partner?"

I see Henry coming out into the back yard behind Caleb, Jackie on his heels. Caleb's still holding the bottle of whiskey from earlier. I take it from his hand and start chugging. I wipe my mouth when I'm done and hand him back the bottle. The warm, spicy liquid nearly threatens to come back up, but I force it down. Why the hell would anyone willingly drink this shit? It tastes like warm piss mixed with battery acid. I force a flirtatious smile on my face.

"Sounds fun. Lead the way."

He grabs me by the hand and leads me over to the beer pong table.

"Me and my Cali girl Madison have next game," he says. Louder than is probably necessary.

By game two, I'm definitely feeling the whiskey I drank earlier. But what I'm not feeling as much is the anger I felt when I got those texts from my mom and the jealousy I felt when I saw Jackie and Henry making out. Okay, maybe the last part is a lie.

We end up playing on the side of the table that faced Taylor and Jesse, who resumed making out as soon as I left, but they stopped when Henry came back. No surprise, Jackie's with him. I try my hardest not to keep looking over there, but I'm not doing a great job. For someone who's never played beer pong, sorry–Beirut, as they call it here–I'm surprisingly good at this game. Every time I make it in a cup, everyone around me cheers and gets excited and Caleb takes every opportunity to touch me. High-fiving me, hugging me, even picking me up and spinning me around when I make the last cup to win our second game.

When he puts my feet back on the ground, I can feel my phone buzzing in my purse sitting against my hip. I pull it out to check it while Caleb sets our cups back up in the starting position. It's a text from Taylor checking on me.

Taylor: Blink rapidly if you need me to rescue you. Lol.
Me: I'm good for now, but thank you!
Taylor: Anytime babe.

Before I put my phone away, my thumb accidentally hits an app and *that* email account opens on the screen. An old email from Ender is staring me in the face.

To: madisrad@gmail.com
From: ravensfan4lyfe@gmail.com
Date: May 12 07:42:43 CST

Subject: Mads is Rad - A poem

Mads,

Now, you know I'm more of a fantasy writer and poetry is not my forte. But for you, and only you, I've faced my literary fears.

Mads is rad

She never makes me sad
If I ever got to meet her
It would make me oh so happy
And if I hadn't ever known her
Well that would just be crappy.
I know, you're impressed. And yes, I had to google words that would rhyme.

Your Best Friend,
Ender

It was truly an awful poem. But, not so awful it didn't stop me from absolutely swooning. I hit reply on my phone, breaking my–*no more writing Ender pathetic draft emails*–rule. I really must be close to being drunk. I type out a quick email just to get the emotions filling my chest out. When I'm done, I lock my phone and put it back in my purse.

I turn my attention back to the game and Caleb. I continue to giggle like he's the funniest guy on earth and bat my eyelashes, letting Caleb paw at me. The mixture of whiskey and beer threatens to come back up every time he touches me. I drink the cups of warm cheap beer he hands me when the other team sinks a cup. I'm pathetic, and I know I'm pathetic. But when I glance over at Henry, I see him watching us and I know I'm having some effect on him. So I continue putting on the show. Pathetic.

CHAPTER EIGHTEEN

HENDERSON

I finally make my way back outside, but I can not believe Jackie is actually following me right now. All I wanted to do was go into the kitchen and find a soda. I needed a distraction after seeing Caleb so close to the girl I so desperately want to be close to. The girl that I know better than anyone else at this damn party and she doesn't even realize it. Plus, I'm trying to figure out if Madison is actually jealous of Jackie. If she is, what the hell does that even mean? Is it possible she doesn't hate me even after the library? Do I still stand a chance?

When I turned around from getting a soda out of the fridge, there was Jackie. Before I knew it, her arms were around my neck and her lips were on mine. The girl cannot take a hint. Even after I grabbed her and pushed her away. I told her it was never gonna be that way again. She winked and said, "We'll see," and then followed me out here.

I make my way over to Jesse and Taylor, who are in their own world curled up together on a lounge chair making out. Madison isn't with them, but I sit in the chair she'd been in earlier and clear my throat. The love birds untangle themselves and sit up side by side facing me. Jesse clears his throat and wipes lipstick off his mouth.

"Sorry dude. I've been busy with work, classes and football. Just making up for lost time."

He puts his arm around Taylor and pulls her closer, kissing the side of her head.

Taylor and Jesse are the type of couple that no matter how much they're all over each other, it never grosses you out. It makes you jealous.

"Where'd Madison go?" I ask, looking around for her.

"She's, um, playing beer pong," Taylor tells me, not meeting my eyes.

Sure enough, Madison is at the beer pong table... with Caleb. She made her ball in a cup and Caleb hugs her as she squeaks with delight. I want to march over there and punch him in the dick and tell him to get the hell away from my girl. But since Mads thinks we only met a few months ago and we've only shared a finite amount of time together, plus one short kiss that was better than any sex I've ever had, she'd probably think I was insane.

I try to distract myself and chat with Taylor and Jesse. I actively try to ignore Jackie. Only glancing over at Madison occasionally, but also occasionally catching her looking back at me. She looks pissed off anytime I catch her eyes, but there's still that hint of sadness there. I can see it trembling just under the surface of the anger she's directing at me and the show of happiness she's putting on for everyone around her.

My phone buzzes in my pocket and I pull it out to make sure it's not Mom needing me. It's not Mom. It's an email, from–.

What the hell? It's a reply from Mads to an email I sent her years ago. Confused and stunned, I stare at the notification for a while before I even open it.

To: ravensfan4lyfe@gmail.com
From: madisrad@gmail.com
Date: August 21 11:43:32
Re: Mads is Rad - A poem

Dear Ender,

You suck. You sck, you suck, you suc.

I hte that you ruined everything. Why did you have to ask me the things you asked me?

Why did you have to write me the most beautiful email I've ever read in my life? Why didn't you just stick to corny, crappy poems?

You suck. But even though you suck, I miss you.

Yours always,
Mads
P.s What did you add to The Sparrow

What the hell? Did she seriously just send this? I look over at Madison and sure enough, she's trying and failing to shove her phone back in her tiny purse. I read the email again. It's littered with errors, making me believe even more–she just sent this.

Oh shit, she definitely looks drunk now. She looks wasted. It's her turn to throw the ball, and she misses by a mile but still celebrates. Caleb, who despite appearing to have been drinking all night long, is nowhere near as drunk as she is. I look at the whiskey bottle he's been carrying around, and it's still pretty full. Is he pretending to drink? He definitely notices how drunk Madison is and when her celebration causes her to lose her balance a little, he wraps her arms around her waist to steady her.

"Damn, Mads looks like she's having fun," Jesse says, following my gaze.

"What the hell did you call her?" I snap at Jesse.

Jesse recoils and puts his hands up in defense, but I'm not paying attention to him anymore. I notice Madison leaning into Caleb like a limp noodle and I see his hands lower down to her ass. He buries his face in her neck, into all of her soft brown hair that's hanging loose and wild. Fuck this.

Before Jesse can respond to my outburst and before I even realize what I'm doing, I'm on my feet and over to her in seconds.

"Madison, I think you've had enough. Let me drive you home."

She turns her head to me, still in Caleb's grip.

"But I'm having such a great time," she slurs, "and I don't know if there's enough room in your truck for me and Jackie."

"Dammit Madison, I am not dating Jackie," I bite out a little harsher than I mean to.

I don't like being this way. I don't enjoy telling her what to do. But, I think Caleb is trying to pull some creepy predator shit by pretending to drink and she's not in any position to be around him if he is.

"You could have fooled me with the way you were sucking half her face off in the kitchen."

Fuck. She saw Jackie kissing me. A smile tries to break through on my lips. I shouldn't be happy, but I am because her anger means she's jealous. It means she has feelings for me, or at least she has feelings for Henry. I don't know how she feels about Ender. If her email is any clue, maybe there's a chance of salvaging this still. I need to come up with a plan to come clean to her. Obviously not now when she likely won't even remember half of this in the morning. I let out a breath and relax my shoulders.

"Madison, it's not what you think," I try to tell her, my voice calmer and softer now.

She ignores me and turns her attention back to Caleb, whose arms she's still in but who has been smart enough to keep his mouth shut.

"Madison, please," I beg. "Let me give you a ride home."

"No!"

She turns to me, crossing her arms.

"In fact, I think I'll go find another drink."

She goes to stomp off, but sways and almost trips crashing into me. I catch her before she can take us both down. She giggles and tries to stand up again, but is struggling. Caleb goes to grab for her and that's when I lose it. I cup one arm under her ass to make sure her dress stays down and throw her over my shoulder.

"Put me down, you jerk!" she wails while beating her tiny fists on my back.

I walk her over to Taylor and Jesse and a very pissed off Jackie.

"Are you guys ready to go, or can you find a ride home?" I ask, Madison still protesting from over my shoulder.

"Ya know what man, this party blows. Let's get out of here," Jesse says.

"Oh shit. Henry, we cannot take Madison back to the dorms like that. Our RA is such a bitch," Taylor adds, looking a little tipsy herself.

"It's fine," I tell her. "We can all go back to my house. You guys can crash in the basement."

Jesse stands and wraps his arm around Taylor.

"Sweet babe, we can watch the game highlights on his massive tv then fuck on the couch."

"The fuck you will," I say, already walking away.

"Fine. No watching the highlight reel, but we can still fuck, right?" Jesse pleads, as if he's a five-year-old asking to stay up on a school night.

I don't answer him and keep walking as they follow behind me, cackling. We go around the side of the house instead of through it and out to my truck. Madison stopped protesting and is laying limp across my back, her hands gripping me to keep herself steady. Her hands are holding on tight to my sides and I'm trying so hard to keep my thoughts in check.

Trying not to think about the fact that I would barely have to move my hand holding her dress down to slip my fingers under her panties.

I pull open the driver's side door and gently set her down on the bench seat. Her head dips toward me as I buckle the seatbelt around her. Her hair is inches from my nose and I inhale. She smells as intoxicating as she did in the library; like warm vanilla and a scent that's uniquely Mads.

"I don't even like Caleb, ya know. He's kinda a douche," she whispers, placing her palm against my chest.

"I know Mads. I know." I say, sliding in next to her.

Taylor and Jesse climb in, Taylor sitting on Jesse's lap, so we all fit. I normally wouldn't over fill my truck like this, but I haven't been drinking and I make Taylor and Jesse still put the seatbelt on around both of them. The drive home is quick since there's no one on the roads. Madison is leaning into my side, gently snoring. I wrap my arm around her to keep her from falling over. I gently run my thumb back and forth on her bare arm and she cuddles closer to me and lets out a small whimper. God, I wish we were the only ones in this truck, and I wish she wasn't drunk.

I wonder if something more than her being jealous of Jackie is going on because the Mads I know wouldn't get drunk like this. She was never a partier, and she hated what drinking would do to her mom. Then again, I'm starting to wonder how well I actually knew her. No, I know her. I know her better than anyone, just like she knows me better than anyone. Well, she knows Ender. She knows the person I want to be.

The living room lights are still on when I pull into the driveway. Mom must still be awake. I gently cradle Madison in my arms and carry her up to the house. She cuddles into my chest, still asleep.

"Henderson, is that you?" Mom calls from the other room.

"Yeah Mom, it's me. Jesse and Taylor are here too," I respond as I head toward the stairs.

"Hey guys, go say hi to my mom. I'm gonna go put her down and I'll meet you in the basement," I tell Taylor and Jesse before making my way up to my room.

I take Madison up the stairs and gently kick open my bedroom door, grateful I was bored this morning and cleaned up. My room never gets embarrassingly messy, but if she woke up and found a pile of my dirty underwear, I wouldn't want that being her first impression of how I live. I lay Madison on top of the bed as gently as I can, hoping she stays asleep. She stirs a little, but turns onto her side, tucking her hands up under her face and gently sighs. Her hair is splayed out over my pillow and I want nothing more than to climb into the bed with her, but I know I can't. Not when she's been drinking like this. After I pull off her shoes and cover her with a blanket, I head down stairs to explain to Mom why there's a girl she doesn't know sleeping in my bed tonight.

Mom's always been cool about girls. And because she's not an idiot, and she's a nurse, she buys me condoms and makes me get tested regularly. Even if I'm not having sex. We don't actually talk about my sex life, or lack of one, but she's made it clear that she's not naive enough to think I'm not having sex. When my dad left, she made a point to tell me once—anything I'd ever learned or heard from my dad about sex or how to treat a partner was bullshit and to forget it all. She made this statement out of the blue one day while we were driving in the car somewhere. There was no lead into it or follow up statements from her. She just blurted it out. I didn't ask questions or ask her to elaborate. I let her seething comment hang in the air.

That's happened a few times—her randomly getting reminded of something my dad did or said that we all let slide. She acknowledges it, but we rarely talk about it. We let whatever short burst of anger or resentment she has be released into the air and go about our day. I think it's healing for her to talk about it so freely whenever she wants, without any judgment. This is part of why I know I can tell her the bare minimum of what she needs to know about Madison, and she'll trust me to tell her the rest when I'm ready. We've gotten better at being honest but also letting each other take time with our honesty.

CHAPTER NINETEEN

MADISON

My head feels like there are elephants wrestling inside of it and my mouth feels like I've swallowed cotton. I'm awake but fighting the urge to open my eyes because I already know it will be too bright. Cracking open one eye, just a little, I find I'm definitely not in my dorm room. With both eyes open now, my head is screaming and pushing my hand to my forehead isn't any relief. Okay, let's try to get our bearings.

I'm in a queen sized bed with gray sheets and a patchwork quilt on top of me. I can see a desk across from me with a few books and a laptop. There's a shelf above the desk with trophies. They look like they're maybe football trophies. Hats hang on the wall next to the shelf. Now, I'm almost certain I'm in a guy's room. Whose, I'm not completely sure yet. Am I still at Caleb's house? Is this his room? I look behind me on the bed. I'm alone, good sign. I'm still wearing my dress, and my bra and underwear are still on. More good signs.

There's a glass of water on the nightstand and a bottle of ibuprofen. I sit up slowly but drink the water greedily and down three of the pills. A note is sitting next to the glass.

Come downstairs whenever you're ready. Taylor and Jesse are here too.

Henry

Well, that solves the puzzle.

Pieces of last night slowly come into focus. Playing beer pong with Caleb. Henry getting pissed off at me for being drunk and, oh crap. Henry throwing me over his shoulder like a child and carrying me out of the party. I am mortified. I knew I was drinking too much. Still, I don't know if I should be grateful he got me out of there or pissed at him for being so... so... possessive?

What gives him the right? He had multiple opportunities to ask for my number, or ask me on a proper date, and he never did. When he finally did make a move in the library, he ran away without any explanation. If anyone's ever been given a trophy for sending the most mixed signals, it's probably on Henry's shelf, among his others.

I don't rush to go downstairs. Facing Henry and the rest of them isn't exactly at the top of my to-do list right now. I take in more of the room and notice a bulletin board on one of the walls and move to it. It's got concert tickets and photos tacked to it. Several of the photos are of Henry with a beautiful older woman. She must be his mom. The indignation I was just feeling is slipping away as I stare at the photos, his arms wrapped loving around her. That one dimple he has, exaggerated by his broad smile.

There are also pictures with Jesse, Taylor, and Emmett. Even one of all of them with Jackie in it, from what looks like a school dance. They're all dressed up, standing in front of a limo. Henry looks amazing in a tux. Jackie looks alright, I think to myself. Not bitterly at all.

Behind some of the photos, a handwritten note is peeking out. I lift the photos to see it more clearly. It's a poem.

Isn't that a risk worth taking
Confessing all your desires
Setting love free, hoping it returns
When the alternative is an ending

It's beautiful and oddly familiar, but there's no author noted. I turn to face my fate when the door to Henry's room creaks open slowly. I still, like a deer in headlights. What if it's his mom, but wouldn't she knock? Henry's face comes peeking around the door. He smiles softly at me and guilt, shame, lust and a million other emotions wash over me.

"You're awake."

"I am," I say, a small smile on my lips.

He walks further into his room. Still in what I assume are his pajamas. A plain black shirt and flannel pants. He hasn't done anything with his hair and a few pieces are sticking up in weird directions. He looks completely adorable, and it makes me want to cuddle up with him on a couch in front of a fireplace with hot chocolate. One glance at him and I forget I'm supposed to be angry with him.

"How are you feeling?"

I take a seat on the edge of his bed, crossing my legs at my ankles.

"Not nearly as bad as I deserve," I admit. "Thank you for letting me sleep here. I'm sorry I was such a mess."

He doesn't give my apology any acknowledgement. How awful was I last night?

Henry rummages around in his dresser and pulls out a pair of jeans.

"I'm gonna go get changed and then I can take you home."

"Okay," I say, not making eye contact with him.

I'm feeling pretty embarrassed right now. I think about sneaking out and walking back to the dorms while he's in the bathroom. When Henry gave me a ride on my first day in Easton, he said he didn't live far from campus. It would only be fair, right? He disappeared from the library and I'll disappear from his bedroom. But before I can decide, he's walking back into the bedroom. He's wearing jeans now, but still has on the black t-shirt.

"I forgot a shirt," he admits while he goes to his closet and pulls a button-up off a hanger.

It's green like the flecks in his eyes. His back is to me and he pulls the black t-shirt up and over his head, tossing it in the corner. His back is what you expect to see on the covers of romance novels—muscular and tan, with broad shoulders that have perfect divots you could sink your hands into. The tattoo I noticed before I can now see is definitely a script. He rarely lets it show, always wearing shirts with sleeves that cover it. The words go from his left arm and all the way across his upper back and wrap up around his other shoulder. The font is too small and delicate for me to read from here, but when he turns around, he's still finishing buttoning his shirt. I can see it continues across the front of him, ending over the left side of his chest where there's what looks like a bird flying out from the words.

"Madison, how much of last night do you remember?"

My cheeks burn with embarrassment when I realize he's caught me staring. Then again, if he didn't want me looking, he could have gone back to the bathroom to finish changing. I wrack my brain, willing it to repeat the question he just asked me. He was asking about last night. *How much do I remember from last night?*

My skin prickles and I break out in a cold sweat. Oh no. Memories of last night are definitely hazy, but the way he's looking at me has me worried. Did something more happen between me and Henry, or even worse, me and Caleb? I don't remember anything that bad happening. I remember finding Henry and Jackie making out in the kitchen. Playing beer pong with Caleb, he was a little handsy. But the end of the night is just out of focus.

"Things are a little fuzzy," I admit. "Did we–"

I don't finish the sentence hoping he'll understand and answer without me having to say it out loud.

"I slept downstairs in the basement with Jesse and Taylor. You slept up here alone. Madison, I would never, ever take advantage of someone."

I'm relieved by his answer, but I can't help shoot myself in the foot.

"I mean, I remember seeing you and your girlfriend–"

"Jackie is not my girlfriend."

"Okay, I remember seeing you and–"

He cuts me off again, looking a little defeated.

"Look, Madison, yes. I used to date Jackie, but we've been broken up for a while now. She and I will never get back together. Never. She kissed me and I pushed her away. You just clearly didn't see me push her away." His voice is getting louder and his body language is more animated and frustrated. He runs a hand down his face, sighs, and comes to sit next to me on the bed.

My body instantly feels warm with him being so close. I shift on the bed and our arms brush. Even with his shirt between our skin, I feel heat where our bodies touch. Anytime I've got close to him like this, my senses go into overdrive. I lean into him, just a little. I feel him lean into me just a little too.

After a long moment of silence that seems to go on forever, he continues.

"I'm sorry," his voice is quiet now, quieter than even his normal speaking voice. I can tell he's working to control himself and his emotions.

He's not looking at me. He's looking down at the gray hardwood floors of his bedroom.

"It's okay, really. I should be the one who's sorry."

"No Mads, you have nothing to be sorry about."

Did Henry just–did he call me Mads? Did he hear Jesse calling me that? He must have. It's the only logical explanation for why he would call me Mads. For just a second, one tiny second, I think of Ender. I like Henry a lot, even if we haven't had the smoothest road of interactions. It's hard to admit, but my heart is still in so many pieces and so many of the pieces are sitting in email drafts.

"I think you better give me a ride home now. I have a ton of stuff I should probably be doing."

We leave his room and make our way downstairs. Henry's house is nice, but he's obviously not rich. Upper middle class maybe, but if his parents are more well off, they don't flaunt it. I've only ever heard him talk about his mom. I wonder where his dad is. As we walk through his house, I notice a few pictures hanging on the wall. All of them of Henry by himself, no family portraits.

When we make it downstairs, Jesse and Taylor are sitting at a breakfast bar in the kitchen eating donuts and drinking milk, talking to the woman from the pictures, Henry's mom. Nothing like coming downstairs from their son's bedroom in last night's clothes to make an impression on a mom. I wonder what Henry told her about me and why I was staying here, in his bedroom, and not wherever everyone else slept.

"Hi there. It's Madison right?" Henry's mom greets me with a soft smile.

"Yes Ma'am. Thank you so much for letting me stay here. You have a beautiful home."

"Oh no problem sweetie, the kids all know they're welcome here anytime and that includes you now, too."

She's sweet and beautiful, but there's a strange sadness to her. Like she's grieving or lonely. Henry pulls two donuts out of the box and hands me one. It's a green tea donut, my favorite. How in the hell does he know it's my favorite? Most people hate these donuts or have never even heard of them. I look at him curiously, but he's distracted by something. He walks over to his mom and gives her a kiss on the cheek.

"I'm going to give everyone a ride home. Can I use your car?" He asks her.

"Sure hun," she says and we all start making our way toward the front door. "Oh, and Henderson, can you pick up some more milk on your way home, please?"

"Yeah, Mom."

Henderson? Is that Henry's full name? I let the name roll around on my tongue silently. I guess you could get Henry as a nickname from Henderson.

I actually think I might be sick now, and not from drinking too much last night.

You could also get Ender.

Chapter Twenty

Henderson

Madison is quiet on the car ride home. Even when Taylor tries to talk to her, she's answering in *mmhmms*, and one-word responses. I'm pretty sure she even tried to sit in the back seat with Taylor, but Jesse beat her to it. She doesn't seem to be *mad*; she seems preoccupied, distracted. I wonder if it has anything to do with whoever was texting her at the party last night. Maybe she's still upset with me, or maybe she's just hungover. I should stop trying to guess and ask her. But, I'm apparently a chicken.

I drop off Jesse and Taylor at Jesse's apartment. Madison tries to get out and says she'll just walk across the street to campus, but I convince her to let me drop her off closer. She doesn't say a word on the short drive over to campus. Familiarity strikes as I pull up to the curb. It's so much like the day she arrived in town. Except, everything has changed since then. I remember thinking about my Mads being off somewhere, starting at her college–thinking back on it now makes my brain hurt trying to reconcile the fact that while I was thinking about her, I was actually staring at her. Admiring her beauty, her sexiness, and lusting after her perfect lips.

We're in my mom's car this time, and there's an obnoxiously huge console between us now. I want to rip the entire console out and pull

Madison on top of me. Just so I can hold her. I want to run my fingers through her hair and tell her everything is going to be fine. Whatever has her upset, we will work through together. I want to tell her it's me, Ender, and I'm here for her. She knows me. She trusts me. I understand her, and she can tell me anything. Even if what she needs to say will hurt me. I do none of this because–chicken.

Madison doesn't even give me a chance to ask if she's okay. She gives me a curt *thanks for the ride* and is out of the car and halfway to the building entrance before I can even form a coherent thought. Something is definitely wrong. I briefly consider parking the car and chasing after her, but at this point I think I've done enough. I just head home. Maybe I should give her some time, let everything from the library and the party settle more. Then try talking to her again.

The whole drive home, I keep having to talk myself out of turning the car around, asking Taylor for their room number and banging on Madison's door. Telling her everything and begging her forgiveness for not telling her sooner. I keep driving though because I'm selfish, and right now, apologizing for what happened at the party seems easier than apologizing for lying to her since the day she arrived in town.

I finally make it home after stopping to get milk for Mom. I find her and Emmett sitting together at the kitchen bar. They abruptly stop talking when I walk in. I get the weirdest feeling that I interrupted their conversation.

"Don't stop talking on my account," I joke.

No one laughs. What is going on?

"I, uh, picked up the milk," I say, lifting the gallon of milk for show before putting it in the fridge.

"Thanks, sweetie," Mom says. "I think I'm gonna go lie down and read for a bit. Enjoy my day off."

She gets up and starts heading toward her room. Leaving Emmett and I alone.

"You come to see me or my mom?" I ask Emmett, throwing in a half-hearted laugh, trying to ease the tension.

"You, of course, dumbass. You wanna go play some Xbox?"

"Yeah, let's do it."

We head down to the basement. I'm not fully convinced the weird vibes I felt when I came into the kitchen are just in my head. Then again, I've got so much on my mind and I'm so damn paranoid about Madison and what she's thinking. My intuition probably can't be trusted right now. I flop down onto the couch while Emmett turns on the console and grabs the controller, starting up Madden.

I pull out my phone while the game is loading, and re-read the email I got from Mads last night. She probably doesn't even remember she sent it. If I respond, will it dig the hole I'm already in deeper? If I don't respond, will she assume Ender moved on finally? When I click into my sent folder, I don't have to scroll far to find the email I sent the night I came home to find my dad was a bigger piece of shit than I ever expected. It's the same email I'd found in my car that she printed. The one she's clearly read and by the state of the paper—torn and creased—she's read it a lot more than once.

To: madisrad@gmail.com
From: ravensfan4lyfe@gmail.com
Date: August 8 11:27:43
Subject: Confession

Confession:

I'm done pretending. I'm done acting like I haven't wanted to tell you this for years now. This is going to change everything and I am fucking scared. I am scared for so many reasons right now, most of which may scare you. But here goes anyway...

You are the most incredible person I have ever known. I have never even seen your face but I know you're beautiful because your soul and your heart take my breath away with every email I read. Your poems set my skin on fire, your banter keeps a huge goofy grin on my face for days at a time.

I have never, in my life, felt more connected or more drawn to someone. I have never wanted to be with someone more than I want to be with you Mads.

I love you, I have loved you for so long it hurts. I want to be together and I really hope you feel the same. I am praying (to who I'm not sure) that you feel even an ounce of what I feel for you.

I will come to you, or you can come to me, I don't care. I will do whatever it takes to get the chance to touch you, feel you, hug you, hear your laughter — because thoughts of you have completely consumed me. Please say you will... say you hear me and I'll know this isn't one sided.

Yours,
Ender

As I read this email back now, after spending time with her, after kissing her–all of those feelings I had, ring true even louder. They're deafening how true they are, like standing inside a bell tower while it rings. The sounds reverberating all around you except the sounds are my feelings and I'm stuck in my own mind. I knew even when I wrote this letter, Madison was beautiful. What I wasn't prepared for was how incredibly sexy she can be. The way she bites her lip or the way she lets all of her emotions show when she's sad or angry. Everything about her turns me on the moment I'm in her presence.

"You've had your nose in your phone for a while. You reading porn?" Emmett asks.

"No, Emmett. I am not reading porn," I sneer.

"Okay, okay. Seriously, are you okay, man? What's going on?"

I make a snap decision and spend the next twenty minutes telling Emmett everything. I tell him about Ender and Mads emailing for years, about the kiss in the library, the party, everything.

Emmett spends the next five minutes laughing, and I want to choke him.

"I'm sorry, I'm sorry," more laughter, "but, that is the most bad reality television, 2000s soap opera, bullshit I have ever heard. You are totally fucked."

"Seriously Emmett. You suck," I groan, dramatically falling back and laying across the couch. I kick him with my foot.

"Okay, I'll be serious. Look, you've clearly got two choices. Tell her who you are and risk her hating you. Or don't tell her, and she eventually figures it out. But then for sure hates you if you wait too long. But you already know that. And I think you already know what you need to do. Tell her the truth, Henry, just... tell her the truth."

Emmett has such a look of sincerity on his face, but I can also see a hint of sadness.

I've known Emmett almost my whole life and I have never once seen him actually sad. He didn't even cry when we were kids. If he got hurt while we were playing football, he'd get angry, not sad. Something is definitely going on with him, but he's like a cat. If I approach too quickly, he'll make a break for it.

"Yeah, you're right. I need to figure out the how and when of telling her the truth."

"While you figure that out, let's play," he says, handing me a con-troller.

We've been playing for close to an hour when I casually ask him where the heck he disappeared to last night at the party.

"I had something to take care of. You know how it is."

"Something or someone?"

He looks at me and winks, and doesn't answer my question. Well, that went well. I learned nothing. I'm not giving up, though. I will find out why he's been acting so strange.

Emmett has always been a bit of a lone wolf. He's never had a real re-lationship. Just a seemingly endless string of flings and one-night stands for the past few years. We all give him shit about it, but Emmett is a solid friend. He was the one who picked me up from the police station after I was arrested. His parents had paid my bail. He was also at every court hearing, even the stupid ones which only lasted five minutes. He even wrote a three-page letter to the judge in case I needed character witnesses. The guy who spends more time flirting with girls so they'll do his homework, than actual time doing his own homework–wrote a three-page letter. Thankfully, it never got that far. I've never properly thanked him for how much he was there for me through all the bullshit. I hope he knows though how much I appreciate him.

A few hours later, Mom comes down to the basement and asks if we want to go get something to eat at the diner. Emmett fires off a yes before I can even consider it and is up turning off the game console and bounding up the stairs. Taylor had told me Madison has today off, so I know she won't be there working. I follow them out to the car.

The diner is busy when we get there, but Joy gets us sat in a booth and brings everyone water. We order our food, Emmett orders half the menu. When our food gets here, we all dig in. I have no appetite so I only ordered eggs and toast. Emmett is halfway through his feast before I'm even done with one of my eggs.

"Emmett hun, slow down. I know you haven't had an appetite, but you'll make yourself sick."

Emmett looks at my mom wide eyed, but sets down his fork and drinks some water. Why does my mom know he hasn't had an appetite? Before I can ask, I notice someone walking through the door to the diner. It's Madison.

Chapter Twenty-One

Madison

I spent the whole car ride from Henry's house to campus trying to convince myself I'm being delusional. That there is absolutely no way Henry and Ender are the same person. It's impossible. It would be way too much of a coincidence and way too bizarre. When I get into my dorm room, I close the door behind me and lean up against it, rolling my head back until it lightly taps the door. Looking up to the ceiling, trying to keep the tears that are beginning to well in my eyes from falling. This can not be happening.

Think, be rational. If I just think all the coincidences through, I'm sure there are rational explanations for all of them. The more I think about them, the more confused I am. Even from the first day we met, when he pulled his hand away so quickly, it was right after I said my name. When he shared the book of poetry with me in the library, he knew I would love it. The donut. He called me Mads. He called me Mads! That's why he pulled away when we kissed. He knows it's me. How the fuck does he know it's me and I'm just now figuring out he's Ender?

I pace back and forth in my small dorm room, trying not to rip out my hair. My hangover is all but gone and is being replaced by anxiety and anger. I'm seething. He definitely knows it's me and he didn't tell me! Was he planning on ever telling me? I drop to the floor, sitting in the middle of the room. I'm full on crying now, big fat tears dropping onto my legs. After a few minutes of wallowing, I decide I have to make sure I'm right. I pull my laptop off my desk into my lap and bring up google.

I type in "Henderson Easton Maryland" a few articles come up that talk about him and his high school football days. Ender and Henry both play football. The signs I should have seen just keep stacking up. I click a link at random and there he is. It's an article that includes what looks like his senior high school photo. Henderson Adler, quarterback, the caption reads. Well, at least now I have a last name too. I skim through a few more articles. Wow, he is apparently a good quarterback, like seriously good. There are articles talking about him being scouted by multiple colleges and I even find one that says he was practically committed to Virginia Tech. If that's true, then what the hell is he still doing in Easton?

I go back to google and search his full name. An article from almost a year ago catches my eye and I gasp. "Local College Football Hopeful Arraigned on Attempted Murder Charges". This can't be right. My hand trembling, I click to open the article. And there, staring me in the face, is Henry. It's a mugshot. I scan the article faster than my brain can process the words. My already cracked and beat up heart bursting wide open. I let myself feel all the pain he must have felt.

Local Easton high school student, Henderson Adler, was arraigned today on attempted murder charges. Adler, who was arrested on August 8th for allegedly beating his father, Christian Adler, so severely with a trophy Adler, C. was in intensive care for four weeks following surgery for a ruptured spleen, pleaded not guilty.

Adler, H. who will not be charged as an adult as he is still only 17, is currently awaiting his trial from home under house arrest. The teenager, who will be a senior in high school next year, is a local football star quarterback and is said to have recently made commitments to play for Virginia Tech College.

Adler, H.'s attorney provided this comment on the steps outside the courthouse today. "My client has pleaded not guilty today because he acted in self-defense of another. You will see in trial that what this young man did was heroic."

Reliable sources tell us, allegedly, on the night of August 8th, Adler, H. arrived home to find his father, Adler, C. abusing the defendant's mother. The trial is set to begin on September 28th.

I slam my laptop shut and cover my mouth with my hands, trying to understand what I just read. Is this for real? I remember Taylor telling me last night about something happening with him. She said it wasn't her story to tell. Is this what she was talking about? I open the computer again and start searching for more articles. I'm assuming he wasn't found guilty because he's not sitting in prison right now, but I can't help myself from wanting to know more of the details. There are a few more articles that explain he ended up taking a plea deal before the trial even finished. Because he was a minor, the Judge agreed to seal part of the record.

When I scan back through the original article again, the date catches my eye–August 8th. He was arrested on August 8th. The same day he sent me the email telling me he loved me. The same day he pleaded for me and I pushed his feelings aside because I was terrified.

When I read his email, I was overwhelmed. Overwhelmed with emotion and the choice, the choice of accepting his love and meeting him in real life or the choice of lying to him, telling him I didn't feel the same way and everything about our relationship changing. In a panic and in total cowardice, I chose neither option. I chose to ignore it, forever. Or so I thought.

Now, with everything I just learned, I'm reconsidering everything. Somehow, by some crazy illogical fate, we've ended up in the same place, at the same time. We've somehow met so organically it's unbelievable. And yet, even now, I've still kept my distance and ran from my feelings. It all clicks into place. Why I felt so comfortable around him from the very first moments. Why my body seemed to be tied to one end of a tether, his on the other. We've been connected since we were thirteen. I've been in love with him for years, even if I couldn't admit it to myself or him—until now.

I know I love him, which makes all of this hurt so much more.

I pull up my Ender filled email account on my laptop. I see the drafts folder and my heart aches. There are one hundred and twenty seven drafts. One hundred and twenty-seven times I've wanted to break my silence.

I click into the drafts folder, wanting to re-read some of my thoughts, when something horrifying occurs to me. I remember writing a draft at the party last night and it was a particularly unsavory and uncalled for one... and I don't see it in my drafts folder. Panicking, I refresh. Nope, still not there. I click to the trash bin. I must have just deleted it then. Nope, not there either. I take a huge breath, and with only one eye half way open, I click on the sent folder. Fuck. Me.

There she is, sitting in my sent folder. I am never drinking again. How could I have been so careless? Why is there not an undo button? I fall to my back, laying there, I try to calm my racing heart and rushing thoughts. I don't have any emails in my inbox from him, so maybe he hasn't read it. Maybe he doesn't even check that account anymore or he could have deleted it all together. No, I think if he deleted it, I would have gotten an error message. I'm not that lucky. There's still the chance he hasn't read it yet.

I briefly consider breaking into his house and stealing the laptop I saw on his desk and deleting the email. It's not the worst idea I've ever had. Then I wonder, if he *has* read it, why hasn't he replied? And if he got it last night and read it, is that why he took me away from the party? My head hurts, not because of the whiskey and beer I drank, but because it's getting too difficult to reconcile all of my thoughts. I am almost completely certain Henry knows exactly who I am. There are just too many coincidences for him not to. I give up on trying to come up with a way for him to not read the email I sent. Instead I focus my limited energy on attempting to find out for sure if he knows who I am or not.

After a few minutes, my stomach growls and I know I need to eat something. I'm suddenly starving. I shower and put on a clean pair of leggings and a plain white T-shirt and start walking toward the diner. I need a good plate of greasy diner food and the school dining hall just will not cut it. Plus, the walk to the diner will be good for me. A chance to clear my head and try to sort out the overflowing emotions I'm dealing with.

CHAPTER TWENTY-TWO

HENDERSON

Madison doesn't notice us when she walks in. We're at the far end of the diner and she takes a seat at one of the counter stools closest to the entrance. One turn of her head is all it will take for her to see me. I'm contemplating if I should stay sitting just where I am or if I should go to her. Say hello and check on her. I stay stuck to the vinyl booth seat.

I am a coward.

What is it about this girl and her ability to make me go weak at the knees and lose all sense of direction? She makes me absolutely feral. I act on instinct around her even though half the time I realize too late my instincts are total garbage. Kissing her and running away, not asking for her number on any of the occasions when I should have–I wouldn't be shocked if she thinks I want nothing to do with her.

I must have been staring at the back of her head too long and she sensed it because she turns in her seat. I duck my head and scrunch down in the booth, making myself smaller. I don't know if she saw me because when I lift my eyes again she's facing away from me talking to Joy.

I pull out my phone and do something stupid. Something risky and chaotic. Something I may regret. I apparently never learn.

I reply to the email she sent in her drunken haze at the party.

To: madisrad@gmail.com
From: ravensfan4lyfe@gmail.com
Date: August 22 2:47:32
Subject: Re: Mads is Rad - A poem

Isn't that a risk worth taking
Confessing all your desires
Setting love free, hoping it returns
When the alternative is an ending

That's all I write. I don't even sign my name. I send only those four lines of poem verse. The one single stanza. Because I promised her I would and because she asked for it. Whether she meant it when she asked for it or not, I may never know. I haven't taken my eyes off her since I hit send. I'm waiting–trying to catch any part of her reaction. She still hasn't taken out her phone and seen the email as far as I can tell from here. For all I know, she could have notifications from me muted or even blocked.

Her food arrives and I can't help but laugh at how adorable she is as she devours the bacon. There's nothing adorable about how she sticks her finger in her mouth to lick the syrup off it. It's sexy as fuck.

Emmett loudly clears his throat and I bring my attention back to the table I'm sitting at. He and Mom are both staring at me. Him with a knowing smirk and Mom with a curious look on her face. My cheeks burn with embarrassment.

"Isn't that your friend Madison from this morning?" Mom asks, jutting her chin toward her.

I smile back at Mom sheepishly.

"Um, yeah. It is."

"Why don't you go say hi while I pay the bill?"

"Yeah, Henry, why don't you go say hi?" Emmett says with a cocky grin.

Asshole.

Mom and Emmett get up from the booth and head toward the register. I stay where I am, still stuck to these stupid vinyl seats. The seats aren't stupid, really, and I bet Madison loves them. She was probably giddy when she found this place. I inhale a deep breath, hoping it will help my currently tiny balls inflate and give me even an ounce of courage. I exhale and walk toward her.

"Hi," I say, taking a seat on the stool next to her.

She startles just a little before turning to me. That's when I notice her phone is in her lap and she has tears running down her face. She looks at me with so much pain, but I can also see anger and maybe pity? I have no idea what she's thinking or feeling and it's killing me. My stomach turns and the food I just ate threatens to come back up.

"Mads, I am so, so sorry," I say, because it's the only thing I can think to say.

She stares at me for a long time, tears still dropping silently. When she speaks, it's only a few words, but those few words feel like a punch to the stomach.

"Fuck you, Ender."

Now I really am going to be sick.

She gets up and rushes out of the diner before I can even react. My current reaction is to just sit here, jaw on the floor, feeling as if time just stopped. The world around me is silent and everything is out of focus.

She knows. She knows who I am and I am so completely fucked. After the initial shock wears off and my brain starts functioning again, I get off my ass and start after her. When I make it outside, I don't see her at first.

When I spot her, she's several blocks away already. Is she actually *running* away from me? Damn, she's fast.

I jog after her, calling her name in the middle of the street on a Saturday afternoon. I must look like an idiot. An idiot who has no idea how he's going to salvage any of this. I don't need a plan. I just need to be honest and tell her everything. When I finally catch up to her, it's only because she had to stop and rest, catch her breath.

She must have been running at full speed because she's panting and doubled over on the sidewalk.

"Madison, please. Let me explain! It's not what you think. Actually, I have no fucking idea what you think any of this is, but please, just let me explain." I've reached out and put my hands on her shoulder, trying to get her to look at me and she violently shakes free of my touch.

"How long?" She asks.

"What?"

"How long!" she's shouting now. "How long have you known who I am? Since the day I got here? Because I just fucking found out today and I have a feeling you've known a lot fucking longer, Ender."

Ender comes out in two distinct syllables, with an extra "d". *End-der.* I hate hearing her say that name like that.

She's mad. No, she's pissed. She's standing there with arms crossed and I can't help but notice it makes her tits squish together and look double their size. Fuck. I am being a total douche, again. I run my hand over my face, trying to stop being such a horny asshole and answer her.

"You dropped a copy of an email I sent you in my car the day I gave you a ride to campus from the bus station."

She gasps and covers her mouth with her hand. I know she knows exactly what email it was.

"Why didn't you tell me you knew?" She asks.

"Because I'm an asshole." It's the first thing I can think of to say, but it's honest. I should have told her from the very beginning. But, I was selfish. I wanted more time with her. I wanted to be in her presence and sneak touches of her soft skin and smell her warm scent. Even if it meant keeping things from her, even if it meant she didn't know who I was.

"And because I was confused and scared shitless of losing you–again." I admit. "Look, can we please just go somewhere and talk and I will answer whatever questions you have?"

I'm practically begging her now and wonder if it would actually be more effective if I got down on my knees.

"I think I need more time. I can't right now." Her eyes are filling with tears again.

"Okay. Will you email me when you're ready to talk? Please?"

She nods her head slowly and turns away from me to walk the rest of the way to campus.

I stand here rooted to the same spot for a long time, watching her walk. I am terrified she is heading back to her dorm room to pack up all her shit and get as far away from me as possible.

I can't let myself believe she doesn't have feelings for me, that she hasn't had feelings for me this whole time, even if those feelings got muddled together. The parts of her feelings for Ender being ripped into by her feelings for Henry. If I let myself believe she doesn't care about me, my heart will break into a million pieces, and I don't know if I'll ever be able to cobble those pieces back together.

A horn honks on the street. I don't even turn to see where it comes from. I'm standing completely still and feeling completely numb.

The horn honks again.

Mom and Emmett have pulled up, Mom giving me a sympathetic smile. I jump in the back of the car and sink down into the seat.

"Wanna talk about it?" Mom asks.

"No."

I've been laying on my bed, torturing myself by reading over old email conversations between me and Madison since I got home. Mom tried one more time on the ride home to get me to talk about what happened. Emmett did me a solid and helped change the subject.

I'm scrolling through the emails on my phone and picking ones at random. I just read a conversation which spanned two weeks where we argued about which was better on a peanut butter and jelly sandwich; smooth or chunky peanut butter. I argued for smooth and she argued for chunky. I don't even care for peanut butter. I just liked the banter when we had these little debates. They always started and ended the same way. One of us would email on a random afternoon something along the lines of "smooth peanut butter has no place in this world" and the debate would ensue. It always ended with me conceding. I relished in making her happy, even if it meant telling a little white lie and letting her think I agreed with her when she argued Thor was the best Marvel super hero when clearly its Captain America.

I know I'm throwing myself a pity party by holing up in my room, reading these emails rather than trying to talk to her and deal with the mess I created. I tell myself I'm giving her space to process everything and I'll come up with a plan tomorrow. I suck at making plans though, clearly. Even if I come up with a plan, I'm sure I would just go rogue and do whatever stupid thing came to mind first.

I could always call Taylor and ask for her advice. Maybe she'd let me into their dorm room and I can fill it with hundreds of roses. No, that's stupid. Madison's not the type who can be won over with cheesy gestures. We had more than one conversation about how we got second hand embarrassment when we saw things like prom-posals or public actual *marriage* proposals.

Madison had stopped replying to my emails by the time I went to winter formal with Jackie, so she doesn't know about the cheesy and pathetic way I got roped into asking her. I was class president and nominated for formal king, and even though Dad was out of the picture by this point, I still succumbed to the pressure of doing what was expected of me.

Taylor's ears must have been ringing because her name flashes on my phone screen with a new text. Maybe she heard what happened and is coming to me with a great idea on how to fix this. I click the text message to open it, nope not a way to fix this, but it is a problem I'm gonna fix.

CHAPTER TWENTY-THREE

MADISON

I slam the door to the dorm room when I get inside and start pacing around the small space. My eyes are welling with unshed tears and I look to the ceiling to try to keep them from creating a puddle on our floor.

"What's wrong?" Taylor says, jumping up and coming to me, grabbing onto my arms to stop me from pacing.

I keep staring at the ceiling, trying to gather my thoughts and wondering if I'll be able to tell her without sobbing. I take a deep breath and recount everything. I tell her about Ender first, so it makes even an ounce of sense when I tell her Henry *is Ender.* I confess how I accidentally emailed him at the party and how he had the audacity to respond to the email, even with everything he knew. Everything he knew, I didn't know. I lose my battle with my tears halfway through the soap opera sounding tale.

At some point, we ended up sitting on the floor across from each other, legs crossed like you did when you were little and it was story time in preschool. Taylor nods at all the right parts and hugs me occasionally. She gets mad with me and is overall sympathetic to my current mess of a situation. I've almost finished telling her everything when my phone starts ringing. I look at it and see *Mom* flashing on the screen. I hit ignore.

She is the last person I want to deal with right now, especially after the texts she sent last night.

I continue telling Taylor all the wild, heartbreaking, and unbelievable details of everything I know. My phone rings again, Mom again. I hit ignore. I finish telling her everything and she just hugs me for a long time. Letting me cry onto her shoulder. My phone rings *again* and I answer without even looking at the screen.

"What?!" I yell into the phone.

"Uh, is this Madison?"

I look at the screen and see it's my mom calling, except it's a man's voice on the phone.

"Yes, who is this? Where's my mom?"

"This is Gary, your mom's boyfriend. Your mom is in the hospital. She says she needs you to come down here right away."

"What?! What do you mean, Mom's in the hospital? I'm across the country at school? What's wrong with her?"

"Your mom just said to call you and tell you to come. I gotta go, sorry."

The line goes silent.

What. The. Hell.

"Madison, is your mom okay?" Taylor asks, concern splashed across her face.

"I don't know. I guess the guy who called was her boyfriend. She's in the hospital, but he wouldn't tell me why or if she's even okay. I have to get there, but dammit, it's going to take all of my savings just to get a last-minute plane ticket out to California."

I sob into my hands more. I'm angry at Henry, I'm angry at whoever the hell this Gary guy is for giving me zero information. I'm actually worried about my mom. I'm more than overwhelmed.

I jump up and pull out my backpack, shoving my laptop and some clean clothes into it. Taking my suitcase seems like too much of a hassle.

Taylor is typing on her phone, but she sets it on her nightstand and walks over to me.

"Here, let me pack for you. You sit down."

She takes my backpack from me and nudges me toward a chair. I sit reluctantly as she packs my toiletries for me.

"Taylor, I've never bought a plane ticket before and I'm not sure I know how. Shit. I've never even been on an airplane. Where is the nearest airport? Can I just buy a ticket at the counter?" I say through sobs I'm still struggling to control.

There's a sudden, very loud knock on our door. Startled, I flinch. I don't move to answer the door because moving seems like a lot of effort since I sat down. Taylor doesn't move either. I look at her and she has a worried look on her face.

Bang. Bang. Bang. More loud knocking, followed by a familiar voice only slightly muffled by the door.

"Taylor, open the fucking door."

Taylor and I both jump and look to our door, where the yelling just came from.

"Madison, I'm sorry, I had to," Taylor says, moving to open the door.

She looks terrified, her eyes are glossy. I'm scared she might cry and even more scared of why she might cry. What did she do? Taylor opens the door to our room. Henry comes charging in as soon as Taylor's out of the way. Or is it Ender coming through the door? Before my brain can even process anything, he's to me and has me wrapped in his arms. Pressing his mouth to my ear.

"I am so fucking sorry, Mads. I promise, I will tell you absolutely everything. I will answer every question you have, but for right now just please, please let me help you."

I'm just standing here like a limp noodle, my arms hanging at my sides, trying to process what's happening. I can't deny it feels good to be standing here in his arms and I'm desperate to ask a million questions. In a moment of clarity, I realize I know, deep down, I can still trust him.

Slowly, I bring my hands up and wrap them around his waist.

Hugging him back, I whisper, "okay".

Henry releases his arms around me but brings them up to my face, cupping my cheeks. He brings his forehead down to mine and just breathes for several moments.

"Emmett just texted. He says everything will be ready by the time you get there."

I had almost forgotten Taylor was even in the room. Henry and I separate and she's standing there holding my backpack. He takes it from her and starts to leave.

"I'll be downstairs. My truck is right outside waiting," Henry says, slinging my backpack over his shoulder.

He gives Taylor a quick hug. I hear him tell her, thank you, before he leaves our room.

I turn to Taylor now and she has tears bubbling in her eyes.

"Please don't be mad at me. I knew you needed help, and I knew he would help," she says, not quite meeting my eyes.

"Taylor, it's okay, really. But how exactly is he helping?" I ask, a little confused.

"Just go with him Mads, he's gonna help you get to your mom. Henry is a good guy Madison, but you already know that. And I think you already know you can trust him."

I nod and Taylor moves to hug me and we hug just a little too tight.

"Thank you," I say before releasing her.

My body is on autopilot. I'm not in control as I leave the dorm room, walk down the four flights of stairs and out to the parking lot. Henry is standing at the open passenger door of his truck parked along the curb. I get in without saying a word and he shuts the door behind me. He drives away and I don't even ask questions. I'm assuming he's taking me to the airport, but I don't even know where the airport is in this town, so I couldn't say for sure.

We've been driving for about ten minutes when we come to a red light. My head is leaning up against the window, tears I have no control over are still slowly dripping onto my jeans. Henry unbuckles my seatbelt from his side of the truck.

"Scoot over," he says.

I look at him, not understanding.

"Just scoot over, Mads."

His expression is soft and pleading. Not having enough energy to argue, I scoot to the middle of the bench seat. He wraps an arm around me and pulls me to his side. I let my head fall, and it lands perfectly on his shoulder. Even though I'm still angry with him, hearing him call me Mads causes a fluttering in my stomach. Traitorous hormones. His thumb brushing up and down on my arm causes goose bumps and makes my whole body tingle.

We drive this way for another fifteen minutes, not saying anything, when we finally pull off the main road. We pull in past a gate and I sit up, looking around and trying to determine where we are. There are several airplanes and large metal buildings, but this doesn't look like any normal airport I've ever seen. We're driving right up to one of the airplanes, a large white one that has a set of stairs down and the door open. He parks the truck a short walk away from it.

Henry reaches across me and grabs my backpack and a small duffle I didn't notice before from the floorboard. His hair is just beneath my nose now. I can smell his shampoo and I inhale, missing the scent as soon as he sits up. He gets out of the truck and extends his hand to me. I take it and scoot out after him. He doesn't let go of my hand when my feet land on the ground, but I don't mind. It's nice having someone to help me feel anchored right now.

As we're walking toward the plane, Emmett appears in the airplane's doorway and comes down the stairs. What is he doing here? They do one of those bro-slap half hug things, but Henry never releases my hand.

"The pilot is in there, ready when you are. Just go up front and tell him where you need to go. He'll find the closest airport and then wait to take you home when you're ready."

"Thank you so much. And, thank you parents for me. I owe them—again," Henry says.

"You owe them nothing. You owe me a beer," he laughs but cuts it short when he notices me.

I probably look as if I've been to hell and back by the nervous smile he gives me. Plus, he hasn't looked at my boobs once.

"I hope your mom's okay, Madison," he tells me.

My voice catches in my throat. I just force a small smile and nod, hoping he'll understand my appreciation for his sincerity. Emmett surprises me by giving me a hug. It's not handsy. It's warm and friendly and tight. It feels as if maybe he needed this hug more for himself than for me. Emmett releases me and Henry takes my hand again, leading me onto the plane.

Chapter Twenty-Four

Henderson

I'm flying by the seat of my damn pants here. When I got the text from Taylor, I shoved some clothes in a duffel bag and broke every speed limit to get to their dorm room. I knew if I called Emmett, he would help me. Having a best friend whose parents own a jet is a privilege I am so grateful for right now.

Madison hasn't said a word since we got on the plane. I've got her settled in a seat and put our bags on another. I'm about to go talk to the pilot and tell him we're ready to leave when I realize I don't know where we're heading. I don't know where home is for Madison.

I squat down in front of Madison. She's looking straight ahead, not saying a word.

"Mads, where am I taking you? What hospital is your mom at?"

She looks at me and I notice her lip is trembling slightly. I want so badly to cover her mouth with mine and hold her in my arms.

"Hope Hospital, it's in Oceanside, California," she says, looking at me finally.

I give her hand a quick squeeze before leaving her to talk to the pilot. When I come back, she's brought her knees up to her chest in the seat, her arms wrapped around her legs. I slide into the seat next to her and get comfortable. The pilot announces for us to put our seatbelts on so we can depart. I put mine on, but Madison hasn't moved.

"Madison, we're getting ready to take off. You need to put your seatbelt on."

She doesn't answer me. She's pale and there are little beads of sweat on her forehead.

"Madison, are you okay? Did you get a text about your Mom? Is she okay?" I ask, trying to decipher why she looks so scared.

"I've never been on an airplane," she confesses.

I have to bite back a laugh because I don't think laughing when she looks absolutely terrified would win me any points right now. She looks incredibly cute though, like a cat who's seeing the outside world for the first time and doesn't know what to do about its vastness.

I reach over her and buckle her seatbelt around her. Then gently take her hand in mine. She turns to look at me now. She looks at me, at our hands, and back up at me with a look that says *I'm scared, so I'm letting you do this, but I'm still fucking pissed.*

"Statistically, airplanes are one of the safest ways to travel. We are going to be fine, I promise," I say.

I can tell we've just been making our way to the runway by the sensations of the moving airplane. We start to take off. Madison squeezes my hand tighter and pinches her eyes closed.

"Babe, what can I do to help you right now?" I ask her, brushing a piece of her hair out of her face.

Her hair is so soft, and I've been dying to run my fingers through it, but if I do, I won't be able to stop myself from wanting to do more and that's not what she needs right now.

"I'm a writer. I like to know things. Can you just tell me what's happening so I can visualize what I can't see happening?"

Anything Madison ever asks me to do, I'm going to do it. This girl has had me wrapped around her finger for longer than she even realizes. So I explain to her we're taking off. The sounds she's hearing are the plane's wheels being lifted and put away, and we are in fact turning, but it's a slow, deliberate turn. When we've been in the air for about an hour, she starts to relax and look around. I'm pretty sure this is the first time she's actually seeing where we are.

Emmett's parents' airplane is stupid nice. I've only been in it once before when I went to Disney World with him for his twelfth birthday. There are four rows of seats on each side of an oversized aisle, only two seats per row. The seats are a lot bigger and a lot nicer than on commercial airplanes. The bathroom is three times the size of the shoe boxes I've had to piss in on your standard plane and one of the best features of this plane, a queen size bed in the back of the plane.

I don't think this is the time for me to be thinking about joining the mile high club and my chances of it happening are pretty much zero with how pissed off Madison is with me. Although she hasn't let go of my hand yet, even though she seems to be much calmer.

"Henry."

Hearing my name jolts me out of my inappropriate daydreaming about Madison and the bed.

"Yeah, Mads?"

"How rich *is* Emmett's family?" She asks, her eyes wide as she takes in the opulence we're surrounded by.

I do laugh now, just a little.

"Well... I don't know for sure because they're not braggers despite owning a personal jet–but if I had to guess, I would definitely say they've got more money than we will ever even see in our lifetime, rich. And that's including if I ever sign an NFL deal."

She nods, says nothing, and gets a little more comfortable in her seat. The pilot announces we can take our seatbelts off, and Madison realizes she's still holding my hand. She jerks it away. The spell is broken.

"I really wish I would have used the restroom before we left. How long is the flight?" Madison asks me, her knee bouncing up and down.

"There's a bathroom on the plane. It's at the back. We should land in about four hours."

She turns in her seat and looks to the back of the airplane, biting that damn lip of hers again. I get lost in thought, staring at it. I'm pretty sure my jaw is slack and drool is threatening to escape my mouth. I pull myself together.

"Would you like me to walk back there with you?"

She nods and I stand and hold out my hand to her. She takes it hesitantly and I walk her back to the bathroom.

Another hour passes and we've been sitting here in silence, mostly. I'm hoping I'll magically grow some balls big enough to ask her if she wants to talk about the fact I lied to her—well, that I wasn't honest with her. Nope. I lied. It was a lie by omission. Madison apparently has bigger balls than I do—.

"Why didn't you tell me who you were when you found the email in your truck?"

She's not looking at me when she asks this. She's sitting with her legs crossed and tucked up on the seat, her hands in her lap, fingers fidgeting.

I guess we're having this conversation now, and I need to do my best to be honest with her.

"Well, at first I was in shock. I mean, what are the odds of you ending up in my hometown? The odds have to be even lower that I'd run into you on the day you arrived. And then the paper must have fallen out of your bag—it was all way too crazy to even believe at first."

I pause, gathering my thoughts, knowing I have to be honest with her, but my honesty may end up pissing her off more. She doesn't push me to keep talking. She sits there patiently, waiting. I'm so scared of losing her, even though I've never really had her.

"When the initial shock wore off I–I got it in my head, if I could get to know you in real life as Henry, and you could get to know me–maybe you'd care enough for me as Henry I wouldn't have to tell you, or if I told you eventually, you'd somehow get over it because you'd already fallen for me. I know, it's stupid and wrong and deceitful. I just —"

I hang my head, rub the back of my neck, and let out a sigh.

"Once I had you here, in real life, right in front of me. I didn't want to give you up. I didn't want you to run for the hills–or I guess the beach since you live in California–"

She gives me a half smile, almost a pity smile, at my joke. Trying to be funny right now probably won't work in my favor. Get it together, dude.

"When you stopped responding to my emails, I was gutted, Mads. I left everything on the table and you walked away from it. You just fell off the face of the earth. When I felt like I had a second chance, I ran with it. I know this isn't fair, but I thought, if I could get you to love me as Henry, maybe–I don't know. And then the kiss —"

I let out a rough moan without even thinking. I look at Madison. Her eyes widen and she sucks in a breath. I notice, but just barely, when she flexes the muscles in her thighs. Our eyes meet but she averts hers, turning her attention back to her hands in her lap that are still twisting around each other. Just being in her presence, breathing the same air as her, sets my skin on fire.

I take a deep breath and try to finish my thoughts.

"I know not telling you right away was wrong, and for that I am truly so sorry, Mads. I'm not sorry though about anything I wrote in that email because I still feel all of it. I feel it even more now. And I am sorry for running away like a little bitch, but I'm not sorry for kissing you. I could never be sorry about kissing you."

It's been nearly five minutes, and she still hasn't said anything. It's been too long for her to think I may have more to say, and while I'm sure there is plenty more I can and need to say–I'm out of words for now. Mads shifts in her seat and brings her legs down in front of her.

"I'm not saying I'm not still mad, but I understand you and I appreciate you being honest with me. I'm gonna want to talk about this again, but for now, I think I need to just think about things."

"Completely fair," I say.

We still have a few hours left until we land, but at least the conversation seems to have distracted her from her fear. She fell asleep a few minutes ago on my shoulder. I haven't moved a muscle because I don't want to risk waking her and not having her touching me anymore.

Even with all the mistakes I made, all the times I thought with the wrong freaking head, I might actually still have a chance with her. I plan on doing anything and everything from here on out to prove to her, I love her, that I'm *in love* with her.

Chapter Twenty-Five

Madison

I wake to Henry gently shaking my shoulder. My head is in his lap and I'm pretty sure I can see my drool on his pants. After so much crying, I was exhausted, mentally and physically drained. I feel anything but refreshed as I sit up and look around, remembering where I am. The past twenty-four hours crashing back down on me.

Henry's smiling sweetly at me, holding my gaze intently. He reaches forward and tucks a strand of hair behind my ear and on instinct I lean into his palm, releasing the air from my lungs I didn't know was trapped there. I pull away sharply when the pilot's voice comes over the speakers.

"If you'll please fasten your seatbelts, we will be landing soon."

I sit up properly in my seat and click my seatbelt into place. Henry does the same. I can feel the plane pitching forward and my stomach drops like it does on roller coasters. Without even thinking, I reach for Henry's hand and grip it tightly, squeezing my eyes closed. He leans toward me and presses his forehead against the side of my head.

"I'm scared," I say.

He inhales sharply and lets out his breath slowly.

"I hear you," He whispers into my ear.

My breath hitches, then calms. I concentrate only on the sound of his breaths moving slowly in and out.

Against my worries we would suddenly drop from the sky; the plane lands smoothly. We're in an Uber on the way to the hospital. Henry and I are no longer seated next to each other, our bodies no longer pressing against each other like they were on the airplane. It's as if we stepped off the plane and a bubble we were in burst. The realities of our situation and why we're in California flooding in and washing out the temporary truce we'd called.

Looking out the window, I see familiar places, one after the other. We drive by the dance studio I went to when I was seven and my favorite burger place. Good and bad memories try to permeate my thoughts at the same time. I didn't expect being back here, where I grew up, to give me so many conflicting feelings.

When the driver finally pulls into the drop zone at the hospital, I want to tell him to turn around and take me back. That would mean getting back on the flying death trap, but it's a fate I might take over dealing with whatever is waiting for me inside this hospital.

Taking a deep breath, I wipe my sweaty palms on the front of my pants and exit the car. Henry's already grabbed both our bags and is coming to stand next to me. Extricating myself from the car was as far as I got. I haven't made a move to actually go inside the hospital.

"Are you ready?" he asks.

"No."

But I take that first step and head into the hospital.

The waiting room is packed; people taking up nearly every chair and kids running around, their parents not caring. I guess when you're dealing with something serious enough for someone you love to be in the hospital, you tune out a lot. The smell of antiseptic is strong and all the lights are too bright. I've never been inside a hospital before. When Dad was in his accident, Mom left me with the old lady who lived next door and went to the hospital alone. He died before she even made it there. Neither of us got to say goodbye.

I make my way to the receptionist's desk and tell the cheery woman sitting behind a computer who I'm there to see. Her bright smile is a stark contrast to my current mood.

"She's in room 407. Take the elevator to the fourth floor and turn left. Put this on," she tells me, handing me a visitor's badge.

I slap the sticky badge on my shirt.

"Does your boyfriend need one too?" she asks.

"He's not my–"

"I'll wait here Mads," Henry says.

He moves to sit in a nearby chair between a man who looks to be in his seventies, clutching a woman's purse, and a middle aged woman reading a book. I give him a half smile and make my way to the elevators. I look at all the signs on the walls and placards labeling the different departments, searching for any clue why my mom is in the hospital. Intensive Care is on the second floor and she's on the fourth so she can't be too hurt or sick. The maternity ward is on the third floor. Thank God she's not on the third floor. Fourth Floor—general care.

Well, that's helpful.

After I find her room, I stand outside the closed door for a few minutes. Preparing myself to see Mom for the first time in months. I'm trying not to have any expectations. I can't help but let my mind wonder about a few things. Will she be nice to me? Is she sober? I stop trying to guess and push the door open.

Mom is sitting up in her big hospital bed. She looks thinner than I remember her last. Her skin is a funny color and there are heavy dark circles under eyes. Tubes and wires are attached to her arms and chest, connecting to big machines that are rhythmically beeping. The cadence reminds me of an Elvis Presley song. There's a man sitting in a chair in the corner I don't recognize. He's wearing an old pair of jeans and a long-sleeved shirt, even though it's probably ninety degrees outside. Neither of them have noticed I entered the room, their attention on the television hanging from the wall.

I clear my throat.

"Hey baby, you came," my mom says, her smile wide.

The man in the corner sits up in his chair staring at me, but doesn't introduce himself. I slowly move closer to my mom's bed. Cautious though, like she's a wild animal who might attack at any moment. She doesn't look great, but she also doesn't look like she's dying.

"Someone called, told me you were here, but nothing else," I say, my voice lilting at the end of the sentence like it's a question.

I have questions, lots of them. I can't get my brain to function well enough to ask any of them. I'm still so overwhelmed.

"Oh, it was Gary, my boyfriend," she says, pointing at the man in the corner and looking at me like I should know who he is.

I don't. I have never seen this man in my life. I blink rapidly at them, trying to gain some composure.

"Are you okay? Why are you here? What's wrong? Are you sick?"

All the questions start coming out at once in a pile of word vomit. Mom just stares at me for a few minutes, then makes room for me to sit on the edge of her bed and pats the blankets of the now open space.

I sit.

"Well sweetie, I was having a hard time breathing and my stomach hurt something fierce. Thought I was having a heart attack. So Gary called an ambulance, and they brought me in."

"You had a heart attack?" I ask.

"No, no. But, they had to do some blood work and other stuff. Turns out I had an enlarged gallbladder, so they just took the thing out."

I stare at her dumbfounded, replaying her words in my head, trying to find the part where she told me she had cancer, a tumor or some other serious disease.

"Wait, so you're gonna be fine?"

"Well, yes, but I could have had a heart attack or died in surgery," she says, defiantly.

I jump to my feet and start pacing back and forth, running my hands down my face. I stop and face her, arms crossed over my chest.

"When did you have this guy call me? Before or after you knew you were going to be fine?"

"What do you mean?" she responds, not quite meeting my eyes.

I exhale slowly, trying to keep the anger bubbling up in check. It doesn't help.

I stare at her, biting out every word. "When did you have him call me, before or after you knew you were going to be fine? Answer the question!"

"Well, we didn't have a chance to call until–"

"You've got to be kidding me!" I stomp my foot like a child, because I'm frustrated and feel like I'm dealing with a child. In reality, I'm dealing with my own mother. A grown woman, who is being incredibly childish and selfish. Does she have any idea how worried I was, what it took to get here?

"I jumped on a plane and flew all the way here, and you're fine? When are you getting released?" I question.

"Tomorrow," She starts, "but since you seem to be doing so well you can afford a last minute plane ticket. Can I borrow a few hundred dollars? I'll pay you back."

She's kidding, right? She is not asking her eighteen-year-old daughter for money after she just flew all the way across the country for no damn reason. I don't even bother answering her. I clench my fists at my side, dig my nails into my skin and squeeze my eyes shut.

"Fine," Mom says, "But if you want any of your shit, you should probably go get it out of my storage unit. They're locking me out of it tomorrow and I don't have the money to pay for it."

She's dropped the fake pleasantries now that she knows I won't be giving her any money.

"Why is my stuff in a storage unit?"

"My stuff is in there, too. I had to put it there when we moved out of the house," she says with the wave of her hand like this is old news.

"When did you move out of the house?" I ask, my eyes protruding in surprise.

"A few months ago," she says. She's twisting her hands together in her lap and continues, "I couldn't keep up with the payments."

She lost the house. I wish I could say I'm surprised, but I'm not. I am absolutely fuming, though.

I take her storage unit key from her and agree to pay the next month's fee. I let her know I'll be going by today to take my things. I'm not hopeful about what she kept or what condition it's in. Mostly, I just want photos and sentimental items. I'm sure there's nothing of value in there. If there was, she would have sold it by now.

By the time I make it back downstairs, Henry has made friends with the little boy sitting next to him on a woman's lap. He's playing peek-a-boo with the toddler and all three of them are laughing. I stop a few feet behind them and watch for a few moments, not ready to face Henry just yet, but also enjoying watching him interact with the kid. It's sweet, and I'd be lying if I didn't admit it makes me a little less mad at him for everything.

I suck a breath in and out through my nose and tap Henry on the shoulder. He waves bye-bye to the little boy and his mother and follows me out of the hospital. I grab my phone from my pocket and order an Uber to take us to the storage unit a few miles away.

"My mom is actually fine, she's just a selfish bitch," I bite out.

Henry doesn't ask questions but can see me ordering the car from over my shoulder.

"Why are we going to a storage place?" he asks.

"Because–" I start, ready to just get the hard part over with.

I turn to face Henry and spit everything out.

"Because my mother is an addict, blew all her money on drugs and lost our house. She put everything she had left in this storage unit and she stopped paying the bill and if I don't go pay the bill, they're going to lock her out of it and there might be things of mine in there I want. I promise I will be as quick as I can and we can get back on the death trap some people like to call an airplane and go home."

I'm breathing a little hard and my heart is racing. I just spilled everything I'd been avoiding telling Ender and then some all over him. Let all the dirty laundry fly, right here on the sidewalk outside the hospital. I'm waiting for him to bolt or tell me he wants nothing to do with me and my baggage and that he's leaving and I can find my own way home. He doesn't do either of those things.

He slowly takes the phone I'd been holding between both my hands and wraps his arms around me. Pressing my face to his chest and squeezing me firmly. Any self control I had is gone. Tears come flooding out from my eyes and big sobs escape from my throat. The anger I'm feeling toward my mom and toward Henry/Ender collides with the sorrow and shame I've tried to keep buried. Henry says nothing, he just holds me until the Uber arrives.

Chapter Twenty-Six

Henderson

Madison is still sniffling and a few tears are rolling down her cheeks occasionally when we're dropped off outside the storage unit. She makes her way down the rows of padlocked metal roll up doors. I rush to cut her off and stop her from walking, placing my hands on her shoulders. I keep looking down at her until her eyes lift to meet mine.

"Why don't you let me rent us a couple of hotel rooms and we will stay overnight and deal with this in the morning?"

I'm worried she's doing too much at once. Worried she's overwhelming herself and is going to actually break down at any minute. I know she's strong, hell she'd have to be to handle everything she just admitted to me without any help from anyone. It seems like she's been hiding that secret for a long time. My heart is hurting so much right now; not just for her, but for us.

Her not responding to my last email is making more sense as the day goes on.

"No, I just want to get this over with Henry," she pleads.

I nod once and move to her side to help her continue the search for unit 324.

I try, and fail miserably, to hide my reaction when we find the unit and roll up the door. It's packed full of furniture, boxes and trash bags. None of it stacked neatly and almost all of it looks to have just been thrown in here. I look to Madison, trying to gauge her reaction.

"Are you sure you don't want to get some rest before tackling this?"

"No," she says defiantly and grabs for a box.

We've been sorting through things for over an hour and it's getting dark outside. I'm getting a little worried we're in over our heads. I notice Madison sat down in front of a box a little while ago and is reading little black notebooks she found in it. The box looks full of them, all the same little black notebooks with handwritten notes in them.

Suddenly, she gasps and draws my attention. I watch as she brings her hand to her mouth as she reads. Her eyes begin to well with tears and I'm only slightly worried she'll end up with permanent tear stains on her cheeks after today. She snaps the book closed and throws it against the storage room wall.

"Is everything okay? I ask hesitantly.

"She lied to me. She fucking lied to me," she says, never meeting my eyes, just staring at the wall.

"Who lied to you, Madison?"

"Just read it. Fourth page. I need to go for a walk."

She stands up and starts walking down the row of storage units. I pick up the notebook she's thrown and open it. It looks like it's a journal. I read the entry on the fourth page.

March 4th

Today I had my baby girl. Happy Birthday sweet Madison. I am terrified. I am too young to be a mother, but I don't have any other choice now. She will be so loved, because even though Eric knows now this baby isn't his, he's agreed to be here for both of us. To raise this baby as his own. Being a mom at eighteen is scary enough, I'm just grateful to not be doing it alone.

Sure, deep down I'm worried being a mom and committing to a guy at this age is ruining my life, but no one but you little journal needs to know that—

I stop reading. One can only assume this diary belongs to Madison's mom and Madison's world just came crashing down. I run after her and find her sitting at the end of the row of storage units, knees tucked up under her chin.

"Madison, this is all too much for one day. We're getting hotel rooms and staying the night and I'm not going to argue with you anymore about it," I tell her, trying to control my anger.

My anger isn't at her, and I don't want her to hear it in my voice. My anger is at her piece of shit mother who keeps breaking this beautiful girl's heart.

She looks up at me in defeat and stands up.

"Okay."

Her single word response—*okay*—seems to be saying so much more than just okay.

I open the internet browser on my phone and start looking for a hotel room nearby. It's a small town, so there are only about a dozen hotels, but every single one I look at shows no rooms available. Then I notice on one of the websites a notice about a surfing contest in town this week. Great. I finally find a hotel with one room available but it only has one king size bed. It's a suite and is going to cost me a month's paycheck, but I don't care. I book the room, I'll sleep on the couch.

I put the diary back in the box. Then I stack another box of things on top of it that Madison said she wanted to take with us before locking the storage unit. I don't know if she'll want to read these right away, but I feel she has the right, and I want to give her that option.

When we get to the hotel, we head to the front desk to check in. The woman behind the counter get's our room keys and takes my credit card.

"Oh, the king's suite, you'll love this room. It has a hot tub," she says. The suggestive look on her face doesn't go unnoticed.

"One room?" Madison says.

Of course, now she's alert.

"It was the only room I could find available within thirty miles. I'll sleep on the couch," I tell her.

She doesn't argue or even comment.

When we get to the room, I'm a little embarrassed. This room is really nice and is definitely giving honeymoon suite vibes.

There's floor to ceiling windows with a perfect ocean view, the bathroom has a shower plus a giant tub with jets, and the king size bed sits in the middle of the room across from a fireplace. There's a small desk and somehow an even smaller couch next to it on one wall. I have no idea how I'm going to sleep on that thing. I may just end up on the floor. Madison is taking it all in but pauses when she see's the couch.

"Henry, you cannot sleep on this couch. There's no way. It's too small. You take the bed."

"Madison, my mother would disown me if I did."

"Fine," she says, defiance in her voice, "We will just share the bed. It's a king. We can put a pillow between us or something. It's not as if we're strangers. I'm gonna take a shower first, if that's okay?"

Words won't come out of my mouth. My brain might be malfunctioning. I have an instant hard on. Between the thoughts of sleeping in the same bed as her and of her in the shower only feet away from me, how can I not? I swallow hard and nod my head. Madison turns on her heel, heading toward the bathroom. I can't help my chuckle. She's probably pretty proud of herself for winning that argument.

While Madison is in the shower, I notice our room has a small balcony. I open the sliding door and step outside. Listening to the water coming from the bathroom isn't helping me keep my mind out of the gutter and I don't need her thinking I'm trying to get laid if she comes out and I've got a hard-on.

The ocean breeze coming in is chilly but refreshing; I can taste the salt in the air on my lips and smell the seaweed. Seagulls squawk in the distance and I can just make out the white crest of waves crashing in the dark. I hear the bathroom door open and Madison comes to stand next to me, leaning on the railing. I look at her. She has on pink silk pajama shorts that show off the bottom curve of her ass and a matching top with thin straps and black lace around the edges. My dick instantly wins the hard-on battle.

"Taylor packed my bag, they're hers," she says.

I clear my throat and look back out at the ocean, embarrassed because she clearly caught me staring.

"I'm gonna–I'm gonna go take a shower," I mumble, and leave before I do or say something stupid.

I hear Madison chuckling to herself as I close the bathroom door. At least I got her to laugh a little.

I take my time in the shower, letting the warm water rush over me, dipping my head under the stream. Trying to sleep in the same bed as Mads when she's wearing that little outfit is going to be a challenge. I finish my shower with a blast of cold water to keep my dick in check.

Chapter Twenty-Seven

Madison

I'm feeling a mixture of anger and complete numbness. Trying to be angry at Henry for not telling me who he really was, angry at my mother for being selfish among so many other things, and feeling a loss about my dad–is all too much to feel at once. At least Henry made an effort to explain to me why he did what he did. He's also kind of been my rock all day long. I don't know how I would have handled everything that's been shoved in my face today without him. I'd probably still be sitting in the storage unit crying in the dark if he hadn't forced me to leave. The anger I have toward him starts to slip away, turning to something else the more I think of everything he's done for me since I landed in Easton.

The door to the bathroom opens and Henry comes out wearing cotton pajama pants and a plain T-shirt that hugs his toned muscles perfectly. I try not to stare, but I never knew a guy's pajamas could be so sexy. While he was in the shower, I decided to get into the bed, under the covers. The bed is soft and my body sinks into it easily, the weight of the day making my limbs heavy. I've already taken one of the extra pillows and placed it in the middle of the bed, an obvious barrier. I'm still questioning if what he did, not telling me who he was right away, is something I should stay mad about. The pajamas are currently swaying me in the direction of not being mad.

I sit up in the bed, feeling too vulnerable laying down, but keep the white silk sheets pulled up to my chest and tucked under my arms. The silk sheets, the big luxurious fluffy towels, the ocean view. They all make me wonder how expensive this room was. Even the room itself smells expensive, like citrus and lavender. It's the type of scent you'd expect from a spa. I should offer to at least pay half of the bill.

Henry hasn't moved any closer to the bed since he emerged from the bathroom. I wonder if he's as nervous as I am. Sure; I slept in the same bed as my ex-boyfriend plenty of times, but it was different. I knew exactly what Liam was thinking one hundred percent of the time. Sex, pot and video games were his three defaults.

"Are you going to get in the bed?" I finally ask him.

He rocks back on his heels and stares out the window. I follow his gaze. I left the curtains and the door open, letting the ocean breeze fill the hotel room.

"Madison, I can sleep on the floor. Really, it's no problem."

I can tell he's nervous and chewing on the inside of his cheek. It's comforting to know I'm not the only one whose mind is spinning at the thought of laying in this bed together.

"Fine, but I'm telling you, it's okay to sleep in the bed and you're an idiot if you sleep on the floor."

That came out a little harsher than I meant it to, but I don't apologize. Instead, I turn off the lamp on the bedside table and lay down facing away from him, toward the open door. A few seconds later I feel the dip of the bed as Henry gets in it. My heart rate picks up a little. Even though I told him I'm entirely fine with him sleeping in the bed, I still don't know how I'm going to fall asleep knowing he's so close.

I manage to somehow, but I wake a few hours later, my mouth dry and uncomfortable. I must be dehydrated from all the crying I've done today. Before I go to get out of bed, I'm reminded I'm not alone when Henry lets out a sigh. Is he still awake? The room is dark. He must have turned off the rest of the lights after I fell asleep. I move to sit on the edge of the bed and peek behind me. He appears to be fast asleep; his eyes are closed, hands tucked up under his head and his lips are gently parted. This is the first time I've seen him look peaceful all day, and it's hard to look away.

I get up from the bed to find a glass. There's a wet bar in the room with a mini fridge but I know better than to take anything in there. I don't want to pay fifty dollars for a three ounce bottle of water. There's a glass on the counter, I grab it and go to fill it from the bathroom sink, padding across the cool tile floors. Within minutes, I've filled and drank the entire glass three times before I make my way back to bed. I've almost made it back when I crash into the desk I didn't see in the dark, making a loud bang and adding to the noise when I throw out a few expletives.

Henry shoots up out of his sleep and sits up.

"Are you okay? What's going on?"

There's a noticeable panic in his words, his breathing is loud and heavy.

"Sorry, I ran into the desk."

"Are you okay? What were you doing?"

I can make out his form in the dark sitting in the bed and I suppress a gasp when I recognize he's no longer wearing a shirt. It's so dark I didn't notice at first, but now I can tell his muscles are a million times more on display than when he had the T-shirt on. Saliva collects in my mouth and I swallow it down, gathering some semblance of composure.

"I was thirsty. Sorry, go back to bed," I tell him as I find my side of the bed and slide back in under the covers.

My back is turned to Henry but I realize the pillow that was dividing us before is gone, it must have gotten pushed down or kicked off the bed. I don't want to turn to find it and put it back in place. I tell myself I don't want to because it would be awkward, but I think deep down, I don't *want* the barrier between us anymore. Henry has settled back down into the bed. The room is now still, and quiet. The only sounds I hear are the waves crashing nearby and Henry's breath, slow and steady, behind me.

I lay there for several long minutes listening to him breathing; I can't fall back asleep. I reposition myself and let out a huff.

"Can't sleep?" Henry asks.

"No."

"Want to talk about what happened with your mom?"

That's the last thing I want to do. I notice I can feel Henry's breath on my back now, just below my neck. It's faint, but I feel a rhythmic warmth. It's sending shivers down my entire spine.

"I really don't. I will, though, not right now," I tell him.

The room is quiet again, but I can feel the bed shift. Henry's breath on my back gets more noticeable, warmer. He's moved *closer* to me. I shift just a little, moving closer to him, wanting to feel more.

"Madison," he whispers.

I respond to him with a *hmm* not able to form any coherent words at the moment.

"Turn over."

His voice is deep and rough, his tone demanding. I don't even hesitate for a second. I turn over and face him, finding him practically in the middle of the bed now–where the pillow barrier used to be. My arms are curled up, clasped under my head as I lay on my side facing him. He's on his side facing me, one hand cushioned under his pillow, the other splayed flat on the bed in the small space between us. The sheets are pulled up only halfway on his torso so I can see his bare chest now, the curve of his muscles in his shoulders and the dips and divots surrounding the muscles. I can only make out part of his tattoo, but what I thought I saw before is definitely a bird. Not just a bird, but a *sparrow.*

I gasp when I see it and strain my eyes, trying to read the text that falls lazily across his chest, meeting with the bird over his heart. I meet his gaze and I can see fire burning in his eyes; longing, desire. I scoot a little closer and Henry takes in a steady, deep breath. Slowly, I stretch out my hand toward his chest, my eyes darting back and forth between looking at him and looking at the tattoo. He never takes his eyes off mine.

My hand finally meets his smooth skin. Henry lets out the faintest moan, and my entire body reacts to the sounds. My toes curl at their own volition, goosebumps spread across my skin and a pleasurable burn-ing starts low in my stomach. I begin trailing my fingertips across the words—my words, my poem.

"When?" I ask him, still staring at the tattoo, still running my fingers lightly across it.

"My eighteenth birthday."

That was at the end of February, which means he got it *after* I stopped responding to his emails. I haven't stopped running my hands over the tattoo and Henry brings his hand up and lays it gently over mine. He follows my lead and traces along the words and the sparrow with me. We're staring right into each other's eyes, our breaths syncing up. They escape our lips lazily, in and out. Henry grips my hand a little tighter, holding it still over the sparrow, over his heart, and pushes it flat against his chest. He pulls his hand away from on top of mine and I instantly miss it, miss his touch.

Hesitantly, he reaches across the small gap between us and runs a strand of my hair between his fingers, letting his hand linger next to my face. My breath picks up as he moves his hand down painfully slow, barely touching me with the very tip of his fingertips. First my cheek, now down my neck–I tilt my chin up. Giving him more access, more freedom to touch me.

"Is this okay?" he asks, his voice laced with desire.

"Yes!"

I'm barely able to get the words out, but when I do, my voice is pleading. I'm practically begging him for more. To move faster.

He makes it to my shoulder, hooks the strap of my top and drags it down with his fingers as they keep making their descent. A whimper escapes my mouth as the side of his hand brushes the silk nightie covering my breast.

The whimper is a catalyst–his hand has moved behind my back in mere fractions of a second and he's dragging me across what space is left between us. Our bodies collide in the center of the bed. Our noses are touching now and our breaths intermingle between us. Neither of us moves. We're both lying here with our eyes closed and our chests pressed against each other.

"I want to kiss you," he says.

He's not asking me, but I give him permission anyway.

"Please."

His lips are pressed against mine before I could even get the word out completely. His hand grips at the back of my shirt. This time, I'm the one to deepen the kiss. I part my lips and slip my tongue between them. Eager to gain access to his mouth. He doesn't hesitate to let me in and meets my tongue with his. A low primal growl escapes his mouth, mine muffling it. I hitch my leg up and over his hip and his hand moves from my back to my ass, grabbing full fistfuls of my flesh peeking out of the bottom of the silk shorts I'm wearing.

I cautiously roll my hips into him, needing to ease the desire building between my legs. His hand gripping my ass helps to push me into him. Laying on our sides this way, I can't feel all of him, but I feel enough through his thin cotton pants to feel his cock straining against the fabric. I don't have to wonder what all of him feels like for long because his other hand slides under me on the bed and he rolls to his back, bringing me with him and positioning my throbbing clit perfectly over his erect shaft. It's thick and hard and takes me longer than I expected to slide from the base to the tip.

I continue rolling my hips over him, quiet moans escaping both of us between kisses. I think we're both trying to control ourselves, but I don't want to control myself. I want to rip all of our clothes off and let him bury himself in me. I need him to. His hands are on my hips and he grips them tighter, pressing me down harder onto him. I gasp and arch my back, coming up to fully sit on his dick now and pressing my hands to his chest.

He stops moving underneath me and stills my hips with his hands.

"Madison, we need to stop or I might not be able to stop."

"What!?" I almost scream, looking down at him. "You want to stop?"

"Mads, no, I don't want to stop. Ever. But I don't know if you're doing this because of the day you've had or–"

I choose to interrupt him by covering his mouth with mine, sucking in his bottom lip and nibbling on it. I earn myself a low moan from him in response. I sit back up and lift the silk night shirt over my head, his eyes widening as I do.

"I want this. I want you, Ender."

A devilish grin spreads over his face when he hears me call him Ender and he tosses me onto my back. Laying on top of me now, he's trailing kisses down the side of my neck, and spreads my legs apart with his knee. One of his hands grips my breast and begins kneading it roughly. I guess he's no longer trying to control himself and it is so fucking hot.

His lips land over my nipple and he sucks it gently into his mouth at first, then bites down on it just hard enough I almost scream out in pleasure. My hands slide into his thick hair and I curl my fingers at the back of his head, holding him to my nipple. I had no idea I could feel this much pleasure and get this close to an orgasm while still being half clothed. I don't want to come yet. I want him inside of me.

"Do you have a condom?" I ask, making my intentions clear.

He releases my now tender nipple from his mouth and looks up at me from behind my breasts.

"Will it make me look like a douche if I say yes?" he asks, actual concern written all over his face.

I soften my expression, "If you don't have one, I'm going to be extremely disappointed because all I want right now is to feel you inside of me."

When did I get so brave? I'm telling him exactly what I want without hesitation. I must have surprised him too, because his mouth is literally hanging open. He nods his head, gives me a chaste kiss on my lips and then leaves the bed, heading for his duffel bag. As soon as he leaves, I feel the loss and I ache for him.

He returns soon enough with a condom. I'm still laying on my back and he uses his hand to pull my knees apart. I'd pushed my legs together to try to get some relief from the aching I feel between them. He slowly crawls up the bed between my legs, laying the condom on the sheets next to me, planting kisses low on my bare stomach.

What is he doing? Why isn't he putting it on? I reach for it, but he closes his hand over mine. I look at him and I'm about to protest.

"Not yet," he says. "I *need* to taste you first or I'm going to lose my fucking mind."

I nearly explode right then and there.

I throw my head back on to the pillows and grip the sheets with both my hands as his mouth moves lower. He snakes his tongue across the top of the silk pajama shorts, dipping it lower with each pass.

He's torturing me and I don't know how much longer I can take it.

Finally, he hooks his fingers into the top of the shorts and starts sliding them down, painfully slow. Kissing me over and over on my hips and thighs as he goes. Agonizingly avoiding my core. He tosses the shorts to the side and brings his head lower between my legs. I'm not wearing any panties under them and can feel the cool air touching my now exposed skin. I can feel his breath now, hot and wet, washing over me. He purses his lips together and blows directly on my clit, and I let out a long moan. Just when I think I can't take it any more he runs his tongue from as low as he can manage all the way up to my clit and covers it completely with his mouth, sucking in hard.

For the next few long minutes, he expertly sucks, nibbles, and rubs his tongue in tight circles around me. My heart is racing and I can barely keep up with my own breathing. Suddenly I feel fullness as he inserts two fingers in me and does a come hither motion with them. I arch my back, raising my chest to the ceiling. My orgasm explodes out of me as I scream his name. My legs are shaking, my stomach muscles have tightened and Ender keeps going until my body relaxes. Dragging out my pleasure for as long as he can.

That was amazing, and the condom wrapper still sits on the bed next to us, unopened. How am I ever going to get enough of this? How did I ever think running away from him was the right decision?

I knew sex with Liam wasn't good, and now I know it's because I never had any real feelings for him. Ender, he makes me feel everything, all at once. He makes me feel sexy and beautiful. I feel in control , but completely out of control. He makes me feel *loved.*

Chapter Twenty-Eight

Henderson

Madison just came on my tongue, and I want nothing more than to make her do it again. I really hope she's got enough energy left for more because my dick is harder than it's ever been.

When her legs stop shaking and her breathing slows down, I finally release her clit from my mouth's grasp and move to lie beside her. She turns to me and lays her hand across my chest, tracing my tattoo again. I had planned to get this tattoo for years before I did, and even though Mads was no longer talking to me by the time I turned eighteen, I still got it. Even if I had lost Mads forever, this was a way for me to keep a piece of her with me always.

"You carried the email. I carried this," I tell her.

She smiles softly.

"It wasn't the only email I carried. It was just the only one that fell out in your car," she admits, laughing.

"Are you still angry? About me not telling you I found the letter?"

She's still tracing my tattoo lazily, not answering me for what feels like years.

"No Ender, I probably would have done the same thing. Hell, maybe what I did–ignoring you after you sent that email was worse because–."

She pauses, her voice cracking.

I grab her hand and turn to her so we're facing each other, laying on our sides and bring her in close. Her eyes are glassy, wet.

"I didn't know Ender. I didn't know about your dad. If I would have known."

Shit. I didn't even think about her finding out about my dad. She must notice my eyes bulging because she continues.

"Once I put the pieces together, I googled you. I found a few articles. I am so sorry, I am so sorry you and your mom had to go through what you did–and I'm sorry I wasn't there for you."

I bring my hand up and brush away a tear that escaped her eyes.

"How did you find out who I was?" I ask.

"It wasn't just one thing, but–the green tea donut was the biggest clue, and then your mom called you Henderson and it all kind of clicked."

I laugh. I didn't even realize I'd bought her favorite donuts. I did it because I knew it was her favorite and I wanted to make her happy. It was a step toward apologizing for being a dick at the party. I didn't even think of the fact it wasn't something I should know. My mom being the one to help me out is ironically funny as well. She's going to love Madison, I know it. I can't wait to bring her home and for them to meet again, with everything out in the open now.

Shit. I'm going to have to compete with my friends and my mom for this girl's time. Well, I'll have to show her as often as I can why time with me can be so much more fun.

I finally stop my laughter and look down at Madison. She has her bottom lips sucked in, nibbling on it.

I let out a groan and push my still rock hard cock against her thigh.

"Madison," I say through gritted teeth. "take your lip out from between your teeth before I come right now."

She gasps and releases her lip, responding to my demand.

My lips crush against hers, hungry to taste her. I wonder if she can taste herself on my tongue. I push it eagerly into her mouth and she lets out a small whimper. She drags her hand down my chest, and fingers the waist band of my pants. My dick flinches with the feel of her delicate fingers so close. I push up against her again, willing her to keep going. Thankfully, she takes the hint and slips her hand inside my pants. Her soft hand easily finds my cock because I'm not wearing any underwear, and she wraps her hand around it at the base, squeezing gently.

I almost come in my pants. I help her by pushing my pants down and kicking them off, freeing myself from the restriction. She stops kissing me and looks down. I try not to smirk when I see her eyes widen. That's right baby. She looks up at me, eyes still wide.

"Is that supposed to fit inside of me?" She asks.

My head falls back and, I burst out laughing.

"Oh, it will fit babe."

She bites down on that perfect, plump bottom lip again in worry.

"What did I say about biting your lip, Madison?" I say, my voice low and laced with desire.

She tightens the bite on her lip, challenging me. Two can play this game.

I grab her around the waist and pull her on top of me, her legs falling to either side of my hips, her wet slit covering my hard cock and pressing it to my stomach. I push her hips back and forth to slide her along my length. Her head drops back and her mouth drops open, her hands grip my chest to give herself leverage.

"Condom," She breathes out, "Now."

"Not yet," I tell her.

I won't last much longer like this, but I need her close because as soon as I push myself inside her, I know I'm going to explode.

She keeps rocking against me, her pace getting faster. I can tell she's getting close. I grab the condom and slide her up so she's straddling my stomach now, she makes little noises of protest that are incredibly sexy. I reach around and slide the condom on.

I look back up at her, waiting for her eyes to meet mine.

"Are you sure?" I ask.

"Yes, please God, yes. Now," she begs, grinding against my stomach, her wetness spreading across me.

I cup my hands under her ass and lift her, positioning her above me and slide into her in one motion, burying myself in her as deep as I'll go. Madison screams out in pleasure and I clamp my mouth down around one of her breasts, sucking in her nipple. She curls her hands around the back of my head, threading her fingers through my hair and pulling. My hands are still cupped under her and I slowly lift her up a few inches, before pushing her back down on me hard. She rewards me with another loud cry. I do this one more time before her muscles tighten around me and I explode, our orgasms rushing over us in unison.

She collapses onto my chest, panting. I'm still inside her and I wrap my arms around her, holding her to me.

"That—was amazing. You are amazing," she says.

I smile into her hair, breathing her scent.

"Ender," she whispers against my chest.

Grunting to let her know I'm listening is all I can muster the strength for.

"Do you want me to call you Ender?"

"Always," I tell her, "Because with you, it's who I've always been."

"I'm glad."

She kisses my chest softly and I smile bigger than I have in years.

We fell asleep with her lying on top of me, naked. She's still asleep when I open my eyes. I stare at her, her hair splayed across my chest, her lips gently parted. I want to stay like this forever–her soft breaths prickling my skin.

Mustering all my will power, I gently roll her off me, kiss the side of her head and go to the bathroom. I decide to shower before she wakes up. If I try to do it after she wakes up, I'll ask her to join me, and I don't think we have time for how long of a shower that would be. Great. Now I'm getting hard because I'm thinking of her in the shower. I almost yell at my dick to calm the hell down. I haven't been this horny or uncontrollable in years. Mads does something to me. She sets every part of me on fire. She makes me want to do things I've never done before. I want to experience everything with her, all at once. All the ways we could touch, or kiss, or–.

My mind trails off again, imagining all the hot sex I want to have with her. The water gets cold, so I force myself to shut it off and get out of the shower. I wrap a towel around my waist. Should I have brought clothes in here with me? I know we had a night of mind blowing sex but we didn't talk about where we stand with each other. I don't exactly know the protocols here.

When I come out of the bathroom, Madison is sitting on the floor in my t-shirt and nothing else and I almost go back into the shower to stand under cold water. It's that or picking her up and throwing her on the bed and making her come again. She's sitting in front of the box of journals, several of them open and spread out around her.

"I wasn't sure if you'd want those," I say sheepishly.

She looks up at me and gives me a smile, which doesn't quite make it to her golden eyes.

"I do. Thank you. Will you help me?"

"Anything. Always," I tell her.

"I'm trying to sort them by date. I'm hoping I can find something in them about who my—what do I even call him? Bio-dad? Sperm donor? Random dude that knocked up my mom who isn't the Dad I know and love—"

"You don't have to call him anything. Let me get dressed and we will do this together."

I put on a pair of fresh underwear and some jeans and drop to the floor with her. I start opening journals to the first entry with a date and laying them out in the timeline she's creating on the floor. Madison's stomach growls loudly and she giggles.

"Shit. We haven't eaten since the diner yesterday. I'm ordering you room service. Anything in particular?"

"One of everything, I am starving," she jokes.

I order one of everything on the breakfast menu. When it arrives, we set up a picnic on the floor and share our feast sitting across from each other. We take bites of omelets, pancakes, waffles, and fresh fruit until we're both full. Madison has a bit of powdered sugar on the corner of her lip. I want to lean over and lick it off, but I just reach over and gently wipe it away with my thumb. Somehow, it's sexier than licking it off. Her lips parted just a little, and she leaned into my hand slightly.

"We should probably finish sorting these," she says.

I want to keep touching her, but I know she's right. What we're doing is important. Hopefully, I have a lot more time in the future to be able to touch her. Right now, I need to help her find answers.

When we're done sorting the journals, she skims through the ones around the time her mom should have found out she was pregnant. I read the ones from a few years after Madison was born, so we can meet somewhere in the middle. From what we've assembled on the floor, it looks as if the journals ended only six months ago. I'm surprised her mom kept writing in them for so long. Maybe Madison has a small thing to thank her mother for, a love of writing.

We read for an hour and I don't find much. In the journals I read, her mom goes back and forth between being a proud, doting mother, and wife–to being resentful for having to handle it all at such a young age. Even though I don't want to, I sympathize with her. I know she had Madison right out of highschool and it couldn't have been easy. Not telling Madison who her biological dad was–even after the dad she loved, her real dad, passed away–that may be unforgivable though. My anger toward her mother doesn't stop me from worrying about Madison reading these, worried she'll lose what love she may still have left for her. I know the feeling of hating a parent and it's difficult. It's confusing and heart breaking. It can be all consuming, trying to reconcile the two warring emotions.

I finally stumble across an entry when Madison was about three years old that looks like it's what we've been looking for. But, it's not what I wanted to find. I clear my throat.

"Mads," I say.

She looks at me and her eyes are hopeful. I'm about to crush her. This is so much worse than I expected.

"I'm so sorry Madison, but I think he passed away," I say, handing her the journal.

CHAPTER TWENTY-NINE

MADISON

I read the entry in the journal Ender hands me. When I'm finished, I read it again.

October 7th

Susan from high school called today. Clint overdosed. They couldn't save him. He was my first love... but part of me is glad that now he can't ever try to take Madison from me. He'll never find out she's his. I wonder if I wouldn't have gotten pregnant if I would have stayed with Clint. Would I have kept letting him convince me to try this drug and that drug until I was as strung out as him?

But, I got pregnant. If Eric hadn't been there, who knows what my life would have been like. Eric thinks we should tell Madison, now that the risk of him taking her is gone. I won't let him though.

I'm crying, not the big, loud, messy sobs like I have been the past few days. Tears are just falling from my eyes without my control. Ender comes from behind me and positions me between his outstretched legs.

Wrapping his arms around me. I lean into him, letting him take some of the weight of everything I'm feeling.

"Madison, what can I do?" he asks.

"Just keep doing this," I say.

He tightens his arms around me a little, and I close my eyes.

"Mads. We need to check out of the hotel room soon."

How long have we been sitting here like this? I check the clock on the desk. We've been sitting here in silence for over an hour. Ender never once let go of me. I kiss his arm and move to get up. I start packing up the journals, but he stops me, putting a hand over mine.

"Why don't I do this and you pack up our bags and order an Uber?"

I nod my head and release the journal.

The car picks us up twenty minutes later outside the hotel. I almost begged Ender to rent the room another night so we could lie in the bed naked all day. I know I need to finish taking care of business, though, and we need to go home.

Home.

It's the first time I've ever thought of Easton as home. It's true though. Easton is my home now. Taylor, Jesse, everyone at the diner, even Emmett who I don't even know very well, are my family. And Ender–especially Ender. He makes Easton feel like home most of all. It was easy to fall into the habit of calling him Ender instead of Henry. It feels right for us, it feels natural. I don't exactly know where he and I stand right now, between all the kissing and licking and fucking–we never discussed what this means. Are we a couple now? I guess it's a conversation we'll have to have, eventually. And we will have it because I am done running away from the tough conversations. My parents refused to have the tough conversations with me, and now look where things have landed.

We decide to stop by the storage unit again to do a quick check for anything else I might want, and to put the journals back. I don't want to read them anymore. I've learned more than I ever wanted to from them. We're almost about to call it quits when I hear my mother's voice coming closer. Great.

"Hey baby!" she says when she sees me.

How carefree she's acting makes my skin crawl.

"We were just finishing up. We're heading home now."

"Who's your friend?" she asks, eyeing Ender up and down.

You've got to be kidding me.

"This is Ender. Here's your key back."

I hand her the key and walk away, not wanting to have any more discussion with her right now. Everything is too raw, too fresh.

"Madison, wait," she says, grabbing my arm as I pass her.

She looks at me and I think I see a hint of sadness, maybe even remorse, in her expression.

"Can I borrow some money?" she asks.

Holy fuck. I want to scream and pull my hair out.

"Why, so you can buy drugs for you and your boyfriend?" I bite out.

I have never, not once, acknowledged her problem out loud in front of her. She gasps and tries to feign innocence, mumbling out excuses and denials. I barely hear her.

Ender places a hand on the small of my back and whispers in my ear.

"Go out front, call an Uber. Please."

There's a forcefulness in his tone, but when he says *please,* I hear desperation. I'm sick of looking at my mother, so I do what he asks and walk away from them without another word. As I'm turning the corner, I can hear their conversation still and stop, just out of their sight.

"You're not going to contact Madison anymore. She is not going to give you money. You will not reach out to her unless you've been clean for a year," Ender says.

His voice is low, but even. His anger controlled. It's almost as if he's simply reporting the weather or something.

"And who the hell do you think you are?" my mother snaps back at him.

"I'm the guy who loves your daughter. Who's been in love with her for years. Who almost lost her because of you. Because you broke her heart so damn badly she didn't think she deserved my love. And I'm the guy who's going to help her heal now—now that she knows the truth about her dad."

I hear my mom gasp. I don't even have time to process what Ender said because I hear his footsteps coming toward me. I quickly hurry out to the curb and open the Uber app. While I wait for him to catch up, I replay what he said. He said he loved me. Deep down I know he does, he told me so in his email. To hear him say the words—to really hear them and not just read them. I think it pushed me a little closer to healing. I know I'll have to talk to my mother about everything, eventually. About her problems. About her not being there for me. About her lying to me. Now is not the right time, though. Ender's right, she needs to get help and clean, or we'll never really be able to fix anything.

Ender turns the corner as I finish ordering the Uber.

"Let's go home," he says and presses his lips to mine.

I deepen the kiss, greedy for more.

We make it back to the small private airport and have gotten buckled into our seats. As soon as I stepped into this sardine death trap some people refer to as an airplane—I wanted to turn around, get off and drive all the way to Easton. It would take me the better part of a week to do so, and that's without ever stopping, but it's still a tempting alternative.

The plane begins slowly moving and I reach for Ender's hand, gripping it tightly. I think I hear him wince a little, but I don't care. My fear is too overwhelming.

"Talk to me," I say, not looking at him, looking straight ahead.

"What do you want me to talk to you about?"

"Anything–how did you know?"

"Know what?"

He's running his fingers up and down my arm, sending little bursts of shivers down my rigid spine.

"I stopped responding to your email because I was scared."

I've now basically admitted to eavesdropping, but I don't think he'll mind and I don't want to keep any secrets from him ever again.

He sighs, then chuckles before answering me.

"I didn't know for sure. I was guessing and throwing out what came to mind. I guess I know for sure now, but honestly, I still don't know *why* you were so scared."

I shouldn't be surprised. Ender knows me better than anyone—of course, he knows me better than I know myself. Maybe it's why he didn't give up in his emails so easily. Maybe he even knew, deep down–if he told me right away who he was I would have run. I wouldn't have been able to handle it yet.

"My life was a mess, Ender. My mom had started using drugs and bringing home one loser boyfriend after the other. It got so bad I was staying with friends when I could. When it was awful and I couldn't find a place to stay I even spent a few nights sleeping on the streets," I tell him.

Ender's eyes widen and are blazing with anger. I knew he wouldn't like hearing that.

"I was ashamed," I tell him. "I was ashamed of the situation I was in and I was afraid that if you really knew what was going on in my life–you'd think twice about what you'd written."

"Oh Mads, you know now where my life was when I wrote that email. I would have never judged you for your mother's choices. If anything, now I wish more you would have told me what was going on. I would have–could have helped."

"I know that now. I'm sorry," I say, hanging my head.

Ender tucks a finger under my chin and tilts my head up so we're looking each other in the eyes. He leans forward and kisses me once, softly.

"Is that all you overheard?" he asks, searching my eyes.

I lean forward and gently press my lips to his, pushing my forehead to his when the kiss ends.

"I already knew, but it was still nice to hear," I whisper.

He lets out a relieved sigh and places a long kiss on my forehead.

The airplane has finished its ascent and the roller-coaster stomach drop feeling has quit. I relax my grip on his hand a little. I'm still terrified, but the less I think about the fact we are irresponsibly high in the air right now, the easier it is to breathe. I let Ender know I need to use the restroom and make my way to the back. I sit on the toilet seat and pull out my phone, logging onto the wi-fi.

I pull up my email account–*that* email account. I find the email I need, hit reply, draft out my email and hit send.

As I exit the bathroom that has no business being that big or that nice on an airplane, Ender isn't in his seat anymore and I panic.

"Back here," he says.

I turn around to find him standing in front of a bed I hadn't noticed before. Of course this thing has a bed. Ender is smiling at me with want and need.

"Wanna join the mile high club?" he says.

I smile at him, cross my arms and don't make any move toward him.

"I don't know, I only get one chance at becoming a member and I don't know–"

Ender has his hands under my ass and is lifting me up before I can comprehend what's happening. I let out a laugh as his mouth comes crashing down on mine. My legs go around his hips and I can feel he's hard even through his jeans. He backs us up, sitting on the edge of the bed when he meets it. I'm on my knees straddling him. His hands slide up my sides and go around to my back, pressing me closer to him. They continue their ascent, going up under my hair and stopping briefly at the back of my neck–squeezing gently. God, the way he acts like he wants to own my body is hot as fuck. I am more than ready for every piece of it to be his.

His hands go into my hair and he grabs fistfuls. Tugging on it with enough force that it's just shy of pain but one hundred percent incredibly sexy. My neck and chest are now exposed to him and, he plants light kisses across me. Soon they turn into sucking and licking at my neck and the top of my breasts.

"Take your top off," he demands.

"Yes, sir," I say. Ender practically growls at this.

I cross my arms in front of me and pull my shirt up and over my head, revealing a black lacy bra. I am no longer mad at Taylor for sneaking extra clothes into my bag when I see his reaction. At least this time the bra is actually mine, because Taylor's boobs are half my size and her bra would not have fit.

"Do you want me to be a good girl, or a bad girl?" I say, trying to push him to move faster.

I need him inside of me *now*.

"Good girl," he says. "Always a good girl."

He turns us around, dropping me onto the bed. He leans over me and unbuttons the jeans I'm wearing, pulling them down and off me. He climbs on top of me, grabs the matching black lace panties in his teeth and drags those down and off me too, the stubble on his chin tickling my skin as he does. Once my underwear is discarded on the floor, he climbs back up me, sticks one hand under my back and unhooks my bra, taking it off and throwing it to the side as well.

I'm laying on the bed, completely naked and he's still fully clothed. I should feel vulnerable, exposed, but I don't. I feel adored and desired. The burning in his eyes that look sleepy with desire telling me everything.

"Get on all fours and face away from me."

Oh my God, demanding, in control Ender is incredibly hot and I melt at his words. It's such a stark contrast to his usual sweet, polite and sensitive nature. I didn't even know this kind of play would turn me on, but I am absolutely ravenous for him. I do as he says, not knowing what to expect but knowing he's about to make me feel incredible. Best of all, I know I can trust him. I know I'm safe with him because I love him and he loves me.

Ender is kneeling behind me now and he takes one hand and slowly runs it down my back and then up again. Twisting my hair around his hand when he comes back up and tugging it back, whispering in my air.

"You are so fucking gorgeous."

I clench my thighs together, the tingling building between my legs. He doesn't leave me wanting for long. While one hand is still pulling just hard enough on my hair, the other slips between my legs. His fingertips dipping into me.

"You're so wet," he says.

I let out a moan as he pushes two fingers in at once, not even bothering to start with one. As quickly as they sink into me, he pulls them out. Running them down the length of me.

"Do you trust me?" Ender asks, leaning over me.

"Completely," I say, and meaning it.

He moves so he's laying on his back, his face between my legs. He pulls me down onto him and covers my clit completely with his warm mouth.

He licks and sucks at me hungrily, his hands wrapped up around my legs and pulling me down onto him. It's like he can't get close enough–can't get enough of me. He's worshiping my body in ways it's never been taken care of and it's pushing my orgasm along quicker than I expected. I scream out his name in ecstasy.

He lifts me and slides me down his body, so we're chest to chest and his strong arms envelop me against him. His mouth by my ear, his breath warm.

"I love you, Mads," he whispers in my ear before kissing me.

Chapter Thirty

Henderson

Madison is laying on my chest, dragging a lazy finger across my skin just above my belt. It tickles, but I'm not going to stop her. I'll never stop her from touching me.

The pilot makes an announcement telling us we need to return to our seats. We're getting ready to land in Easton. I completely forgot about the pilot. He definitely heard us back here. I don't care though–that's right, buddy. I made her make those sounds. I smile to myself, proud and arrogant.

Madison gives me a quick peck on the lips and scoots off the bed. I quickly grab onto her hips, pulling her back to me, and bring her lips to mine. I kiss her deeply and she moans into me. I release her, knowing we do actually need to go to our seats. She smiles at me and I want to capture her smile in my memory forever.

We make it back to our seats and get buckled in.

"You don't seem to be as nervous," I tell her.

She turns to me and takes my hand gently in hers.

"Airplanes aren't quite as scary anymore," she says and winks at me.

I feel the plane descend and Madison's grip on my hand tightens.

"Okay. Maybe they're a little scary still."

I put my hand under her chin, turning her face to me, and kiss her. Softly at first, but then I take my tongue and glide it along her lips, asking for permission to enter her mouth. She parts her lips and our tongues meet, swirling around each other. She kisses me back with urgency for a long minute, then pulls away, her breath heavy.

"That helps, thank you," she says, leaning her forehead against mine and releasing a sigh.

When we land in Easton, I thank the pilot and shake his hand. He gives me a knowing smile, but I keep my face stoic. Madison is turning me into a cocky asshole.

We find a bench to sit on and wait for Emmett to pick us up. I check the time on my phone wondering what's taking him so long and notice I have an email notification. I click it open.

To: ravensfan4lyfe@gmail.com
From: madisrad@gmail.com
Date: August 23 02:17
Subject: Re: Confession

I hear you. I love you.

I turn to Madison. She's staring at me and I know she can see what I just read. I run my fingers into her hair and curl my hand around the back of her neck, bringing her forehead to mine.

"You have no idea how long I've been waiting to read those words," I say, my voice low.

"I'm sorry I didn't send it sooner."

I pull away to kiss her and see a tear rolling down her cheek. I brush it away with my thumb, then kiss the streak it made. I've seen her crying so much in the past forty-eight hours and I never want to see her cry again from pain or sadness. Madison has my whole entire heart and I will do everything I can to protect hers.

Emmett finally shows up almost an hour later and we both hop into the back seat. I tried getting an Uber and called my mom, but we only have like two Uber drivers in town and my mom wasn't answering her phone. I normally wouldn't treat Emmett like a driver and would insist one of us sit up front with him, but I'm not ready to be so far away from Madison yet. Emmett thankfully doesn't complain.

"Dude," I say. "What the hell took you so long? We landed an hour ago."

"I am so sorry guys. I got caught up at an appointment."

"An appointment with who, your attorney? Someone trying to sue you for breaking their heart?" I tease.

He laughs, but it doesn't sound sincere. He ignores my prodding and drives away. I have Emmett drop Madison off first. It's agonizing saying goodbye to her. I want to drag out the time I've had with her. I'm panic-stricken that we were in some trauma-induced bubble that will burst when she has her first moment of alone time. I walk her to her dorm room, carrying her bag and the box of things she brought home from the storage shed. We're standing outside her dorm room door now. So much still left unsaid between us.

"Thank you Ender, for *everything*."

"Anytime," I say and lean in to kiss her.

When the kiss ends, she unlocks her door. Before she can get inside, I turn her back around to face me. I'm nervous and I don't know why.

"Mads?"

"Yes?" She looks just as nervous as I feel.

I shove my hands into my front pockets and rock back and forth on my heels, trying to get the courage to ask her what I need to.

"Will you—will you go out to dinner with me tonight?" I finally ask her.

She chuckles quietly, and I'm about to puke or run away. I've seen, touched, kissed and licked almost every inch of this woman, but I'm still terrified of her rejecting me.

"I would love to," she says.

I let out the breath I was holding.

"I'll pick you up at eight?" I ask her.

She nods. I give her one more quick kiss, then press my lips to her ear and whisper.

"Don't wear any panties," I say.

She lets out a small gasp. I pull away to see her eyes wide, her lips parted. I turn on my heel and walk away, back to Emmett, waiting to take me home.

When Emmett drops me off at home, my mom's car is in the driveway. I wonder why she wasn't answering my calls. I make my way inside the house and find her taking her shoes off in the hallway. She's in her scrubs and looks like she just got home. Weird, she doesn't normally work on Mondays.

"Did you have to cover someone's shift?" I ask.

"Oh, Jesus, Henderson," she shouts. "You startled me."

I can't help but laugh. I apologize and go to give her a quick peck on the cheek.

"Um, no, I just had some things I needed to take care of," she says, dumping her shoes in a nearby basket. "Are you hungry? Can I make you something to eat?"

We move to the kitchen and I let her make me a sandwich. It's already after five, so I need to get ready for my date with Madison, but I'm starving. We hardly took any time to stop and eat while we were in California. Mom's just finishing layering on the tomatoes for my turkey sandwich when I speak up.

"Mom, I have a date tonight."

"With the pretty brunette from the diner?" she asks, not even looking up from the sandwich as she wraps in a paper towel.

She hands it to me and gives me a pitying smile.

"Henderson, I'm your mother, I know things. Where are you taking her?" she asks.

"I was thinking, Olivers."

She nods in agreement. It's the only nice restaurant we have in town. A small Italian place that has linen-covered tables and is lit mostly by candles.

"I think Olivers is perfect," she says, patting my arm in the reassuring way mothers do.

She heads to her room as I devour the sandwich she made me.

"Oh and Henderson—I actually have to be on call for the next forty-eight hours, starting at midnight. I think I'm just going to go stay at the hospital," she says, turning again to continue toward her room.

"Just remember, I'm too young to be a grandmother," she yells from down the hall before closing her door.

My mother is a saint. I make a mental note to get her an exceptionally good mother's day present.

I've just gotten out of the shower and am trying to decide what to wear. I've never actually taken a girl on a real date before. With Jackie, it was always with a group of friends or a party. Never a fancy dinner, just the two of us. I decide to play it safe and wear black slacks with a black button-up shirt. Rolling the sleeves up to my elbows to make it a little more casual.

I grab my phone and text Taylor, letting her know my plan for dinner so she can help Madison pick out an outfit appropriate for the restaurant. I also tell her I'm gonna need her help because I want this night to be perfect. Mads deserves perfection.

I'm running late to pick her up because my truck was on empty. Jesse picked it up from the private airport for me when we left for California and of course didn't think to tell me he left it on empty. When I finally get to her door, I have to wipe my hands on the front of my pants. My palms are so sweaty. I knock quickly three times and suck in a breath.

Taylor opens the door and is beaming at me.

"Well, hello handsome."

"Hey, Tay."

I am not prepared for what I see when she opens the door the rest of the way. Madison is standing there in the middle of the room in a short, tight black dress that hugs her body and her curves perfectly. The top of the dress is rounded and dips perfectly low enough to show off only the top curve of her breasts. Her hair is down in big soft curls and she's added just a touch more makeup than I'm used to her in. Her lips, that I love so much, are painted a soft pink and are shiny, making them look fuller and more supple. She's wearing a pair of black flats and I'm glad. She'd look amazing in heels, but they just don't seem like her style. I'm glad she's still being herself.

"Do I look okay?" she asks, tugging at the bottom of her dress.

"If Taylor wasn't here right now, I would rip your dress off you so fast," I say.

I'm pretty sure my mouth is stuck permanently open and I'm drooling.

Madison's cheeks turn pink and Taylor hoots and claps her hands together.

"Damn Henry, you sound like me. I approve," Taylor says. "Now get out of here, you two. You're going to be late."

I reach out my hand for Madison's and she gives Taylor a quick hug before she slips her fingers through mine as we head out the door–for our first real date.

Chapter Thirty-One

Madison

Ender told me when he picked me up, our dinner reservation wasn't until 9:30, but he had plans for us until then. He won't tell me what those plans are. I secretly hope they involve me ripping off his shirt because he looks absolutely delicious in his all black ensemble. His button-up shirt fits his muscles perfectly, and his slacks let me see more of the curves in the front of his pants than a pair of jeans would. I am turning into a horny teenage boy.

As soon as he asked me to dinner, I went into my dorm room and called Taylor so she could help me get ready. I was ready almost an hour early because I was so nervous. I borrowed the dress from her and it's a little shorter than I prefer, but Taylor said it was perfect. I did as Ender asked though, I'm not wearing any underwear. Making the problem of the too short dress even more nerve-wracking when I got into his truck to sit down and the dress rode up even more. I can feel cool air tickling parts of me I'm not used to having exposed. I even let her do my makeup and I'm grateful she kept it natural. I would have been even more nervous if I didn't look like myself.

While I got ready, I told Taylor everything that had happened over the past day. I left out most of the details about the times we didn't have any clothes on, but I'm pretty sure she still got the idea of how well it went.

She hugged me when I cried telling her about the journals. Re-applying my eye liner three times and never complaining. She squealed and giggled when I told her about sharing the bed in the hotel room. Her begging for more graphic details made me blush, but I still kept most of it to myself.

For the first time ever, I felt I had a best girlfriend. Reliving it as I told her everything made me emotional. I cave and tell her this. She hugs me tightly and says she's so happy we were paired as roommates. I tell her I love her and I realize she's the first person I've said those words to that wasn't family or Ender.

I recognize the direction we're heading out of town from the few trips I've made with Taylor to what everyone calls the big city. It's not much bigger than Easton, but it has more shopping and restaurants. When we pull into the dirt parking lot of the carnival I went to with Jesse and Taylor a few weeks ago, I get giddy. This is better than ripping his shirt off.

My eyes must be bulging with excitement, because Ender is staring at me with a proud goofy grin.

"We can't stay long, but there is one thing I want to do," he says before getting out of the truck and coming around to help me down.

I am so glad I didn't try to go out of my comfort zone and wear heels. I would have fallen flat on my face trying to walk on them in the dirt. Hell, I probably would have fallen flat on my face walking on any surface. Ender takes my hand and speed walks toward the carnival rides. We stop at the Ferris wheel and he hands the ride operator some cash and says something low I don't hear. The carnival is pretty deserted, it's been here for so long most people have already been there, done that—we're the only ones getting onto the ride.

We squeeze into the Ferris wheel, the worker locks our bar in place and starts the ride. As we make our way higher, Ender pulls me closer to him, wrapping his arm around me. I snuggle into him, breathing in his woody cologne. He turns and gives me a quick kiss on the side of my head.

The memories of riding the Ferris wheel with my dad come flooding in again and I try not to get emotional. I want to enjoy this time with Ender. I can't help but think of everything that's happened though and everything I've discovered since I was last on this same ride. Since I found out yesterday the man I grew up knowing and loving wasn't my biological dad, I've done a lot of thinking about what it even means to be a dad. I know my mom is my biological Mother–it doesn't make me any less or more angry with her. My dad loved me, he loved me and knew I wasn't his blood. I will continue to think of him as my dad.

I'm not angry with him, even though I wish he would have pushed harder to tell me the truth. I have to believe in my heart he was doing what he thought was best, protecting me. I am still livid with my mother, but not just because she lied to me and apparently manipulated my dad. No, there's so much more to be angry with her for. I just hope with time, the anger will subside. I hope in time she will get the help she needs and we can somehow repair our relationship.

I think that's what had me so worried when I thought she was in the hospital for something awful. I was scared she was dying and there wasn't enough time to heal things between us. I know not a single day is guaranteed. I learned that when my dad died. But I was relieved when I found out she was going to be fine, even if all I could feel in the moment was anger and annoyance.

Our Ferris wheel basket makes it to the very top of its rotation and we slowly come to a stop. I look at Ender and he's smiling sweetly at me.

"Did you do this?" I ask.

"I may have slipped him some extra cash," he admits.

We're staring into each other's eyes and I wonder what he's thinking. He doesn't keep me wondering long.

"Mads, I am so sorry for everything you've been through. Not just what you've been through the past few days with your mom and those journals. I'm sorry for what I've put you through. I hope you'll let me spend every day trying to make it up to you. I'll do whatever it takes to show you how much I want to be with you, and not just physically the way we have been. Although, that's amazing too and I will always want to rip your clothes off—"

He's tracing his thumb across my jaw now, stopping at my lips and running the calloused skin across them, then continues his trail down my neck and over my collar bone. It's giving me butterflies and goosebumps, making my heart race. I'm grateful for the distraction when he continues talking.

"I want to be able to show you every day how much I love you–how madly in love with you I am. If you'll let me."

I wish I could record everything he's just said to me and carry it around the way I did his letter. I'm not too worried about it though because I have a feeling I'll be hearing things like this from him a lot more often now.

"I love you so much Ender."

He lets out a breath he was holding and leans forward, covering my mouth with his. The kiss isn't needy or hurried. It isn't filled with the same "I want to be inside of you" passion like other kisses we've shared. This one is soft and slow, with just our lips parting. His lips ever so gently sucking on mine. This kiss is showing me his love, not just his desire. This kiss is the perfect top of the Ferris wheel kiss.

The restaurant Ender takes me to is really nice, one of the nicest I've been to. I have yet to admit to him this is my first date. We order dinner, and it's incredibly delicious. I think Ender's nervous too because we haven't really talked much since we sat down at the restaurant. Even though the date started before we got here, this part is so much more formal than the carnival, so much more typical of a first date. We've just finished our entrees when the waitress comes over, a beautiful blonde girl about our age with sparkling hazel eyes. Her figure is like the ones you'd find in fashion magazines.

"Can I get you guys some dessert?" she asks.

Ender never takes his eyes off mine, doesn't look at her once.

"We'll take the chocolate cake with a side of your homemade chocolate syrup and some strawberries," he says assertively, staring at me with a hunger in his eyes. "To go please."

I squeeze my legs together because the look he's giving me is nothing short of smoldering.

Ender reaches across the tables and takes my hand, slowly rubbing circles on it with his thumb.

"You haven't talked much," I say.

"Did you do as I asked?"

My cheeks burn and I push my legs together tighter as he reminds me I'm not wearing anything under my dress. He gives me a knowing smirk and leans toward me.

His voice is low and husky.

"If I start talking they'll kick me out for the things I want to say to you."

I let out the faintest moan, unable to control myself. He moves to the empty chair next to me so we're sitting side by side while we wait for our dessert and the check. He scoots closer to me, placing an arm around me on the back of the chair.

His other hand goes to my bare knee under the table. He slowly moves it up my leg, veering inward when he meets the hem of my dress. I can barely breathe. I can not believe he's doing this here.

"Ender!" I mutter under my breath

"Shhhhh."

How is he able to hide any emotion from his face? I fear if you take one look at me, you'll know exactly what is going on. I look around the restaurant frantically. There are only a few tables occupied, and they all seem to be paying no attention to us.

His hand makes it past the bottom of my dress and I part my legs almost against my own will. His fingers meet my sex and he leans his lips to my ear.

"You are dripping," he growls.

I don't say a word. I'm too busy focusing on controlling my breathing.

One finger dips into me slowly, and the faintest moan escapes me.

"Here's your dessert and your check. Thank you guys so much."

I nearly pass out at the waitress returning. Ender doesn't even flinch. He gently removes his hand from between my legs and grabs the check off the table. He thanks the waitress and drops cash on top of the bill, never taking his eyes off me.

"You ready to get out of here?" he asks me after she's gone.

"Yes please," I pant.

CHAPTER THIRTY-TWO

HENDERSON

"Ender, why are we at your house? Is your mom okay with me being here?" Madison asks when we pull into my driveway.

I put the truck in park and kill the engine. She's sitting right next to me in the middle of the bench seat, and I turn my head to look at her. I give her a delicate but meaningful kiss, only using my tongue to taste her briefly. I pull away from the kiss and bring my hands to either side of her face, making sure she's looking at me.

"My mom won't be home all night. She's staying at the hospital for forty-eight hours."

I steal another kiss and then open my truck door, letting us both out on my side. We walk up to the house and barely make it inside the front door before I'm grabbing her under her ass and pulling her up to wrap her legs around me. Our lips never leave each other's as I carry her upstairs to my room. She works on undoing the buttons on my shirt as we make it over to the bed.

I sit on the edge of my bed and her knees fall to my sides so she's straddling my hard on. She finishes unbuttoning my shirt and pushes it off me, attacking my neck and chest with wet kisses. I kick off my shoes and move to pull at her dress and she swats at my hand.

"Hey, what was that for?" I ask.

"It's my turn to make you feel good," she says as she slides off me and onto her knees on the floor.

Holy fuck yes. I have been dreaming of those beautiful cupcake icing lips doing this since day one. I let out a moan as she unbuckles my belt and she giggles.

She undoes the button on my slacks and hooks fingers into the front of both my pants and underwear, pulling them down. I lift my hips to help her and she finishes pulling them completely off me. I'm sitting on the bed completely naked and she's on her knees in front of me, staring at my cock.

"I've never done this before," she says. "I mean, I wasn't a virgin–I've just never done *this*."

"Baby, you don't have to–"

"No, I want to, I really want to. I just need–maybe a little guidance. I don't want to be bad at it," she says, chewing on her lip, still staring at my erection.

I don't think it's even possible for her to be bad at it and I tell her this. I stand up in front of her. On her knees, she's the perfect height for her mouth to meet me.

"Drag your tongue along the side and follow it with your hand wrapped around me," I say.

My voice came out deeper than I expected. Fuck, this is going to be the best blow job I've ever had, and she hasn't even started.

She does as she's instructed, wrapping her right hand around the base, turning her head to the side and dragging her tongue down me.

"Like that?" she asks.

"Yes, baby. Do it again."

She does and my dick twitches getting impossibly harder.

"Wrap your lips around just the tip, suck on it and swirl your tongue around it," I instruct her.

She smiles at me and opens her mouth, bringing me to her. Her tongue on the tip of me feels better than I could have imagined. I tip my head back, letting out a long, low growl of pleasure. Her hand is still gently squeezing my base. I wrap my hand around hers and gently start guiding it, both of us pumping me. I'm not going to last long.

I reach down with my other hand and push the thin straps of her dress off her shoulders and down, releasing her breasts. They sway with her as she starts to follow our hands with her lips, taking more of me into her. Just a few inches at first, but soon she gets ambitious and takes more and more of me into her mouth. My free hand instinctively threads through her hair and lands on the back of her head. I gently push her, seeing how far I can go. She takes her hand off of me, grabbing the back of my thighs to steady herself, and lets me push into her, taking almost all of me.

I reach down, twisting one of her nipples. She moans, actually moans around my dick and I lose all control. I pull out of her quickly and grab my shirt from the floor, releasing everything into it.

She sits back on her heels, looking up at me.

"You are so fucking beautiful," I say, leaning down and kissing her. I can taste myself on her lips mixed with her usual sweet vanilla taste.

"Did I do okay?" she asks, looking up at me through her long eyelashes.

"Fucking phenomenal," I tell her, putting my finger under her chin and guiding her to stand up. "Now, can I finish taking your dress off and fuck you?"

She pulls her dress down her body, letting it fall to the floor. I spin her around and push my cock to her ass. I'm already fully hard again. She leans back into me, bringing her hand up and wrapping around the back of my neck. My hands reach in front of her. First I toy with her nipples. Rolling them between my fingers and tugging on them. She thanks me with little whimpers. I let one hand travel south, palming her between her thighs. My middle finger glides up her wet slit, swirling her clit when I reach it. She pushes her ass back against me.

I grab a condom from my nightstand, tearing the package open with my teeth and sliding it on with one hand. Never letting my other hand leave her warmth. I sit on the edge of the bed and slowly pull her back to me, lowering her onto me until I'm buried in her as deep as I can go.

"Fuck, Ender," she breathes when she's fully sitting on my dick.

I love the way she says my name. I love when she calls me Ender. I hold her there on top of me for a few moments, neither of us moving. I enjoy the feeling of being in her, filling her completely. I reach around her and find her sensitive spot between her legs. Working it slow at first, then faster. Her breathing picking up. I grab her by the hips and push her up and off me a few inches, then gently slide her back down onto me. I do it again, just as slowly. She matches my rhythm, leaning forward and putting her hands on my knees to help her stay steady as she slides on and off my lap up the length of me.

I start pushing her to pick up the pace, bringing her down onto me harder and faster. She follows my lead and starts moving faster, slamming back into me harder, chasing her orgasms. I can't take it any more when she clenches around me and my orgasm pumps through me. She pushes herself back down on me one last time, her legs trembling and shaking as she comes.

I fall back onto the bed, bringing her with me. I wrap myself around her as we both come back down from our highs.

We stay this way, wrapped up in each other's arms for a long time. Not talking, just breathing together. I almost fall asleep when she begins talking.

"Ender?"

"Yes, baby."

"Thank you for a perfect first date," she says.

"It was perfect for me too and there will be many more," I tell her.

"No–I mean, that was my first, first date. Ever."

I chuckle at the irony and she pouts. I kiss her hair. She thinks I'm laughing at her.

"It was my first real date too," I say.

She turns in my arms to face me.

"What about Jackie?" she asks.

"I never took her on a real date. It was always a group thing, never just the two of us. I never wanted to put the effort in. Really, I think I knew I was waiting for you."

I hate to let her out of my arms but I really have to piss and get this condom off. I excuse myself, promising to be quick. When I come back I find her wrapped in a blanket looking around my room.

"Snooping are we?" I tease.

"No, I snooped last time I was here."

She smiles at me and my dick twitches. I didn't even know I could get a boner this many times in one day.

"I loved the poem," she says, nodding to my cork board where I have it written out. "Have you been writing much? I feel like it's been forever since I've read anything new you've written."

"Actually, I hadn't written in a long time but was inspired recently and picked it back up. I even shared it with my mom."

"I'd love to read it sometime if you'd let me."

"You can always read anything I write," I tell her.

She sits down on the bed. I stay across the room and lean up against my desk. Every time I get close to her I get more turned on and I don't want her to think sex is all I ever think about.

"Hey Ender?" Madison says, suddenly looking shy.

"Hmmm."

"Where did the chocolate sauce go?"

Chapter Thirty-Three

Madison

Ender runs out of the room faster than he would after the snap when he's being rushed on the field. Yes, I've been studying and watching more football since I went to practice with Taylor than I ever have in my life. I'm becoming slightly obsessed.

He comes back into the room only a little out of breath, holding the bag of chocolate sauce, cake and strawberries. His eyes are searching mine. I won't give him any clues to what I have planned. I drop the blanket from around me and saunter over to him, butt naked.

"Drop your pants and lie on the bed," I tell him as I take the bag from him.

His eyes widen and he hurriedly does what I ask. I think I'll make a few demands of my own.

I take the strawberries out first and pull the leaves off of one. I take it and the chocolate sauce over to the bed, setting them next to him. Straddling him and running my hands up and down his chest, dragging my nails across his skin. He grabs at my hips.

"Nope," I tell him. "No touching until I say you can, please."

He smirks at me but relaxes his hands back on the bed at his sides. I feel him harden beneath me and have to will myself to concentrate, to focus on the task at hand. The goal—make him scream in pleasure. It's not easy when all I want is him inside me. I bring the strawberry to my lips and gently suck on the tip of it, making a pop with my lips as I pull it out. Ender growls below me and takes fistfuls of the sheets in his hands. I know how much he loves my lips. I caught him staring at them even before I knew he was Ender. I run the strawberry along his lips now and they part. I push the strawberry gently, halfway into his mouth.

"Suck it," I demand, trying to keep my voice low and sultry.

I'd worry I'm making a fool out of myself, but the sounds coming from Ender and the constant twitching I feel from him between my legs tell me I'm doing something right. He sucks eagerly on the end of the strawberry. His mouth making the most sexy sounds. I can't help myself. I rock my hips on him, just once. Letting my wetness run across him. He sucks on the strawberry harder in response.

"Bite it," I tell him, and he makes a show of biting off half the strawberry.

I lean down and kiss him, enjoying the sweet taste on his lips. I put the rest of the strawberry between my lips and feed it to him. He eats it hungrily. I lick the sweet fruit juice from his lips and drag my tongue down his chin and throat, feeling his prickly stubble as I do. I slide down further on his legs, releasing his cock from beneath me. It springs up. It's practically throbbing and I can tell he's more than ready, but I want to make him wait just a little longer.

I pick up the small jar of chocolate sauce. Ender gives me a devilish grin.

"What are you going to do with that?" he asks.

I ignore him and just smile down at him.

I start by dipping my finger into the sauce and slowly bring it to my mouth. I close my eyes and suck the rich chocolate off my finger, letting out an exaggerated moan.

"Would you like some?" I ask.

Ender nods slowly. I dip my finger into the chocolate again and bring it to his mouth. He slowly sucks in my whole finger, swirling his tongue around it just like he'd had me do to the tip of his cock. I pull my finger out just centimeters at a time until he's licked it completely clean.

I'm almost ready to let him have me, almost. My finger pushes into the dark sauce one last time and I bring it to first one of my nipples, then the other. Spreading it around them leisurely, as if I have all the time in the world. I'm doing this all while staring directly at Ender. He swallows, his Adam's apple protruding in and out from his neck.

"Lick them clean," I tell him.

He's sitting up faster than I can even finish my sentence, his lips wrapped around my right nipple. He sucks on it, swirls his tongue around the point and kneads his hands into my hips. I let him roam my body with his hands now, first my hips, then moving back to my ass where he grabs onto my cheeks. He spends more than a minute on just that one nipple, and by the time he moves to the left one I'm already close to coming.

"Faster," I demand.

He flattens his tongue against my nipple, moves his hands up my back, and pushes my breast to his face. I grab the back of his head and hold him there. The shock waves of pleasure overtake me and I start rocking back and forth on his lap, grinding into him. I rock backward and forwards only a few times before I'm screaming out his name and coming.

He never even touched me anywhere between my legs. I am stunned.

Ender is clearly done letting me be in charge and flips me onto my back, the pleasure of my orgasm just barely waning. He doesn't waste any time and quickly grabs a condom, pulling it on over himself. He finds my entrance right away and pushes into me hard and fast, causing my entire body to jerk upward at the force. The headboard slamming into the wall.

I am so glad we have this entire house to ourselves, because it's about to get loud.

Our grunts and moans mix in the air around us. He doesn't take it slow at first, the way he has before. He grabs onto the headboard above him for leverage and starts drilling into me over and over. His grunts and groans are getting louder. I'm practically screaming. Saying his name over and over, begging him not to stop. I wrap my legs around him and it allows him to push into me even deeper, his balls pressing up against my ass with every thrust. In this position, he's able to bury himself in me completely and the fullness is deliciously agonizing. I can feel another orgasm coming and I slide my hand between us, rubbing at my clit.

"Fuck, Mads, that is so damn hot," he says, picking up his pace even more.

He kisses me, first on my lips, then my neck and breast. It's like he's trying to taste every part of me and can't get enough. I find what I was chasing after and tighten my legs around him even more, holding him as deep as he'll go in me. He grunts and I can feel his cock pulsing inside me as we finish together.

The best part though—when our orgasms have faded, and he's disposed of the condom, he comes back to the bed and turns me on to my side. Sliding in behind me, he wraps me up in his arms, giving me soft gentle kisses on my back and shoulders. We lay there, our legs tangled together, and talk for hours.

We talk about how amazing the sex has been, of course, but we talk about serious things too. We talk about my mom and my dad, we talk about his dad, and he tells me all about being on probation. We talk about our friends, school, work—everything. We lay there, exposed and vulnerable, in more ways than one. I'm an 'everything happens for a reason' girl, but I'm struggling to find the reason why I wasn't brave enough to let myself have this sooner. I'm just glad I have it now, and I promise myself to do everything I can to keep it.

CHAPTER THIRTY-FOUR

HENDERSON

Mads is sitting on the sidelines with Emmett at football practice. He's not practicing because he's been bitching about his knee hurting. I have this sinking feeling he's lying. It's another thing to add to his string of weird behaviors over the past few months.

Madison charmed the pants off the coach and convinced him to let her sit right on the sidelines for practices. Coach Davis, a six foot five and over two fifty pounds of muscle man–has been swindled by a girl. I have a feeling he's going to regret the decision. She's become a football fanatic. I'd complain, but she always gets really worked up after she watches me play, in the best way. Then, when we're done having sex, she wants to talk about strategy and what I could improve on the field, it's hilarious and adorable.

It's a stark contrast of support from the way my father supported me. Madison makes me feel proud of what I can do on the field. She never makes me feel like I'm not good enough.

It's been three weeks since we got back from our impromptu trip to California. Fall classes start Monday. Our first regular season football game is next weekend, against our biggest rival. It's a home game and Madison has already worked out her strategy on how to get front row fifty yard line seats. I hope I can keep my head in the game and not be distracted by how cute she is when she gets excited, or even better, when she gets mad.

In the three weeks since we've been together, I've probably had more sex than I have in my entire life. Madison and I can't seem to keep our hands off each other. I thought I'd live at home for the next four years of school, but I'm really re-considering it right now. The freedom of not having to wait until Taylor's not in their dorm room or my mom's at work–would be incredible.

My mom and Madison got to meet again last week. I asked Mads for permission first, then told my mom the whole saga. Everything from meeting Mads online at thirteen to me being a total douche and lying to her when I discovered who she was. I left out almost every detail of our trip to California, though. She did not disappoint and lectured me for ten minutes about talking to strangers on the internet. There were several, *Henderson, you did not's* and some pearl clutching. Of course, when it came down to it, she welcomed Madison with open arms. They've even taken to ganging up against me, which I did not see coming. If I had, I wouldn't have ever told my mom about Mads.

They're pushing me to change my major. They got to talking about my writing and think it's something I should pursue. Or even getting into the world of writing by working for a publisher or something like that. I haven't agreed yet but I haven't said no either. The problem is, I'm still working to evict all the garbage my dad filled my head with. He hammered into me for so long what a real man should be, it's not easy to dismiss all of that in just a year.

My mom said one night when we were eating dinner, if I didn't love football anymore, I should quit. I thought long and hard about her offer. I almost took her up on it. In the end though, I do love football when I'm playing for me, or now, playing for Mads. She's made it fun again. Too bad I can't convince her to wear a short little cheerleading skirt when she's standing on the sidelines. She actually gagged at my even suggesting it. She's right though, it's not her style. And I love her style.

Shit, I love everything about that woman.

Madison says her mom hasn't called or texted once since we saw her. We talked about it though, and Madison says she's going to look into different rehab programs and send her the information. She's going to include a letter, telling her mom how she feels about everything that's happened over the past few years. Telling her she's forgiven her for lying to her about her dad. But she can't have a relationship with her again until she's clean and has been clean for a time. I am so proud of her.

She's been working to find out more about her biological dad. She hasn't liked much of what she's found, but she found someone online she thinks is her aunt. The decision on whether to reach out to her has been weighing on her. If I could protect her from everything the discovery of her dads has brought, I would in a heartbeat. I'm learning, not everything is within my control. Some things Madison has to do on her own. All I can do is be there to support her.

We talk a lot about how we both used writing to cope with our problems over the years and how our writing brought us together. I've been writing more fantasy stories to help me deal with my feelings about my dad. Madison always reads them as soon as I'm finished, so does Mom. They both usually end up in tears even though I don't always mean to write sad stories. It's felt good to enjoy writing again, and not have to do it in secret. To be able to release some of the shame surrounding it.

I think back to what my life was almost a year ago and I wish my mom never had to go through what she did, but I'm grateful for where we all are today. And, I'm grateful I walked in on them when I did because who knows how long she would have hid what was happening trying to protect me. It's not something I enjoy thinking about and my therapist says dwelling on it isn't productive.

Madison starts therapy next week. The school offers free counseling and when I told her how much therapy has helped me to deal with everything; she said she would try it. She doesn't have high hopes yet, but I think she'll find it rewarding. Just being able to have someone on the outside to remind her she is worthy of love and she didn't cause any of the trauma she's experienced. I want more than anything for Madison to believe what I know. That she's strong, beautiful and talented.

I glance over at Madison on the sidelines, her and Emmett are talking and laughing. Emmett's pointing to different players on the field. I wonder if he's just shit talking them to her, or actually explaining things to her. She looks like she doesn't like something Emmett is saying. Suddenly, she gets up and goes stomping off toward the coaches. Oh no.

I jog over to her before things get out of hand. I can't control everything, but I can stop her from pissing off the coach. He won't take it out on her because he's too charmed. I know Coach Davis has a soft side even if he doesn't show it in practice. He took me aside at the beginning of the summer and told me he wouldn't let my past stop me from being great. He believes in me, and that means something. He won't, however, hesitate to make us run drills for the next hour if Madison puts him in a bad mood.

CHAPTER THIRTY-FIVE

MADISON

"Hey coach."

"Yes, Ms. Cartwright?" he says, not looking up from his clipboard.

"Did you know you have your fastest player on the team on defense?" I ask him, my arms folded across my chest.

Ender is standing behind me now, his hands on my shoulders. I don't know why he thinks he needs to be over here. This conversation has nothing to do with him. Ender is nearly perfection on the field.

"Is that so, Ms. Cartwright?"

Is the coach even paying attention to me? He hasn't looked up from his clipboard once.

"You know, you might intimidate the boys on the field, but you don't scare me," I tell him, my arms crossed in front of my chest. I stand as tall as I can.

"Ms. Cartwright, I know they're hard to see because my skin is getting older, but these tattoos on my arms–they each represent a pro-bowl or super bowl where I was part of the winning team. There's over eight of them there."

I look at his muscular arms and sure enough, the right one is covered in roman numerals. I don't care how many games he's won, it doesn't make him impervious to error. I'm about to tell him what a colossal mistake he's making having Josh on defense when he would do so much better as a wide receiver on the offense, but Ender is pulling me away.

"Hey! I was trying to have a conversation with the man," I tell Ender.

"Babe. You know I love you, and I think all your ideas are brilliant, but you can not tell the coach that he's doing his job wrong. Please, for me, go back and sit with Emmett and you can complain all you want to me later."

He gently walks me all the way back to the bench and I sit, only throwing a small tantrum. Ender shakes his head at me, gives me a quick kiss and runs back onto the field. Emmett just sits there laughing at me.

"What?!" I ask Emmett.

"I did not say a word," he says, trying to contain his laughter.

"You're the one who shared everyone's speeds with me! Did you not expect me to try to do something about this obvious oversight?"

Emmett hangs his head, no longer able to control his laughter. I ignore him. I peek back over to coach Davis, who is shaking his head and laughing too! I pout some more and turn my attention back to practice. Their first game is next weekend and I'm not sure we're ready. Ender, of course, is ready and has been doing amazing at practice all week. Some of these other fools still look like they should be on a peewee team. The rest of practice goes fairly smooth, and by the end of it I'm at least a little more hopeful for our game.

Ender makes his way over to us, sweaty and without his shirt on, his shoulder pads in his hand.

"You did great today, baby," I tell him, kissing his sweaty cheek.

He grabs me around the waist and pulls me to him. I squeal in protest but he leans down and kisses me on the lips. There's nothing quick about it.

"Okay, you two, get a room," Jesse says, joining us, "Emmett, you picking me and Taylor up at 9 tonight?

"Yeah, you'll both be at your place?" Emmett asks.

"Yup, sure will."

Jesse and Emmett both give us a wave. Jesse heads to the locker rooms and Emmett to the parking lot.

Ender goes to talk to the coach before we leave. We're planning to go back to his house. His mom won't be home. She's on a week-long vacation that Emmett's mom is treating her to.

Ender and I have been taking advantage of having the house to ourselves and spend all of our free time either having sex or laying together naked and talking. After practice, I'm always extra horny. Those tight pants and him getting all sweaty does something to me. One time, I couldn't stop myself and started taking off both our clothes in his truck before we even made it home. Luckily it was after a late practice and all the neighbors were asleep so we were able to run into the house half naked before anyone saw us.

Tonight we're meeting up with our friends at the Barn. It will be my first time there and the first time all of us hang out since Ender and I got together. My relationships with Taylor, Jesse and Emmett have all gotten stronger over the past three weeks, each of them being supportive of everything I've been going through in their own ways. Emmett and I have gotten especially close since he's been sitting on the sidelines at practice. I've enjoyed his company, but I'd be lying if I said I wasn't nervous he won't be playing for the first game. He says the team doctor hasn't cleared him yet, but I don't understand because he doesn't seem to be in any pain.

Ender comes back over to me, takes my hand and we walk to his truck.

"Babe, you've gotta leave the coaches alone or they won't let you sit down on the sides during practice anymore."

I start to protest but admit defeat and tell him I'll keep to myself. As much as I've grown to love football, I never want to even come close to being the overbearing supporter Ender's dad was. That wasn't support, that was a demand for unrealistic perfection. My priority is ensuring Ender continues to love playing, and me causing trouble with the coaches wouldn't help.

When we get back to his house, we take a shower together and then get ready to meet up with our friends. While I'm putting on a little make-up–Taylor's been giving me a few tips on how to apply things–Ender makes us something to eat. He's shuffling around the kitchen in just a pair of gray sweat pants assembling sandwiches when I come down stairs. I slide my arms around his waist from behind him.

"I could get used to this," I say.

"What, me making you food?"

"Yes. But also, this," I say, squeezing him tighter. "Spending time with you doing the mundane things like eating sandwiches."

He leans back into me and inhales deeply.

"Me too, Mads, me too."

We're all sitting around the television in the barn while Jesse and Emmett play video games. Taylor in a big cozy chair, Emmett and Jesse on the couch and Ender and I are lounging on a loveseat.

"So this is the infamous barn?" I say. "Taylor, you kinda hyped it up–"

"Hey, tonight is a quiet night. We've had some much more wild nights here," Taylor fires back.

The group shares stories of some of their favorite memories in the barn. Sometimes I'm a little sad I didn't get to meet all of them sooner.

They're more than friends to me now, even in such a short time. All of these people are like family to me, which I was in short supply of before moving to Easton. Even Bev, Joy and Chuck–who has officially warmed up to me–treat me like family. I'm really lucky to have found such a great support system and I wouldn't have made it through the past few weeks without all of them.

Taylor has been my shoulder to cry on and my voice of reason. Jesse has made me laugh so hard when I was down for too long, I've nearly peed my pants more than once around him. I don't think I could ever repay Emmett for letting us use the plane to go to California. He's also never complained once when I ask him a million questions from the sidelines of practices. Then there's Ender–Ender is everything.

He's given me back my best friend, he's given me back my greatest confidant, and he loves me through all of my emotions. He loves me fiercely and deeply, without judgment or criticism, even when I allow my anger at my mother to cloud my judgment. He's my biggest supporter, but he also pushes me to do things that terrify me. Like his encouragement for me to go to therapy even though I'm more than hesitant. I never doubted Ender's care for me in all the years we were just friends online but now, being able to feel and hear his love for me daily. My world has changed.

"You know, your boy Enderrrr, had many of his own nights making a fool of himself here," Jesse says, dragging out the *r* in his name.

When we told them all our story, everyone instantly started calling him Ender. First as a joke, poking fun that Ender was his sexier, brooding, alter ego. Eventually, the name I love him as most, stuck with everyone. Jesse still likes to tease him about it.

Chapter Thirty-Six

Henderson

"You know guys, we're going to make so many wild memories in Mexico next month," Emmett says.

The trip Emmett told me he wanted to take is actually happening. We all have a week off classes for some professor training week, so we're taking advantage of it.

"I can not wait!" Taylor squeals, raising her red cup in the air. "I'm the last one to get to ride in the family jet!"

"You're not missing much," Madison groans, "The things a death trap."

"Oh, I don't know–I thought it had some pretty awesome perks," I say, winking at Mads, not so subtly.

"Y'all did NOT get it on in my plane," Emmett scoffs.

"No," Madison starts, "I mean, we're not official mile high club members."

She giggles and buries her face in my chest. I stroke her hair, loving the way my fingers feel gliding through the soft strands. Emmett rolls his eyes and Jesse goes to give me a high five. I shake my head at him and slap his hand away. I would brag all day about how amazing sex is with Madison, but I know it embarrasses her, so I try to keep it to myself.

"I don't think we've ever gone on a trip, just us before," Taylor says, "Why the urgency to do it now, Emmett?"

I haven't told anyone about our trip to the water tower, not even Madison. As much as I want to tell her everything, there's something that's telling me, that adventure should be kept between just Emmett and I, for now at least. Everyone else has noticed that Emmett hasn't quite been himself and now they're questioning why he pushed us all to go on this trip. He's footing the bill for the whole thing, or rather, his parents are. He even offered to make up for Madison's wages she'll miss out on when she tried using that as an excuse to not go. Of course, she would never in a million years let him do that. Jesse, Taylor and I were all quick to joke that he could send us checks for the hours at work we'll miss.

Emmett doesn't answer right away. He must be lost in the video game he's still playing. Eventually he answers her, though.

"It's just time is all."

"Well, as long as you don't get so wasted, you injure yourself more," I tell Emmett, "I need you on that field with me sooner rather than later."

"Well, Henderson, you may need to start thinking about trusting your new tight end."

There he goes again, calling me Henderson like he's my mother.

"Why? Is the doctor not going to release you?" Madison says in a panic.

Emmett puts down the video game controller and wipes his hands on his jeans. He takes a deep breath, exhaling loudly.

"No, he's not going to release me because I'll be in treatment at least until the end of the season, if I make it that far," he says, looking down at his hands.

We all look at each other. What the hell is he talking about?

"You'll need to rehab the injury that long? What the hell?" Jesse says.

Emmett looks up at us and his eyes are glassy.

"No, not rehab. I have cancer."

Afterword

I Need You
The Easton You Series: Book 2
Emmett's Story
Coming Summer 2023

As an indie author, reviews mean so much to me and is a great way to help others to find this book! A review on Amazon and/or Goodreads is always appreciated.

ACKNOWLEDGMENTS

To my wonderful, amazing, and selfless Husband. Thank you for reading this book no short of half a dozen times in total. Thank you for reading many romance books in preparation of being asked to read mine, staying up late arguing over grammar and massaging my shoulders when I refuse to sit in a proper chair while writing all day. We somehow manage to work together on all of the wild adventures I dream to take us on, and still love each other deeply. You will forever be my person. I hear you.

To my mother, Lyn. Thank you for helping me explore my love for books throughout my life and always having lots of books in the house. P.S. I'm sorry for all the naughty words and sex.

To my mother-in-law, LeeAnn, thank you for always believing in me and cheering me on every step of the way.

To my bestie, Jacque/Jackie, thank you for letting me steal your name for the character we're all not really supposed to like. Thank you for not being that character and thank you for being such a great cheerleader through this whole process. I love you oodles.

Thank you to my BETA readers for catching what my eyes could not. And my ARC team, thank you for taking a chance on a newbie.

To my therapist for keeping me mostly in one piece and pushing me to do this.

The One's Who Show Up—You know who you are. Thank you for letting me take over our group chat with my book stuff. Love you all.

To every single person who reads this book. I love you. Publishing a book has been a dream of mine since I was a little girl and I let one too many people convince me I couldn't. If you enjoyed this book, you've made my dreams come true. At 33 years old I finally learned to chase all of my dreams. To ride the Ferris wheel to the top and not be afraid. To be able to enjoy the beauty brought to me by doing the scary things.

ABOUT AUTHOR

Kay Mitchell has hot pink hair that makes up seventy percent of her personality and is equal parts nerdy and girly.

She has spent the better part of her adult life as a professional wedding photographer and wedding planner but has had a passion for books since she was young. She was stealing Nicholas Sparks books from her Mother as soon as she was just barely old enough. When she's not helping couples have kick-ass weddings days, reading or writing—she's spending time on the beach with her Husband and their two dogs, Bella & Betsy.

Kay also enjoys finding every opportunity she can to give back and has mentored several aspiring photographers in her free time. She approaches all of her endeavors with a community over competition mindset.

Although she talked about writing a book "someday" for years, she had began to believe it wouldn't ever happen. Thanks to a few special people who believed in her, some epic timing and a hell of a lot of hard work, I Hear You became a reality and will soon be accompanied by other books in The Easton You Series.

Content Warnings

This book includes the following content:

Sex (On Page, Descriptive)
Grief – Loss of Loved One
Addiction
Domestic Violence (Not between main character love interests)